IN MY ATTIC

A Magical Misfits Mystery

Lina Hansen

Literary Wanderlust | Denver, Colorado

In My Attic is a work of fiction. Names, characters, places, and incidents are the products of the author's imagination and have been used fictitiously. Any resemblance to actual events, locales, or persons, living or dead, is entirely coincidental.

Copyright 2020 by Lina Hansen

All rights reserved. No part of this publication may be reproduced, distributed, or transmitted in any form or by any means, including photocopying, recording, or other electronic or mechanical methods, without the prior written permission of the publisher, except in the case of brief quotations embodied in critical reviews and certain other noncommercial uses permitted by copyright law.

Published in the United States by Literary Wanderlust LLC, Denver, Colorado. www.LiteraryWanderlust.com

ISBN Print: 978-1-942856-51-1
ISBN eBook: 978-1-942856-56-6

Cover design: Pozu Mitsuma

Printed in the United States

1

ARRIVAL

My aunt lay dead and I was lost in her life. It came complete with auntie's beloved bed and breakfast fully booked and brimming with guests. Too bad, since I slung a mean tea bag but was a hopeless cook. Instead, I was a murderess. Well, okay, call it guilty of failing to render assistance, but it felt worse.

Yesterday, Aunt Eve had rung me, panic vibrating in her voice.

"Myrtle, I need your help. This is getting out of hand."

"What is? Listen, I'm so sorry, but there's a faculty meeting in two minutes and—"

"I can't do this on my own."

"Daisy—"

"Not for this. I need you. I won't let him win." The last bit came out as a wail and triggered my monumental mistake. Aunt Eve was the most rational person on Earth, though she had her wild moments. I decided this was one of them, made soothing noises and promised to ring back.

I never made that call.

Now, on a deceptively pleasant Tuesday afternoon, I found myself standing in the kitchen of my aunt's bed and breakfast, caught in a haze of loss and anguish, assaulted by the lingering aromas of fry-ups gone by. To make matters worse, the Witch's Retreat was also overrun by the police in their size elevens.

Bang on cue, a copper tramped in from the corridor and pushed his way through the saloon-style swing doors, his helmet under his arm.

He beamed at me. "Hi there, any chance of a cuppa?"

Such a simple request. Aunt Eve would have had the kettle boiling in no time. Why was I still standing there, the strap of my purse cutting into my shoulder, the industrial-sized fridge humming away in indifference?

"Give me a moment." I dumped my suitcase onto terracotta tiles as immaculate as the cupboards with their glossy eggshell finish. Illuminated by ceiling spots so bright they out-dazzled the watery April sunlight, the doors of the cabinets reflected my haggard face, colorless and distorted as if I were a specter haunting auntie's world. Everything looked like it did in November when I visited this place for the last, and first, time. My scruples had nothing to do with the old house. The renovations did the Georgian elephant proud. The village it stood in was a different matter.

Don't be such a Moaning Myrtle, my inner voice scolded.

True, this mawkishness was not my style. I heaved a shuddering breath and searched my surroundings. In a corner, close to the steel double sink, I spotted a toaster and the kettle. Tea bags were nowhere in sight, but then the blasted tears were once more blurring my vision. I searched my pockets for a tissue, wiped my eyes and blew my nose. All the time, my uniformed companion was tactful enough not to comment.

Trying to calm my breathing, I focused on the flowerpots lining the windowsill from the back entrance to the sink, their occupants the only sign something was amiss and must have been for a while. Aunt Eve took good care of her green boarders. These plants, primulas from what I could make out, were as shriveled and dried as last autumn's leaves.

Fabric rubbing on fabric reminded me of the young police officer still waiting, his helmet now parked on the quartz countertop. His eyes narrowed and he cleared his throat. "Uh,

I'm sorry. You're Mrs. Coldron's older daughter, correct? Or would that be niece?"

The bloke was as well informed as he was nosy. "Take your pick," I said.

"Ah. Put my foot right in it, then. Thought you might be another helper. My apologies. The ladies who do the cooking are ever so good with the drinks and sandwiches."

Had this place turned into a police canteen?

"You seem to be familiar with the arrangements, officer."

Policeman Plod snapped his heels together in a mock salute and bowed. "Constable Alan Hunter, at your service. Actually, I'm one of the houseguests. Just transferred to Swindon. I'm still looking for a flat, so I booked a room here for the time being. It's a great place." His gaze slipped aside. "Well, it was."

The bloke was easy on the eyes in his natty uniform, and his voice sounded genuinely contrite and well educated, so I forgave him.

When he spoke again, he addressed his helmet rather than me. "I'm sorry about...what happened. You must be in shock."

Polite despite the thing with the helmet, "shock" was not the word I would have used. One moment all I had to worry about was a mountain of essays for English Lit and A-grade German that needed correcting, wondering what the girls might be commenting on. It didn't sound at all like the set novels. Moments later, the headmistress had called me in, the lines in her sourpuss's face distorted by what I only afterward identified as concern. She had passed me the phone and my world went black.

"I'm afraid Mrs. Coldron met with a fatal accident," the female voice on the other end of the line said. "In fact, we are treating this as a suspicious death. Can you come?"

I packed my case in a daze and spent a tortured hour in the teachers' wing, the headmistress having stopped me from belting up the motorway to Avebury. Instead, a colleague was to drive me in my car and return by train. The headmistress had been surprisingly compassionate; she granted me a week's leave and had given me tea and a pat on the back before I set out. I understood this to mean the job that meant so much to me—despite the crappy essays—might still be waiting once I escaped from this nightmare.

Auntie was my anchor, the one person who had always been there for me. She took me in when my parents died in an awful accident.

Now I was grieving for her.

My vision wobbled, and I sagged onto the rubber gymnastic ball auntie used instead of a kitchen chair. She insisted it did wonders for her spine and, whenever excited, bounced up and down on it like a toddler. Tears burned the back of my throat.

No more bouncing.

"You all right?" The copper's voice dragged me back to the present. "Need some tea?" That was the UK for you. If in distress, stay calm and switch the kettle on. To tell the truth, I was thirsty. And hungry. My body craved sustenance, no matter what was going on and whether or not I liked it.

"No, thank you. If you don't mind, I'll unpack in Number Seven and then..."

No idea what to do then. My aunt was gone. Neither tea nor tears could bring her back.

"Room Number Seven?" my police officer asked. "I thought it stood empty?"

"It's a spare, for emergencies," I said. "It suits me."

That had been an odd thing to say, so I changed the subject. "Any suggestions where my cousin might be?"

The constable shook his head. "The other Ms. Coldron suffered a breakdown when she heard the news, and the doctor gave her a sedative. She's not in the house for sure."

Yup, that sounded like something Daisy would do. If she was not at my aunt's place, she had most likely returned to her room in the pub where she tended the bar. Running a B&B was beyond her, coping with emergencies was beyond her—in a way, life was beyond her.

As usual, it was all up to me. Not that she would appreciate my efforts.

The ball hurt the small of my back, and I dragged myself up. "Can I talk to your superior? I still don't understand what happened. Is he around somewhere?"

Constable Hunter pushed the blond fringe from his face and twinkled his baby blues at a point somewhere over my right shoulder, which was an improvement over the helmet.

"She," he said. "The Sarge is upstairs with the SOCO. They should be done soon. I'll tell her you've arrived." He bounced a smile in my general direction and trooped off, the doors swinging shut behind him.

Upstairs with the what? SOCO sounded ominous. And where upstairs? At least he didn't mention pathologists. That was the last thing I needed now. What I needed was a porter, but even if the Witch's Retreat was reasonably upmarket, it was no five-star hotel.

With every step I took up treads carpeted in midnight blue, my battered suitcase got heavier. The big three-oh was recent, so I shouldn't wheeze like this. Not that I did, usually. Back at the school, I bounced up and down stairs along with the girls. Here, I felt like I was climbing Mount Everest without a Sherpa.

The first landing gave me an excuse to let go of my luggage and catch my breath. The silent corridor, with the pine doors mirroring each other on both sides, seemed to have slipped out of the time stream and I with it. No creaks, no groans, none of the noises old buildings tended to make. Even the guests remained mum. The result was an oddly appropriate otherworldly stillness. Aunt Eve's brilliant mind had created this place. Here, her memory would live on. I could almost see her smiling, her tall figure striding along the passage.

The phone at reception downstairs rang once, twice, then stopped. The spell was broken, and I loosened my death grip on the blond wood of the handrail.

Something, probably a window, banged shut in the bedroom closest to the stairs, telling me the guests were awake after all. Perhaps the police had forced them to stay, and those innocent-looking doors hid a killer.

Despite the plushy comfort offered by my favorite moss-green fleece jacket, a breeze sneaked along my spine. I was overwhelmed by an urge to scamper back down and keep running. Instead, I forced my unwilling legs to hoist myself and my luggage to the top floor. Whoever had so diligently vacuumed below had capitulated here. Footprints marred the dark blue of the carpet leading up the steps and into the upper corridor.

The cold spread from my spine to my arms and drew goosebumps. I must be close to the crime scene. No sooner had the thought chilled my brain than I heard voices on the draft coming from the door at the end of the corridor. It led to a little landing with Aunt Eve's room on the left and Daisy's on the right. Both door and landing were half-hidden by a curtain featuring tiny mauve roses. Where the furnishings chosen by my parents had been all about angles and squares, Aunt Eve's taste in interior decoration had leaned toward the floral, although she restrained herself to her private sphere. Her Wiccan spleen she had vented openly when she chose this village, of all places, for her business, naming the bed and breakfast "Witch's Retreat" and hanging kitschy ceramic tiles displaying the room number and a witch motif on the doors to the rooms.

When I reached for the brass knob of Number Seven, featuring a teal-colored seven and a broomstick, I caught movement from the corner of my eye. A blue and white plastic band, unnecessarily labeled "POLICE," barred access to the private part of the corridor.

Had my aunt been killed in her bed?

The carpet was even dirtier up here, showing the evidence of many a booted foot trudging to and from the makeshift but ominous barricade. For a moment, I considered searching for another place to stay. Unfortunately, apart from the Witch's Retreat, Avebury offered little choice of accommodation. Next on the list was the Crystal Dawn, a quixotic New Age B&B down the road, a flat over the Magic Mushroom Café, available only during the summer months, and the few rooms at the Whacky Bramble, the pub where my cousin worked. If I had any home in this village, this would be it, crime scene or not. At least my aunt's remains had been removed. The disembodied voice on this morning's phone call had told me that much.

When I entered Number Seven, the room welcomed me with the sweet perfume lilies release into the summer skies.

Aunt Eve must have refreshed the potpourri before she died. Sobs tickled the back of my throat, but I slammed the door before they escaped. I dumped my luggage to fumble for a box of tissues on the nightstand of the nearest twin bed.

Several sniffles later, I opened the suitcase. My packing had been hurried, and it showed. I could only hope the motley collection of charity rejects would yield some useful items of clothing. First things first: I needed a shower before confronting Constable Hunter's sergeant.

The moment I entered the bathroom, a knock sounded on the door to Number Seven. I cracked it open and beheld the same lantern-jawed face and roving gaze I had encountered earlier.

"Sergeant Widdlethorpe can talk to you now if you like. She's got to leave soon to attend the—eh, never mind. She'll be back tomorrow. You can meet her then if you prefer." He looked at my ear expectantly. We were making progress.

I opened the door farther. "For how much longer will I have the pleasure of a police presence?"

"You mean the on-site investigation? They're almost done, don't you worry."

The urge to talk to Constable Hunter's superior became overwhelming, so I stepped into the corridor. "If your sergeant is ready, I wouldn't mind having a word with her now."

Hunter nodded and led the way. Ever the helpful neighborhood bobby, he lifted the plastic strip for me to bend under and pushed the curtain aside so I could enter the landing. Fluorescent lamps threw their glare into what used to be such a cozy place, illuminating a figure in a white hooded suit next to an aluminum stepladder lying on its side. A young woman in street clothes leaned against the wall opposite the entrance, her neck craning toward a trapdoor in the ceiling. The tips of her shoes rested inches away from the chalked outline of a person with one arm reaching out, knees pulled up.

My stomach lurched.

Dried red rose petals lay strewn about the grisly smear, flattened and crumpled in places. They clustered in the part marking the splayed fingers.

Bile rose in my throat. Those dark splotches half-hidden by the wilted and crushed petals could only be blood.

My aunt had not died in her bed.

She had plummeted from the attic.

Killed by a bouquet of roses?

2

INCIDENTS AND ACCIDENTS

A wave of pain washed over me, broke with a thunderous roar and left me stranded in a whimpering limbo. From somewhere among the turbulence frothing in my brain surfaced the sharp voice from this morning's phone call.

"Constable, what on Earth is she doing here?"

When a warm presence put its arm around my shoulders, I clung to the reassuring human contact and allowed myself to be pushed onto a saggy surface reeking of mothballs. The arm slipped away, and in its stead fingers found the top of my spine and pressed downward until my head hung between my knees. The fiendish surf ebbed away. Unfortunately, my nose was now inches away from a floor stinking of Clorox. I gagged, and a hand patted my shoulder. Grounded once more, I identified the thing under my buttocks to be the wonky settee, which once belonged to my grandmother. The heirloom was both uncomfortable and hideous, probably the reason it got parked up here.

"But Sarge, you said you wanted to talk to her." Hunter sounded aggrieved.

The young police officer released a sigh that seemed to come from very deep down. "Hunter, I appreciate your reporting for duty on your day off. Let's discuss this back at headquarters."

From a brief glimpse, Hunter's sergeant was everything I was not: well-groomed and slim with short dark hair gelled into spikes and a hungry expression on her narrow face.

"Ms. Coldron?" The voice took on an urgent undertone.

"I'll be all right," I mumbled. Once I had prised my nose away from the floor, the police officer extended her hand, well-manicured with elegant, cool fingers. I gripped them once, and then let go.

"I'm Sarah Widdlethorpe. We spoke earlier. Sorry for giving you such a fright. I'm sure Constable Hunter meant well, but I guarantee you it is not standard practice to expose relatives to, uh, scenes."

I could only marshal a nod.

Sergeant Widdlethorpe swung away from me to address the constable. "That'll be it for the moment. Please wait for me in the car as I asked you. Do you need help?" With that, she addressed the hooded figure, a man to judge by the bulk. He shook his head in response, grabbed a large plastic container and preceded the constable through the door.

"What happened here?" My eyes were magnetized by the faint outline on the floor and the floral confetti so out of place. The tears welled up again, but I blinked them away.

The sergeant stepped closer to the trapdoor and gazed into the attic. In doing so, she blocked my view of the grisly outline.

"I suggest we go downstairs," she said.

I shook my head. Having seen the worst, I wouldn't budge before I got answers. "Please."

Sergeant Widdlethorpe cracked the knuckles of her fingers. "Well, then. From what we know about the accident—"

"But you said my aunt's death seemed suspicious." Yes, I was impolite in cutting her off, but so far, the local fuzz had underwhelmed me.

"Trouble is, we lack evidence of third-party involvement. Ms. Coldron, let me explain. I understand this must be very hard for you."

The inner turmoil attempted to break out again. *No, you don't,* I wanted to scream.

I breathed in and let the air flow back out on the count of four, a useful trick I had gleaned from a yoga program I once watched, briefly, before flipping channels to *MasterChef*.

With almost uncanny timing, Sergeant Sarah spoke the moment I was once more ready to listen. "Let me summarize for you. At first, we figured your aunt must have been in the attic before she dropped through the trapdoor. However, that scenario isn't consistent with the injuries. I'll have to wait for the results of the, eh..."

She regarded me with a sheepish expression on her face. Perhaps the woman was not as experienced as I had thought. Or more human than I had deemed her to be.

"Autopsy?" I asked.

"Eh, yes."

"But how can this be suspicious? Did you find an imprint of a hand on her back?"

My comment reaped a blank stare. Perhaps the young sergeant was unused to the newly bereaved going cynical on her.

"No, it wasn't that. According to the first response team, Mrs. Coldron lay next to the fallen step ladder, with the trapdoor bolted shut above her." She looked at me expectantly.

I didn't get it. "Auntie closed it, climbed down, and toppled the ladder? What about those petals?"

"She was stretched out on top of them, her palms pricked and bloody, but we found no stalks or flowers anywhere. Instead, a dishrag lay on the threshold to her room. My best guess is she dropped the petals before she even climbed into the attic. I wonder whether she might have surprised a burglar. The buggers have been all over the area in the last few months. Your aunt liked potpourri, didn't she? However, the ladder scenario bothers me."

What the sergeant had said about the petals made sense, but her last sentence didn't. "Care to explain?" I asked.

"Mrs. Coldron's injuries are consistent with having dropped from a great height. See, your aunt was a tall woman, like you, and the trapdoor opens sideways. To close it, she needed to have been no higher than the second or third rung on the ladder. Falling from there should have given Mrs.

Coldron a broken wrist or a sprained ankle at the utmost. At least, that's what the doctor says. But her injuries are much more severe."

"Hmm." I pushed myself off the sofa to examine the sunlit rectangle above me. The trapdoor was fastened by three hinges to the right side of the opening, a copper bolt on the left, with handles fixed to both sides of the panel. "If I understand correctly, this door cannot be bolted from inside the attic?"

The sergeant nodded. "Just the one lock on the outside. Plus, the whole thing's pretty heavy and hard to push up. Next to the ladder, we found a wooden pole your aunt must have used to shut the trapdoor."

"Are you telling me she plummeted through the hole, injured herself before she got back up, bolted the door, climbed down and—died?" I had difficulty saying the word, but it was necessary if I wanted answers.

My comment was rewarded with an economical smile. I knew that one. I used it on my brighter pupils. "As I told you, the situation appears suspicious. At least it does to me. But unless I can prove somebody else was involved..." Sergeant Sarah shrugged.

"Who found her?" I asked. "That person could have closed the darned thing."

The sergeant's nostrils widened, and for a second she held me pinned in her gaze as if conducting a full soul scan. I must have passed muster because she reached into the pockets of her well-cut navy blazer to pull out a notebook.

"One guest, a Mr. Chris Lentulus, stated he heard a crash while climbing the stairs. He raced to the top floor, found your aunt, called 999 and administered first aid with the connection still open. When the first response team turned up, they checked the upper rooms and the attic to make sure nobody was hiding up there."

"Is that man a suspect?" I asked.

I had crossed an invisible line, and the notebook disappeared into the pocket.

Sergeant Sarah checked her watch and straightened. "Right now, I can't tell you more. Let's talk again when I have a clearer picture. How can I reach you?"

"I guess I'll be around for the next few days."

When reality hit home, the crooked finger of fear twanged on my nerves, already strung tight like piano wire. I would be trapped in the village that had killed first my parents and now my aunt.

I exorcized the thought, but something must have shown in my face. The sergeant gave me a penetrating look before pointing at the exit. "After you. Until the official ruling, this part of the house will be closed off."

Once we had crossed the plastic barrier, I raised my chin at the keys. "Are those my aunt's?"

"Yes. You'll get them back eventually, don't you worry."

I had my own set, but that was something Sergeant Sarah didn't need to know.

"Where are you staying?" she asked.

"Over there." I pointed at Number Seven.

A graceful eyebrow rose. "Will you be okay up here?"

"I'll cope, thank you." To be honest, I was glad my police escort had locked the door on the scene. A firm handshake later, I was on my own and could wash the shock and grief from my body.

—

Much refreshed, physically if not mentally, I decided I needed calories and padded downstairs in slacks and ski socks.

The first door I passed after doglegging the reception desk belonged to the breakfast patio, a winter garden on steroids added by my aunt. Every room had its designated table, each of them decorated with a cute ceramic sign that matched the ones on the room doors. Colorful numbers were paired with cartoon magical objects including a raven, a kettle, a pointy hat, a cat...

Oh, my gosh. Cat.

Where had Tiddles got to, my aunt's geriatric pet? She was not my biggest fan, and the antipathy was mutual. For my aunt's sake, I would have to make sure old grumpypants could live out the rest of her life in peace.

But first I had to find the dratted animal. I decided the sitting room was my best chance and marched toward the pine door at the end of the corridor. Marked "Private," it led to auntie's private parlor also known as the arena where back in November I had taken my stand. When I grabbed the door handle, scraps of our argument zinged through my brain.

"I won't be back. I'll do anything for you, but just thinking of those standing stones makes me feel guilty. I know I should visit, but I can't."

Aunt Eve dropped her knitting into her lap and regarded me with the same pale gray-blue eyes that smiled in my mother's portrait and scowled at me from the mirror. "I know. It hurts being here."

"Eh? Why open up a business in a place you don't even like?"

"As long as you associate Earth powers with hydraulic equipment, you won't understand."

There had been no winner. Only an uneasy truce, and a peeved Daisy who had wanted to watch the latest beauty contest, dance show or whatever caught her fleeting fancy. A few days later, she moved out. Well, mostly.

When I opened the door, Tiddles was nowhere in sight, nor was the knitting basket the crafty beast used for a cat bed. Odd. I could have sworn my aunt kept it next to her favorite cherry-red armchair or, failing that, the beige settee. Calling Tiddles wouldn't work either. Could she be in the dinky office from where my aunt managed her business? It was connected to the sitting room by an open archway, so I rushed across, tripping over the threadbare Turkish carpet that was another of grandma's bequests and in no better shape than the sofa upstairs.

When I peeped around the corner, I hit pay dirt in the form of an open wicker basket filled with half-finished fluffy creations and knitting needles pointing every which way, the balls of wool themselves missing in action.

"Tiddles?"

A sleeve, draped across the hairy jumble, moved. Next, a face covered in tortoiseshell fur peeped from under my aunt's handiwork, gracing me with a throaty sound that could pass for a purr.

The cat came out of hiding and, stretched, brushing her silky fur past my ankles, tufts of hair floating to the ground. No doubt the feline instinct for survival had alerted the crafty old animal to the change in can opener arrangements, and she chose to behave.

Tiddles farted. Not so clever after all.

"Phew." I picked up the less than sweet-smelling but surprisingly light bundle of fur and pressed her against my cheek.

More purring.

With the cat draped over my shoulder, I searched auntie's desk for a personal message. I had cut short Aunt Eve's call, and she never gave up. Neither draft letters nor emails were to be found on the computer, the password of which had been stuck to the back of the monitor. I retraced my steps to the sitting room and the shelf crammed with reading matter, paperbacks mostly, with a few old treasures hiding among them.

Call it disrespectful, but I still groaned. If Aunt Eve had hidden a message among the literature, finding it would take me ages.

But why would she do such a thing?

My fingers slid over the dusty spines of auntie's collection until they stopped on the ribbed ridges of the biggest treasure of them all: the recipe book. Its leather warm to the touch and velvety smooth, the book snuggled into my palm and, almost by itself, found its way into my hand. Pages torn from cookery magazines stuck out on all sides, and one dropped to the floor. When I picked it up, a spicy scent wafted into my nose.

Auntie's recipe for her special apple pie. I would never taste it again.

The tome slipped from my hands onto the coffee table, and the cat half dropped, half jumped from my shoulder. With an indignant hiss, Tiddles stalked off, her claws clicking on the floorboards until the sound was swallowed by the old carpet.

This time I lost the plot completely. Curled up in auntie's armchair, grief wracked my body and would not release me from its grip for what felt like a lifetime.

Eventually, I ran out of tears and blew my nose on a crumpled tissue from the pocket of my fleece jacket.

Another accident. By now, this village had swallowed up most of my family. Only Daisy and I were left behind. Who would be next?

Once I had wiped my eyes with the heel of my hand, the recipe book swam back into view, now spotlighted by a ray of sunlight piercing the glass of the latticed window pane. Unlike my aunt, I had never believed in the supernatural. On any other day, I would have called the setup cheesy. Today, the sunbeam called to mind a beacon and my blue funk lifted.

"I'll find out what happened."

I whispered my vow into the empty sitting room, my voice still hoarse from crying. There was no heavenly choir bursting into sound or string orchestra going nuts over the violins, only the ormolu clock ticking away the seconds on the mantelpiece and the sound of my breath, finally becalmed.

This time, I was no longer fourteen. This time, I wouldn't wallow in my grief. Instead, I would unravel this mystery. Even if it was the last thing I did.

3

DINNERTIME

"Mrrp." Tiddles had returned and looked up at me with rheumy greenish eyes.

"You think that was weird?" In hindsight, my whispered vow to the sitting room might have been a tad bizarre, but I felt better for it. "I mean what I said. Moreover, I'll prove it to you. Let's see if the chap with the funny name is around, shall we? I want to ask him a few questions."

A pink tongue rasped rhythmically over a beige paw.

"First, I need food."

The cat must have heard "food," because she belied her age by cannonballing into the kitchen. The animal's antics made me smile for the first time today. I chased after her, too fast to stop when a dark shape popped through the swing doors.

"Oof," it said when we collided.

I broke contact first. "Oh, sorry."

"It's a pleasure," said my antagonist, a somewhat swarthy young man. From the bluish stubble on his cheeks and his deep-set inky eyes, I deducted the guy's ancestors must have washed ashore with the remains of the Spanish Armada.

Romance alert, my inner voice clamored.

Yes, he was my type. No, I wasn't shopping for men, not

after the wreckage last year and certainly not while grieving.

The fake *señor*, who I took to be a tick older than me—midthirties was my best guess—curled his thin lips in amusement. "What an entrance." The smile faded away. "You must be the niece. The older daughter, I mean."

Here was the second person in this place who was amazingly well informed about my circumstances. "Yes, I'm Myrtle Coldron. Are you a guest?"

I gave him a furtive once-over and observed long, muscular legs clad in tight-fitting black jeans, broad shoulders sheathed in even blacker leather and a general air of fitness, enough to dash up a flight of stairs. Could I be that lucky?

"I'm Chris Lentulus. No, it's not Latin for lentil, in case you wondered." He raised his chin in defiance. Then the rigid line of his jaw relaxed. "By the way, I like the colors you're wearing."

What an off-the-wall comment. Lentulus must have interpreted my expression correctly, for he added, "Don't like people dripping with black for convention's sake."

Then why are you?

I had no energy for arguments. I was after intel. "Thanks. You found my aunt, didn't you?"

Wariness surfaced in those hooded eyes. "Yes. Do you mind if we don't discuss this in the corridor?" Without waiting for my response, he pushed his way back into the kitchen. Once inside, I was greeted with an imperative yowl from the cat who had planted herself next to the fridge.

Lentulus bent over and tickled her under the chin. "Hungry, are we? Hang in there a moment, puss." He straightened and faced me. "I called the ambulance, and I tried first aid with a paramedic on tap. Did a stint with them during my studies, but it's been a while."

My throat had gone dry, forcing me to swallow before speaking. "Did she say something? Anything?"

Lentulus closed his eyes, no doubt seeing a scene that would stick with him forever. When they opened again, they reflected the bleakness of a moorscape in winter. He pressed a "No" past unwilling teeth.

"Mr. Lentulus—"

"Call me Chris," he said, a tick too cheerfully. "Your aunt did." He whirled around and yanked open the fridge, making sure not to bump the cat with the door.

"How about a toast in her memory? I've got some local ale here."

Kind of him, but I needed food, not beer. That was assuming I liked the stuff, which I didn't, less even if the gunk was local. Otherwise, I would much rather have discussed minor details such as what his relationship might have been with my aunt, and not only in the last minutes of her life. I let it drop it for the moment. "Are there any eggs left?"

Chris looked over his shoulder. "You must be joking." He moved aside and waved at the interior of the monster fridge. Stacks of brown eggs filled the shelves, as if Wiltshire's hens kept their produce in cold storage, in case they suffered from laying problems. "There's plenty. Would you like me to make you an omelet?" he asked.

Auntie must have been running the do-it-yourself version of a bed and breakfast. Good for me, because the sheer thought of dinner caused saliva to pool on my tongue. It would also give me an opportunity to fish for more details, so I accepted. "That would be kind of you. I'm not the world's greatest cook, and I guess I should eat something."

My companion shrugged out of his leather jacket and rummaged around the fridge in his black tee to remove six eggs, one red pepper, one green pepper, butter, cheese, and a handful of parsley.

"Can I help?" I asked, hoping he would say no, which he did, politely.

While he clattered about, I eased onto one of two hardwood chairs at the table placed in front of the windowsill. It was either the chair or the orange gymnastic ball, which didn't suit my current mood.

A soft murp at my calf reminded me of Tiddles. Chris was busy cracking eggs into a bowl and chopping peppers and parsley. With practiced movements, he opened cupboards, found paprika, pepper, and salt and seasoned his mixture before turning on the hob. I got up and wondered which cabinet harbored the cat food. I chose one at random and found myself confronted with scouring powder, bleach, and an anti-ant spray.

Chris made the right connection between an edgy feline and a human being searching the kitchen shelves.

"Second to the left. I fed the old dear occasionally when your aunt was busy."

"You must have known each other quite well?"

"Uh, so-so. Been popping in and out since the inauguration." He opened a cupboard under the sink and fished out a pan. "Helped your aunt with her computer projects. I'm an IT specialist."

"May I ask what projects?"

He turned his back on me, and I couldn't see his face. His voice was level enough. "Oh, programming stuff. You'll be in charge of Mrs. Coldron's affairs, I gather? Let's discuss this another time. Finding your aunt was a pretty horrid experience."

Devoid of tears, I shuddered.

Behind the door he had pointed out, I found tins with kitty chow, opened one, gagged at the rank smell and still made an old cat very happy, at least temporarily.

From the hob wafted a delicious aroma. Chris was well on his way toward making good old me a bit happier. Not only was he attractive, but also he knew how to cook. Once more, the inner voice clanged its warning.

I shushed it and sat down again. "Where are the others? This place is supposed to be fully booked, but I've met only Constable Hunter."

With a flip of his wrist, Chris turned the omelet. "Huh. The Retreat was booked out, yes. But Mr. and Mrs. Burns have moved in with her brother. His farm isn't far away. She believed murder was too much for Robbie and Johnnie. Their kids, I mean. They love to ride in their uncle's van. I suspect you'll get to meet them when he does his next delivery. Burns is a tosser. Jenna, his wife, is sweet. No idea where the old folks are. Probably house hunting."

Chris scowled at the omelet. I wasn't sure why since it looked and smelled heavenly.

"Old folks?" I asked.

"Yeah, Damian and Rosie Ragwort." Chris opened the fridge, this time to fetch the ketchup. "They left once the police were done with them, but I think they kept their room. Not sure about Number One, you need to check with the Simpkins sisters. Somehow, this place attracts the last traveling salespeople left in this country."

The housekeepers I knew about. They were hired after I left last November. "You're telling me there are still traveling salespeople out and about?" The aromas of roasting peppers wafted in my direction; it took all my good upbringing to keep me from drooling.

Chris shrugged. "Think of them as being retro."

The resident chef fetched two heated plates from the oven and flipped his creation onto one plate. He then cut the omelet in half and deftly shifted one part onto the second plate. A sprig of parsley went on top, a dab of ketchup was placed on the side, and cheese got sprinkled on top before Chris yanked open the fridge once more. "If you don't drink beer, what do you drink?"

"Champers," I said without thinking. It was true though. Auntie and I, even Daisy sometimes, had polished off the odd bottle or two. Imaginary bubbles tickled my tongue, and I wrestled with a snivel.

Chris removed a dark green bottle from the fridge. "Here we go."

I remembered where to find the cutlery and napkins and laid the table before sitting down again. While Chris popped the cork and filled the glasses, I stared at the garden, waiting for my dinner.

Outside, spring also kept us waiting. After an unseasonably warm and wet winter, we now shivered through an equally unseasonably chilly and blustery spring. As another shower took hold, the wind whipped a cluster of foolish daffodils. Inside, on the windowsill, the sad corpses of the primulas foretold their fellow flora's fate. I reached across and stroked the dry leaves of one plant, wondering what the deuce auntie might have been up to.

A plate landed in front of me, bearing a vision in crispy gold. We drank a toast to Aunt Eve and dug in. Oh yes, the guy could cook. The omelet was fluffy and light, everything an omelet should be and never would be if I were at the hob.

We ate our meal in companionable silence.

"This is lovely." I poured two more glasses. The champagne was making me lightheaded—and ashamed. Here I was, eating and drinking, enjoying myself when auntie no longer could. Suddenly, the omelet tasted of ash, and I pushed my plate aside. It was almost empty anyway.

Chris dabbed his mouth with a paper napkin. Warmed by the food and emboldened by drink, curiosity nudged me in the ribs. "Aren't IT guys supposed to thrive on pizza?"

"Not my style. And I sort of fell into IT. I studied history." Chris bit his lip.

True enough, the man was not your average computer nerd. His expensive clothes, his whole self-assured manner spoke of an upbringing very different from mine. One thing was clear: My aunt, who never trusted people easily, must have trusted him. But then, I had only his word for it.

"May I ask what brought you to Avebury?"

Instead of responding, Chris checked his brushed-metal watch, no doubt worth a fortune, smiled apologetically and stood up.

"So sorry, but I need to leave you," he said. "I'm on a deadline. Let's meet again tomorrow. After breakfast. I'm never at peak performance before I've had my coffee."

That made two of us.

With a sketchy wave, Chris left Tiddles and me behind in a kitchen filled with shadows, savory smells, and dirty dishes.

"I'm not your housemaid, you know," I said to the fridge.

It kept on humming.

Fair enough, the guy had cooked me dinner. One might call it tit for tat, only it was not, but now it was too late.

I sorted out the mess, the conversation replaying in my head and yielding no insights. Once I had dried my dripping hands, I wondered what to do next. A walk in the fields to defog my brain? A sudden gust rattled the windowpanes, scattering raindrops onto the glass. Chancing the great outdoors was not an attractive option. Shame it was too early for beddy-byes. Plus, I regretted those glasses of bubbly. They had left me all hyped up.

At a loose end, I headed for auntie's sitting room, followed by Tiddles.

"Ms. Coldron?"

I started and whisked around. Constable Hunter had returned, this time not wearing his natty uniform but jeans and a sweatshirt with the emblem of the Bristol Seals Ice Hockey Club. He looked as sheepish as he had sounded when berated by his superior and I liked him better. So did the cat, who wove a figure eight around his ankles. The constable bent down and scratched her ears before straightening again.

"I'm sorry about earlier. All I wanted to do was help." Clad in his casuals and with his guileless blue gaze, the man looked like a farm boy. This time, he even managed to keep me more or less in focus.

"No worries. It was probably a lack of food." Thinking of food reminded me of Chris. Would Hunter know about him? "Mr. Lentulus was kind enough to cook for me."

At the mention of the other man's name, Hunter narrowed his baby blues.

"Can I give you a piece of advice?" he said. "I suggest you stay clear of the bloke. At least until we know what he's on about."

My cousin might be the better actress, but after having coordinated the Christmas pantomime at my school I wasn't completely clueless either. I widened my eyes with fake shock and crossed my hands over my mouth. "Oh my gosh, you're telling me he might be the murderer?"

Constable Hunter groaned and slapped his forehead. "I've done it again. Keep putting my foot in it, don't I?"

Now I felt sorry for the poor man.

"Can we sit down somewhere so I can explain? There's nothing to worry about." Hunter didn't wait for my answer. He opened the door to the sitting room and ushered me into auntie's cherry-red armchair. "Please take a seat."

I complied, grappling with the apology that threatened to escape. As sleuths go, I was a bit of a dud.

"I can't disclose details about Mr. Lentulus. Ongoing investigation, see? I'm not even part of it. All I wanted to say—"

"You're not?"

He shook his head. "Was sleeping off a double shift when things happened. I reported for duty as I know my way around here, but since I'm a resident I'm too involved. About that chap, well it's...odd." Hunter tapped his lips. They were well-shaped, with cute dimples in the corners, but the strong jawline saved them from being too feminine. There was an alertness in his face that told me although the man might not be the brightest torch in the cop shop, he was no dimwit.

"What do you mean by odd?"

He must have come to a decision, for he gave me the benefit of a full wattage glare. "Your aunt opens her business and next thing Lentulus shows up on the scene."

I made sure to sound casual. "And?"

"And what? As I told you, even if I knew more, I couldn't tell you."

Hunter was no pushover either.

Note to self: Find a Sleuthing for Dummies somewhere.

Before I could rustle up some annoyance, Hunter raised his hand. "Please, the DI and our Sarge have matters well in hand. No need to worry about Lentulus or any of the other guests."

Oblique it might well have been, but the warning about Chris had come straight from the heart. Now, my friendly copper was putting the barriers back in place. His reticence required a more roundabout approach.

"If I understand this correctly, there aren't many left."

Hunter shook his head and got up. Blast, he was about to escape. "Well, they haven't gone far. The DI would never allow it. If you want details, I suggest you have a chat with the housekeepers. They know everything. And everybody."

He towered over me, so I rose from my seat. "You don't?"

My remark got me a practiced smile. "I arrived only two weeks ago."

Why did I have the distinct impression the guy didn't trust me? Not that I could blame him.

"In any case, I hope you feel better. Don't hesitate to call on me if you feel the need. I'm in Number Three."

"I appreciate your kindness, Constable Hunter," I said,

meaning it. With a police officer under the same roof, I might sleep better.

He must have read my thoughts, for he grinned. He had a pleasant grin. "Call me Alan. Quicker that way." With a nod, he pushed off.

The Witch's Retreat was a big house, but I wondered whether it was big enough to contain all this strangeness: A suspicious death with added complications I still needed to get my mind around and the proverbial dark stranger who must have been on reasonably intimate terms with my aunt. While she had been full of praise for her housekeepers, she never once mentioned her computer whiz. Add a clumsy, but well-meaning, police constable into the mix who warned me off the other guy, echoing my misgivings.

Like a lightning strike on a clear day, auntie's last words flared in my mind: *I won't let him win.*

Who had she been talking about? Until now, I had met part of the male cast, but there were more, their names zinging around in my head. Soon it ached, making any clear thinking downright impossible. I turned on the telly and flipped through the broadcasts of the latest world crises until I hit the weather forecast—more rain, more wind. A rerun of *Gardener's World* was next, but I lost interest and opened a magazine instead. Countless minutes later, I caught myself staring at the wall, listening to the gale that howled through the empty streets, rattling the windowpanes with the impotent rage of a million lost souls.

I gave up and retired to bed, hoping sleep, if not a good night's rest, would banish my demons.

4

SPRING CLEANING

I woke at six in the morning to the homey sound of a hoover. With a growl, I pulled the lumpy pillow over my head, which did little to dull the droning coming from the corridor. It was good to see, or rather hear, somebody tackling the mess the police had left behind. If only that somebody had chosen a more suitable time.

The feeble light of the morning hinted at another overcast day. When they predicted doom and gloom, weather reports tended to be correct.

Silence again permeated my room. The vacuum cleaner had been turned off, but too late, for I was wide awake. The sudden quiet was immediately broken by a series of rhythmic thumps coming from the staircase. That had to be one heck of a heavy hoover.

"Alma?" a female voice hollered from the first landing. I hoped for patient guests. Otherwise, I would need to shell out refunds. Then I remembered. If the Omelet Wizard was right, he and Constable Charming were the sole residents.

I swung my bare feet onto the sanded floorboards. The furniture in the spare room had been upgraded with the rest of the establishment, and the box-spring bed was not the reason I had slept so fitfully. I padded toward the window in my sleep shirt and pulled aside the chintz curtains, which flaunted more pale roses.

Outside, the scenery had changed little since yesterday evening. The wind was marginally less ferocious and the rain had stopped, but the slate roofs of the houses opposite the Witch's Retreat were still as sodden as they looked sullen, and a menacing bank of clouds stalked the light above, threatening to dump more water on us. I would have to brave the weather and the village though. I needed to talk to Daisy. She was at the pub that stood a fair walk away, if I could trust my fuzzy memory, right in the middle of Avebury's gigantic ring of Neolithic standing stones.

The front entrance of the pub faced the one stone I had closed my eyes to when my colleague drove in on the Swindon road.

My stomach froze into a chunk of ice at the thought. The chill had nothing to do with the nasty weather and caused the baby-fine blonde hairs on my arms to rise in unison. How I would have loved to slip back under the warm covers. Instead, I stood under the steaming shower until my eco-conscience ordered me to turn it off.

I was still frozen to the core.

It didn't help that the aftermath of my night still haunted my day. Roses, ladders, and shapeless forms diving through tea-colored waters had troubled my dreams, leaving behind a fuzzy taste on my tongue. Brushing my teeth took care of the problem, but fantasizing about tea reminded me of the housekeepers, so I proceeded downstairs.

"What do you reckon she'll do, Alma?" A female voice with a Wiltshire burr came from the kitchen.

"Sell this place." Same strident tones, different pitch.

"That's our rotten luck again, isn't it, Alma?" said the first voice, defeated.

I pushed through the swing doors and with fake cheer greeted two round faces framed in permed brunette curls. The Simpkins sisters were middle-aged, their stocky forms plain and their suspicion about my plans bang on target.

My mood, which hadn't been the best anyway, curdled.

"Morning, Miss. I'm Cecily, this is my sister, Alma. You be

wanting your breakfast?" She wore a pink acrylic frock, while her sister had chosen sapphire blue. Cecily had to be the older of the two, to judge by the starburst of wrinkles around her birdlike eyes. Both sisters showed careworn expressions from a life full of hard work and few rewards.

"Do you need any help?" I asked.

"Oh no, t'wouldn't be right," Alma said. Her gaze was sharper than her sister's, her mauve lipstick bleeding into the tiny lines framing her lips.

They must have fed the cat. Tiddles was curled up on one of the hardwood chairs, snoozing.

Cecily jiggled the frying pan waiting on the hob. "How do you take your eggs, then?"

Outside the kitchen window, the dark shape of a van appeared, accompanied by the crackle of tires on gravel and a misfire. A car door banged, followed by the hollow roll of another sliding open.

Alma threw open the back entrance to the kitchen to a ruddy-looking youngish man with mud-streaked jeans carrying stacks of cardboard containers on his arms. They were full of eggs, making me wonder whether yesterday's omelet indulgence had caused a catering crisis.

"What's this, Marty? We need bacon and sausages, not more eggs." Alma said. "We're drowning in them as it is."

I tuned out the ensuing argument and instead watched the two small boys who sprinted into the kitchen, one making the sound of an airplane taking off, the other one trying his best to mimic the van's engine. They raced past the cupboards until they nearly collided with a grim-looking Cecily.

"Told you before, stay out of here."

They were identical twins, ginger-haired, freckled and blue-eyed, their small faces alert with ferrety intelligence. I guessed they were around five years old and most likely the Burns offspring Chris had warned me about. Small children had never been my forte; my pupils were in their teens. They gave me a different type of headache—one I was ready to tackle. Still, the noisy twins blew like a fresh breeze through the cobwebs in my brain, and I caught myself smiling. When the one in the blue-striped pullover waved around an object the size of a stick of chewing gum, I stretched out my hand.

"Care to show me?"

"Mine." The boy jumped backward, dropping his toy.

His brother, clad in a green-striped pullover, darted across to snatch it up, howling triumphantly. "Gotcha. Now I've got two You See Bee sticks and you none." He stuck out his tongue and ran outside, pursued by his screaming sibling.

Cecily mumbled something under her breath before she opened the fridge and reached for the sausages.

"Trouble?" I asked.

The pan got banged on the hob. "Hah. Robbie and Johnnie are disaster magnets." Cecily pointed at the farmer who was still sparring with Alma over the groceries. "Marty's sister Jenna is a Wytchett by birth. She moved back here with her family, but the old farmhouse wasn't ready. It still isn't, but who cares." She smacked her forehead with her free hand. "They've still got their stuff in their rooms and haven't paid their bill. You want a chat with Mr. Burns." She made the name sound like an insult.

Two eggs, two sausages, and a tomato landed in the pan, followed by a piece of bread. My lack of response must have triggered the standard cooked breakfast. A quick flip of the kettle switch confirmed my suspicion.

Cecily pulled at the fridge door and addressed its interior. "One of the sales chaps always hands out these computer thingies, says they're porno items."

Alma shouted from the back door. "Promo, Cecily, promo."

Farmer Marty's grin challenged the Cheshire cat.

Cecily shrugged, removed a carton of orange juice and waggled it at me with a questioning expression on her face. I nodded, and she filled a glass. "Mrs. Coldron must have given some to these nippers to keep them quiet."

If that had been her intention, it had failed spectacularly. I retreated to the conservatory to enjoy my solitary breakfast.

An hour later, I was replenished enough to brave the village. I could have taken the car, but I felt safer on foot. The Simpkinses had kitted me out with Wellingtons and an old Barbour jacket of dubious provenance and age, which made me look suitably rustic. I followed their directions and hiked along Wytchett Farm aiming for the tree line that marked the course of the river Kennet. It was raining again, and the wind picked up, threatening to blow the hood off my head. Raindrops and not tears dimmed my vision, turning the gray shape of the distant church into a dumpy lump hard to distinguish from the surrounding huddle of houses. The church tower, squat and square, stretched for the heavens but failed to touch even the low cover of clouds. Thankfully, the stone circle was still out of sight.

Once I sloshed closer, the village reached out for me with fingers of whitewashed, thatched cottages that were giving themselves airs. Their windowpanes seemed to watch me with disdain, telling me I wasn't wanted here. But not only the windowpanes: The odd curtain was twitching, betraying the presence of human eyes. Were Avebury's streets always so empty on a Wednesday morning? It was raining, my reason argued. The lump in my stomach didn't care.

All by themselves, my feet slowed, and I came to a stop in front of a shop window. Orangey streamers snapped in the gale, accompanied by wind chimes jangling under the purple awning. I welcomed both the shelter and the respite and perused the display tastefully arranged around an amethyst geode. Sticks of incense, cute baby Buddhas, perfumes and semi-precious jewels framed various sets of tarot cards. One deck had been fanned out, the Seven of Swords lying on top. Years ago, I had read up on the stuff to impress my aunt—and reaped fake enthusiasm for my efforts. If I recalled things correctly, the card hinted at unknown opponents, theft, betrayal, and sabotage, or something along those lines.

Just what you need now.

A cold drop landed on my cheek. I wiped it off with my palm and pushed on.

When I reached the motley collection of craggy boulders that formed the ancient stone circle, they turned their soggy backs on me as they hunkered under the low skies. Could they have summoned the moaning gusts, which brought the stink of dead earthworms and manure from across the open plain? *Begone, girl, begone,* cried the wind.

I shut my ears to the wailing and headed for the Tudor façade of the pub. No matter how hard I tried to ignore the stone across the road, it kept hovering in my peripheral vision, a blemish on my soul no ritual could ever cleanse.

I made it to the pub and stomped my boots on the mat that promised a welcome. When I rattled the handle, I found the door locked.

Drat. I should have called. Daisy was probably still in bed.

With a bang, a window slammed into the wall on my right. I leaped so high I could have qualified for the Olympics.

"Myrtle?" Daisy's head appeared over an empty flower box. "What are you doing here?"

"I'm absolutely drenched. Care to let me in?"

The head withdrew, and a moment later the door opened, releasing the stale odors of last night's boozing. I followed Daisy into what appeared to be the public bar. While the small windowpanes added to the historical atmosphere, they did nothing to improve the brightness of the room. A single light burned over the bar and lit up my cousin's auburn hair once she had stepped behind the counter.

"I still need to clean. The pub opens at eleven." Daisy grabbed a glass from the drainage rack and started polishing. "Why didn't you take the car? Silly to walk in this weather." In a single movement, she flipped her thick braid over her shoulder.

Somebody had to be the beauty in the family, and it hadn't been me. No hair of mine would ever get flipped—it was too wispy and not long enough. The first white hairs had turned up prematurely, invaders in the strawberry blonde. Where Daisy's eyes were caramel-smooth, mine sported the color of stonewashed jeans. Of course, I would be the one saddled with freckles and a pale complexion. Hers was creamy and stayed that way even without fancy cosmetics. Nor did her luscious lashes need mascara while mine were invisible without. At least I topped her by half a head. In five years, when she was my age, she would find keeping her weight down even more of a challenge than I did.

"I wanted to check whether you were okay," I said. "It's all so surreal."

Daisy dropped her dishrag and disappeared behind the bar to retrieve it. "What do you mean?" When my cousin reappeared, she was wringing the striped cloth between her hands. "Mum's gone forever." Her voice quivered, and then firmed. "The police should leave me alone."

Everything was always about her. "Yes, but what was she doing in the blasted attic?"

Daisy took up her polishing again. "Don't ask me. There's nothing but old stuff up there, right?" She gave me a speculative look and toyed with the chain around her neck where little pendants tinkled under her touch. I spotted a silver bunny, a futuristic key, a sparkly cross and something that looked like the luxury version of a mariner's knot. All very cute.

A frown wrinkled Daisy's smooth forehead. She opened her mouth as if to speak and then closed it again. When words finally came, they were slow and measured, unlike her usual breathless tones. "You should know why mum kept obsessing about the place. You're the one she talks to. I wish she'd found some cash. I'm broke."

Daisy always was broke. My aunt had bailed her out a few times and grown increasingly frustrated with her daughter's shortcomings.

Either I didn't excel at the poker face, or my cousin knew me too well. "You have no idea." She flung her dishrag next to the beer pumps. "If I don't come up with the cash, I'm toast. I was hoping..." The lips trembled and a sob escaped. "Look, it was kind of you to come, but I feel like shite."

Considering her mother died yesterday, she was doing remarkably well. My heart went out to her. "If money's a problem, I can bung you a tenner. Otherwise, you're not alone in this, you know?"

My cousin barked a sharp laugh. Then she straightened. "I'll take anything, thanks." While I fished for the note in my wallet, she dug in her pockets and removed her car keys. "I'll drive you. It's chucking it down out there."

Touched by her offer, I followed my cousin out of the bar

and into a downpour. On the short trip back, the atmosphere in the car was too dense for words, because I was scared, and she was preoccupied. After a short—and thankfully uneventful—journey, we parted with a brief hug that allowed for minimal contact only. Then Daisy returned to her petrol-guzzling wreck and accelerated, gravel spurting.

As I dashed toward the porch, I heard a voice from behind. "Excuse me?"

I swung around and beheld a prim-looking, elderly lady in a hooded mackintosh waiting by the black-and-white B&B sign that guarded the car parking. "Would you be Eve's niece, by any chance?"

"Uh, yes, I am."

She crunched across the gravel and stopped in front of me. A faint sweetish scent I couldn't identify drifted into my nostrils. "I'm Gloria Mornings. I wanted to express my condolences. Your aunt will be sorely missed, I tell you. If you need help, visit me any time. I live across the road." She pointed at a semi-detached built of the local dark brickwork, its garden filled with colorful gnomes arranged in regimental order, their bulbous noses dripping with moisture. Her eyes reminded me of bluebells. But bluebells are harmless. Something in Mrs. Mornings' tense stance told me she wasn't.

She shifted her weight. "Will you be taking over?" she asked in a confidential whisper, her eyes darting first left, then right.

Standoffish earlier, the village now tried to reel me in. "Eh, better not. I'd probably burn things."

She recoiled, her eyes flickering. "Burn things?" The odor thickened and I found it hard to breathe. With a sniff, Mrs. Mornings whirled around and splashed away, never once looking back.

For a moment, I stood in the rain, dazed, until water ran down my neck and I bolted to safety. The over-perfumed old biddy with the gimlet eye had spooked me, but she didn't throw me off track.

Even I could spot a clue when it bit me in the patootie. It was time to explore the attic.

5

JUMBLE SALE

Somewhere a window had to be open—a draft played with the folds of the curtain in the corridor, rustling the police barrier behind me.

Once I had unlocked the door, I slipped into the landing. Everything looked as I remembered it from yesterday: the shape outlined in chalk that had haunted my dreams, the aluminum stepladder, the open trapdoor. Today, no sunlight brightened the rafters. Instead, the small space was coached in shadows despite it being midday, and I fumbled around for a light switch. While the lamp didn't improve the gloom by much, it highlighted the door to auntie's room.

Shouldn't you start here?

Made of honey-warm pinewood, unspectacular regardless of its exquisite carpentry, the panel might as well have been a steel barrier. With death, all privacy ends, and our deepest secrets get dragged out into the open for greedy eyes to see. It's the ultimate violation. I would have to pry if I wanted answers. Auntie might well have hidden a message among the boxes of memorabilia she kept in her bedroom. But not yet, not now. The attic I could cope with. Her room was too much.

I swallowed hard as I positioned the ladder under the trapdoor and started upward, one hand and foot at a time.

Once my head was above floor level, I looked around at a bog-standard attic and a dusky one at that. I flipped on the light switch mounted on the nearest pillar.

A colorful clutter covered the rough wooden planks. From rickety nightstands, trunks, open boxes full of clothes to suitcases, piles of bricks, a broom, and stacks of old magazines, the roof space was crammed with junk.

I pulled myself through the opening, and the floorboards creaked under my weight. Trails tracked through a dark powder mixed in with the dust, which I presumed had been left by the cops. I followed in their footsteps, from the suitcases to a row of old files, and from the piles of firewood (what were they doing up here, other than being an incendiary hazard?) to the magazines and bricks piled against the bigger of the two chimney stacks. Behind it, I spotted an old chair even more hideous than the sofa below, its dusty green upholstering reeking of mildew. The seat sagged in the middle, and when I kneeled, I saw parts of the stuffing hanging out below. A too-obvious hiding place. I sneezed.

The cobwebs made me hesitate, but only for a moment. Surely no self-respecting black widow would take residence in a British attic? I prodded the inside of the chair with my fingertips—and hit a nest of powdery horsehair. Law enforcement had been here before me. Somehow, they had been far more conscientious about their job than I had given them credit for.

I rose again and would have scratched my head had my fingers not been so grubby. What in the world had Aunt Eve been doing up here? Bats perhaps? Endangered species would have ranked high on my aunt's agenda, straight after the plants. However, given the lack of guano, the idea was most likely wrong.

Behind me, a floorboard creaked.

I shot around, but I was alone in the attic, alone with the dust motes dancing in the slight breeze—and my memories.

"You're special," Aunt Eve had said on my eighteenth birthday, the light of the setting sun glittering in her eyes. "You have a gift. We all do."

"We? What gift?" I had braced myself for another lecture

on energy flows and herbal medicine. Occult mumbo jumbo, entirely at odds with the rational person she otherwise was.

When she continued, my aunt was addressing the trees outside, not me. "Your parents didn't want theirs. You're like them. You block your emotions. Too brainy for your own good."

She turned around, those tiny sparks again in her eyes. "I'm sorry, I shouldn't have said that."

She had brought back the pain, and I wanted to hurt her in return. "No. Do me a favor and stop blathering about that hobby of yours."

"Myrtle, I won't force you. I can't. I can't even tell you. It would destroy everything."

Of course. The mystery monger at work.

The vision faded and another one replaced it: flames crackling in my head, distorted shadows writhing in the front seat of a car, the stink of burned flesh.

I bit down on a sob and yanked myself back to the present. Shivering in the draft, I found myself drenched in sweat and with a metallic taste on my tongue.

From somewhere in the attic came a tinkling sound. It was a cheerful mechanical tune, much beloved once, but forgotten since.

The sweat became a coat of ice.

"Hello?"

The music continued unconcerned. It issued from below a curtain of moth-eaten sheets covering the back wall. Reason argued I couldn't be hearing those strains. My ears told me otherwise. Tugged along by an invisible cord, I pushed aside the sheets. The tune petered out.

On top of a box filled with old toys sat my old Playmobil carousel. One of the pink horses quivered, then stilled. The toy had been a bone of much contention between Daisy and me. At ten, it was too babyish a toy for her. She craved it out of sheer spite, knowing how much I cherished the memories of my previous life. Because of our fights, the mechanism broke, and the tune was lost.

I sensed the current again, stronger than before as if I was standing close to a hidden opening.

Now I was imagining things like I had imagined the music. "Pull yourself together," I hissed through gritted teeth, retreating toward the trapdoor.

In the bowels of the house, I heard a rumble of a washing machine going into its final spin. It was a call from the real world. Attic dust in my nose and the echo of my pain in my head, I scrambled down the ladder faster than I should have. Then I rushed back into the corridor without bothering to lock up behind me.

Let the police think what they want.

I wanted to get out.

My legs carried me all the way down to the kitchen, where Alma and Cecily were packing up for the day. It must have been their sensible if penetrating tones that had pulled me here. Alma was carrying a foil-wrapped casserole dish to the fridge when she spotted me.

"Ah, Mrs. Bingham has left this for you. Carrots and beef. She came to pay her condolences while you were out."

"How kind of her. You must be talking about the lady across the road. Gloria, I think is her name?"

"No, that would be Mrs. Mornings. She's a newcomer."

I took that to mean the good woman had lived in the village no longer than half a century.

Alma placed the offering in the fridge. A dangerous pattern was emerging. First, I accepted a casserole; next, I would be decorating the church altar along with the rest of the Women's Institute. But the gift had been meant kindly, and I would need to start a list of people to invite to the wake or whatever it was my aunt had planned.

The Simpkins sisters were shrugging into their coats when I didn't want them to leave. I gave voice to the thought that clamored the loudest, "Will you be back tomorrow? I know Mr. Hunter and Mr. Lentulus are the only guests, but I need you here."

"Of course. And there's three of them. Mr. Norton of VaniShine Triple Glazing is arriving tonight," Cecily said. "He knows his way around. Key is in the hanging basket out front."

Not only was the Witch's Retreat the do-it-yourself version of a bed and breakfast, but it also favored an open-door policy.

"Tell me something, what is Constable Hunter's issue with Chr—Mr. Lentulus? I get the impression he doesn't exactly like the bloke."

Alma buttoned her gray trench coat, shiny at the elbows but otherwise immaculate. "Mr. Lentulus is a gentleman. Bit of a dark horse, but Mrs. Coldron grew to like him, I think. He did stuff for her. In the end, he was around a lot."

"Always bobbed in and out, he did," Cecily said. "He told me his customers are all scattered across the UK. Had to stay in the Crystal Dawn once, for we had no space left."

Alma's bird eyes twinkled merrily. "Served him right."

"Would you have any idea why my aunt hired him?"

Alma shrugged. "She told us she wanted an expert, and there he was. The copper came much later."

What would my aunt need an IT specialist for? That was assuming she had hired the man for his computer skills. "Expert" could mean anything.

Cecily fastened a plastic headscarf over her poodle curls. "You're not fair with the constable. He's spice guy. Helps me with the hoover."

"Nice guy, Cec. Farm-born, that one." Alma said. "He's got ideas above his station. For the likes of him, the only way is up."

Bingo, I had been spot-on with my observations of poor Alan.

Alma tutted. "One of them days I'll forget my head." She removed a sheet of paper stuck to the fridge with a magnet. A witch's pointy hat, why was I not surprised? It was no message from auntie, though. The fridge had been pristine when I arrived. Alma rummaged in her handbag, found her reading glasses and donned them. "There's been a few things going on while you were out." Her intonation made it sound as if my explorations of the attic had taken me to faraway places. Well, it had felt like it.

"Sergeant Widdlethorpe would like to have a word with you at the St. Leonhard's Way Police Station. That's in

Swindon. And your cousin turned up half an hour ago. Wants you to call the solicitor about the will. Anyway, I've noted both numbers."

"Daisy drove me across from the pub this morning. She could have told me."

Alma pursed her mouth but said nothing.

"She keeps forgetting things," Cecily explained. "Poor girl just lost her mother."

"Hah," said Alma and reached for her purse.

This time, I didn't stop them. To fight the oppressive stillness that settled on the house when the front door had closed behind their solid backs, I busied myself with making appointments. The solicitor was flexible. Sergeant Sarah was harder to get hold of.

While I was waiting for a response from the cop shop, my gaze fell on the row of flowerpots with the sad remains of the primulas. The pot on the right, closest to the sink and standing in a puddle of foamy dishwater, showed a tiny nub of green. Could it be possible? I got up and checked. Yes, there was a small sprout on one side where yesterday there had been none. I picked up the watering can and doused all the wrinkled corpses while listening to the white noise coming from the phone.

A disembodied voice eventually confirmed Sergeant Widdlethorpe could see me at four today. If I wanted to give the solicitor half a chance at explaining things properly, I had better get cracking. Back up the stairs I went and was about to reach for the doorknob when I noticed something lying on the floor.

A pink rose petal. Fresh, this time.

The rose petal lay in the cradle of my palm, weightless, its marzipan smoothness full of life. Still, my hand was as heavy as my heart.

"Aunt Eve?" I whispered.

I noticed the door to my room stood open a tiny crack. I had closed it before searching the attic. Or had I? The thoughts darted away when I tried to grab them. I let them go. The petal still in my palm, I gave the panel a push and allowed it to swing wide but waited on the threshold before entering.

The room was tidy, even more than before. While I had been in the attic, the Simpkins sisters had worked their magic and left behind a neat-looking space. But it wasn't their presence I sensed. Something, or somebody, had come in after them and that person had tainted the air molecules. Call me silly, but there was something menacing, spooky.

My gaze fell on the two beds and I froze.

They were covered in a flurry of pale pink petals.

My hands shot up in defense.

The petal I was holding dropped from my palm and sailed down to the floor.

My heart thundered away.

I'm still alive, still here.

Twice, the sun peeped from behind the clouds and disappeared again while I stood in stunned disbelief, not daring to twitch, worrying who might be watching me.

There are no ghosts and you know it. This has to be the work of a schemer.

Slowly, ever so slowly, my heartbeat calmed down.

I should move rooms, shift my belongings downstairs. All I had to do was chuck out the Burns's clutter or nick Number Two from the Ragworts as long as they were gone.

Don't just cave in. Nothing has happened. And nothing will if you remember to lock your frigging door.

Who said inner voices were helpful? Mine was a beast, but more often than not it was right.

I threw open the window, gathered the petals and let the gale blast them all away.

A cat's lick over the sink, deodorant, and a fresh tee took care of my funky odor and a few of the jitters. The cleanup didn't allow me enough time for mascara and makeup. I left my blotchy face *au naturel,* the freckles standing out like bruises. All I did was yank a brush through lanky hair in need of a wash, hairspray, and other things that couldn't be further from my mind.

I swapped my green fleece for a purple cardigan slightly

more presentable, squeezed into black ankle boots that had seemed like a good idea when I bought them and clomped outside. I even rattled the chrome knob twice to reassure myself the door was indeed closed. On the first floor, doubts overcame me, so I dashed back up and rattled some more.

The door was still closed, with the keys weighing heavy in my pocket.

Back on the first floor, I thought of Alan. And Chris, but thoughts of Alan came first. He should know about the petals. I rushed along the corridor, raised my hand to knock on Number Three, only to drop it again.

From the closed door to Number Four, Chris's room, came the plinking of a piano concerto that clashed with the free jazz apparently favored by Alan. It was not their musical preferences that made me hesitate but the imagined conversation with Alan ringing in my mind. I had watched heaps of cop series. I knew the drill.

"Okay, so you found the beds in your room covered in rose petals. Was anything stolen?"

"No."

"Anything disturbed?"

"Nothing I'm aware of. Just the petals. Though this means somebody must have a spare or a skeleton key."

"Are you sure you locked Number Seven before you left it?"

"Eh, no."

"Any idea who might have been in your room?"

"The Simpkins sisters when they cleaned it. But they wouldn't strew rose petals over the beds."

"Why would anybody bother?"

"To scare me, I daresay."

"Scare you why?"

"Don't know yet."

"Can I have a look at the offending petals?"

"No, I threw them to the winds."

Alan's imagined skeptical expression vanished once I reached the sitting room. I searched the shelf for a map of the area because the free navigation app on my phone had the nasty habit of sending me down forest paths, onto railway tracks or into rivers.

A shadow darkened the window to my right. My head snapped up.

A distorted face, nose squashed flat, grinned at me like an evil imp.

My breath stuck in my chest and there was a ringing in my ears.

The face retreated, leaving its impression on my retina. My brain jumped in, helpful for once.

One of the Burns twins.

I sank onto the settee while my lungs released their stranglehold on the air. The tears resurfaced. My aunt was dead, and the remains of her life were dragging me under. Surrounded by mystery, my old friends from uni married and busy with their offspring, and my friendly colleagues miles away, I had nobody to talk to apart from two middle-aged caretakers.

Something clicked along the wooden floor behind me.

A "mrrp?" sounded on my left, followed by a warm body plopping onto my lap.

Sharp claws kneaded my jeans-clad thighs.

An unholy stink wafted into my nostrils, reminding me my count was off by one: Two caretakers and a flatulent feline.

6

CAFFEINE FIX

Aubrey Sneldon, Aunt Eve's solicitor, awaited me in his office that sat tucked away in a winding lane behind Swindon's magistrates' court. What had to be the outcome of many business lunches oozed in layers over the too-tight collar of the man's expensive shirt. While I was trying to get comfortable in the hard steel and leather visitor's chair, Sneldon sank into a padded spaceship. The rose petal incident had pushed aside all thoughts of food, which returned with a vengeance. As I sipped the tepid water provided by the solicitor's secretary, my stomach growled.

The solicitor pulled at clunky cufflinks that reminded me of the metal ice cubes on offer at posh kitchen outfitters. He then straightened the paperwork on his desk and, when he missed the exact right angle, rearranged the files again. Through the half-open window came traffic noise and greasy smells from the pizza place at the corner, which made my stomach even more unhappy.

"Ms. Coldron." It was a statement, not a question. Sneldon's voice was pleasant, a mellifluous baritone. "Please accept my condolences at your adoptive mother's untimely passing."

At first, I misunderstood him and heard "untidy." I bit

off a remark when I realized my mistake. Instead, I plastered an attentive expression on my face that I hoped would pass muster. It must have since the solicitor nodded and opened one of his carefully positioned files.

"Eh, here's your mother's testament. It's not up to my standards, I'm afraid. She first contacted me a few weeks ago and wanted to achieve so much more, but I urged her to at least address a few basic points. In hindsight, I would say a good move, don't you think? Otherwise, she would have died intestate."

"May I ask why that would have been a problem?"

Sneldon leaned back in his chair, which huffed in protest. "In that case, the estate would have been shared between you and your adoptive sister. I understand Ms. Daisy Coldron finds it difficult to, ahem, make ends meet. I also was made to believe things had gone from bad to worse recently. Mrs. Coldron wanted to secure a living for her biological daughter. Unlimited access to substantial funds would not have achieved her goal, or so I understand." Auntie's solicitor tilted his head but didn't get far because his solid neck was in the way.

"What would, then?"

Sneldon leaned forward, and his chair sighed with relief. "You. She wants you to settle in Avebury to manage her estate, the bulk of which also goes to you. The estate includes the bed and breakfast. Your sister is to receive a monthly stipend."

Respecting my aunt's last wishes was one thing, but having my strings pulled something else.

Sneldon must have misinterpreted my expression, for he pushed a green folder at me. "There's no need for you to worry about the business side for the moment. Mrs. Coldron employed a contact of mine as a financial advisor. He's prepared an overview of the assets and will be in contact."

The dossier slid across the desk.

I opened the document, looked at the bottom line and nearly whistled. Those strings came with a hefty bonus. Despite her funny hobbies, Aunt Eve had been a shrewd businesswoman on top of being a gifted journalist. From what I could tell, she had sailed the rough seas of the stock markets and ended up on Treasure Island.

"What if I don't accept?"

Sneldon sniffed as if something smelly was stuck to his precious documents. "You would have to, eh, concede to accept the arrangements for half a year. Afterward, you're free to do what you like with your inheritance, apart from the stipend for your sister, of course. That's non-negotiable. As long as you keep the bed and breakfast, your sister is to be given a room there. That's it. Not entirely to my satisfaction, but then we had merely started working on her estate plan when she left us so unexpectedly."

The headmistress had given me a week, not half a year. "Fine, but let's assume I'm not in a position to stay here. What happens then?" Another sniff followed, more pronounced than the first one. "The estate gets split fifty-fifty. But I assure you, this is not what Mrs. Coldron intended."

At least I wouldn't get disinherited. But that wouldn't have been auntie's style. "Thank you. I need to think things over. Tell me, when did she first contact you?"

"Let me see." Sheets rustled. "Ah, here. She contacted me on the twenty-fifth of March. That's not even three weeks ago." Sneldon looked up, a slight frown on his forehead. "Such a hurry is never prudent."

Dazed, I wondered what could have forced my methodical aunt into taking such desperate measures. That she had not made a will before I could understand. She always wanted Daisy and me to share and took it for granted I would deal fairly with her daughter. I reached for the water, but my glass was empty, much like my stomach, which again rumbled in protest. "Is my cousin aware of these details?"

"Eh, no," Sneldon said. "However, she knows Mrs. Coldron made a will. Actually, she rang me a couple of times. The last time she did so this morning. Mrs. Coldron was very clear here. Ms. Daisy Coldron was not to be informed about the exact nature of the arrangements before you had been briefed."

"Oh?"

"She trusted you to act on her behalf. Mrs. Coldron gave me the distinct impression that by controlling her younger daughter's inheritance, she could protect her from something."

"Or somebody?"

Sneldon inclined his head as far as it would go. "Or that."

What on Earth did Daisy get herself mixed up in? And how could Aunt Eve confront me with such an impossible choice? I found it hard to follow the solicitor's voice when he droned on about probate. The word "funeral" woke me up.

"Your mother made arrangements with a funeral home here in Swindon. Here's the address." He pushed a cream-colored business card bearing a silver feather at me. "They'll take care of, uh, matters once the body is released."

"Thank you," I said.

His duty done, Sneldon steepled his hands once more. "Is there anything else I can help you with?"

I would have to ask, even if it made me sound needy. I pointed at the files. "Is that all?"

The solicitor compressed his small, prissy mouth.

"Not regarding money. I mean, some message for me? A letter or a note from my aunt? She always wrote everything down. Yes, she made a will, but she contacted me the day before she died, and I had no time for her. Somehow, I would have expected a personal note."

The pudgy fingers spread wide but seemed to get dragged down by the clunky cufflinks. "These papers are all I have. If she left further instructions, they are not with me."

I made appeasing noises, whereupon Mr. Sneldon handed over his business card and escorted me to the door. I stepped onto the pavement, and there I stood, watching the pedestrians rush past, my head still in a whirl.

Somewhere, in the distance, a clock chimed the quarter-hour. I looked at my watch. It was time to head for the cop shop. Across the street, a Starbucks beckoned, so I fortified myself with a double cappuccino to go, a chicken wrap, and a croissant filled with nougat before heading out.

Navigation apps can be useful, assuming they are willing to cooperate. For once, mine did. It guided me to St. Leonard's Way Police Station via the main road. When I signaled to turn,

I spotted the empty containers on the passenger seat.

Now you're eating on autopilot.

It was a shame the nougat was now nothing but a sticky-sweet memory on my tongue.

The police were customer-friendly and provided off-street parking, so I slammed the door of my clunker three times until it closed and headed for a nondescript brick building reminiscent of a middle-class enterprise going on shabby. Prodding a stubborn piece of lettuce that had got wedged in my teeth with my tongue, I climbed a set of stairs and found myself in an off-white, air-conditioned environment reeking of old cheese and unwashed bodies.

Constable Hunter, who was leaning against the front desk and chatting with the copper behind it, wasn't guilty of the odor crime. He looked fresh and smelled faintly of apples, which I noticed when I stepped up.

"I'm to be your welcoming committee," he said, a sudden smile crinkling the corners of his eyes.

"Don't tell me you came in just because of me?"

Alan laughed. "Nah, don't worry. We had a bomb scare in the outlet center. Constables have to jump when their superiors blow the whistle, shift or not. A false alarm, fortunately."

Alan was wearing body armor over his light blue shirt and dark blue trousers, the number 322 stitched in silver on his shoulder pads. He looked nice. He had before, but now he looked even better, giving even grieving little me a pang in my heart. I wondered what made men in uniform special.

Alan addressed the bloke behind the counter, a towheaded young man whose nose must have been broken at least once. "Did the Sarge say anything about where to take Ms. Coldron?"

"Nope. But given interview room number one is the only one available, she doesn't have much choice."

"Why's that?" Alan asked. "Two is much more pleasant, I dare say."

"Two's off-limits, mate," the other copper said. "If you read your memos once in a while, you'd know."

"I'm rushed off my feet."

A grin split the other copper's face. "It's a hard life, innit?"

Alan gave him a grim smile.

The cop with the broken nose sighed. "Forget it. Just take her to Number One. A junkie barfed all over the other one. Shouldn't have been in there in the first place, but there you go."

We went into a place featuring scuffed walls, worn gray floor tiles, and cheap furniture. Thankfully, it smelled of nothing worse than stale air and stagnant water. Alan disappeared to fetch first a cup of coffee and then the sergeant. I used the opportunity to prod the obstinate piece of lettuce stuck between my teeth.

When it came, the brew was weak and tasted of curdled milk, so I pushed it away. Sergeant Sarah turned up the same moment, dressed in a smart black pantsuit, her dark hair bristling like a sea urchin. She sat opposite me, placing an anemic brown file on the table.

"Thank you, Ms. Coldron, I'm glad you could make it. There have been developments I wanted to share with you." After promising news, she didn't deliver. Instead, she fell silent and stared at her perfect nails.

I waited, and when nothing happened, sketched a wave. "Hello?"

The sergeant folded her hands, looked me in the eyes and smiled lopsidedly. "You won't like my intel."

We had hardly started the conversation, and we were already heading for the wall. "That's for me to decide, isn't it?"

"True." She licked her lips, her immaculate fingers tapping on the file.

I forced myself not to look at it and concentrated on the policewoman instead. She was likely not much older than me. My guess was early thirties; my aunt must be one of her first cases as lead.

The sergeant spoke again. "You're right. I find this rather hard to do. Please, promise you'll hear me out, okay?"

"Sure."

"I'm very sorry, but our investigations couldn't establish any evidence of third-party involvement in your aunt's death. I want to spare you the details, like the report I got from the pathologist."

"Please don't. I need to know." The dithering made me

edgy and less inclined to cut her any slack—either that or the stubborn remains of my snack were making me cranky.

"Well, if you insist. Tell me if it gets too much, will you?"

I nodded.

"Right then. Your aunt experienced compound fractures of her extremities, consistent with having fallen from a reasonable height. Reasonable in this context meaning at least the attic floor. Or even higher, actually."

"Higher? That's not possible."

"No. But her injuries were severe. Our experts are pretty baffled, believe me."

For a moment, neither of us spoke. I wrestled with the silly vision of my aunt skydiving and crashing through the roof when the sergeant continued. "In any case, it wasn't enough to kill her. Nor was it the internal hemorrhaging."

My gut cramped and the sour sting of bile and half-digested chicken wrap rose in my throat. Fair enough, Sergeant Sarah had warned me. At least the bit of lettuce had lost its grip on my molar.

She must have seen my expression and hastened to add more. "Please, Mrs. Coldron didn't suffer, not much at least. She passed away reasonably quickly after her fall. Also, the shock would have numbed her. I know it's a small blessing, but the doc was clear on that point."

"But she didn't die at once."

"Well, no. Mr. Lentulus tried his best to save her. He told us her skin felt cold to the touch, the pulse was all over the place, and she had breathing problems. Also, your aunt seems to have been unconscious all the time he was with her. She wouldn't have felt much pain. She just slipped away."

I braced myself for the worst while I waited for the response to my next question. "What killed her, then?"

7

SAD TRUTH

"Our doctor thinks she died of organ failure due to septic shock. This, in turn, must have been the result of a skin infection most likely caused by pricking her hands on a thorn. Or digging in contaminated soil. Well, something along those lines."

Another closed case.

Once more, the sergeant proved she was worth her police officer's salary and interpreted my expression correctly. "When searching for evidence of third-party involvement, we found a lot of prints other than your aunt's in the attic. We printed all the guests, but their fingerprints don't match any we found. Most of them are smudged or too old, anyway. Trust me, nobody has wiped anything down either. That happens a lot. People are convinced they're smart, but if there's an attempt at concealing evidence, there's usually a reason for it.

"But the attic itself is not the problem, the trapdoor is. We checked it for DNA and fingerprints. By the way, no, we didn't forget the bolt. Or the pole. Only Mrs. Coldron's fingerprints showed up. Since the thing can only be bolted on the outside, she must have been alone. Suddenly, her blood pressure dropped and she fell. The doc says normally patients are in massive pain and seek medical help. But if other things weighed on her mind, she might not have. Hence the accident ruling."

What the sergeant described sounded familiar. Once, Aunt Eve interviewed a politician while suffering from double pneumonia and running a life-threatening fever. "But I still don't get the bit with the injuries. Like you said yesterday, to bolt the trapdoor she would've needed to stand very low on the ladder."

Sergeant Sarah rose and walked to the bare window. From what I saw through the closely spaced bars painted a dirty white, it overlooked a dingy concrete courtyard filled with three unmarked vehicles in muted colors and a meat wagon.

"Correct."

I tried another tack. "My aunt didn't fight with anyone? In the attic, I mean?"

"She wouldn't have been fit enough. Plus, there's no evidence."

Was that her mantra, or what?

"Other than some plant matter, there was no residue under your aunt's fingernails. No, I'm sorry, but somehow she must have bolted the trapdoor before her blood pressure dropped, she fainted and suffered an unfortunate fall. The doctor thinks the odd injuries might have been caused by cramping, though he didn't want to be quoted on that. That's the only explanation we have. It's not impossible, you know?"

When the sergeant faced me, there was a tick in the corner of her eye. "I'm very sorry to tell you this isn't a murder investigation anymore. I agree it's all rather odd, but there you go."

That comment was one morsel of bad news too many. My head channeled a pressure cooker with a stuck valve, and Sergeant Sarah's last words blew through the blockage.

"Odd? That's all you have to say?"

"Ms. Coldron, please..."

"I find it odd my aunt made a will in a mad rush before she even fell ill. A will where she staggers my cousin's inheritance to stop her or somebody else from getting at the cash. I find it even odder that Aunt Eve rang me on the day before her death, talking about not letting 'him' win. Oh, guess what, the biggest oddity of all: Today when I entered my room at the bed and breakfast, somebody had strewn rose petals over my beds. Given what you told me about the likely causes of the sepsis and the petals I saw on the scene, this can't be a coincidence."

My throat burned from screaming and my environment disappeared into a teary haze. I slumped in my seat and a tissue was pressed into my hand. The next thing I noticed was a door opening while the sergeant instructed somebody in the corridor. The door closed again. I kept sniffling into my tissue.

Firm fingers patted my shoulder.

"Ms. Coldron, please try to calm down. We're aware of the will. And yes, the hurry struck me as weird. Unfortunately, your cousin wasn't available for questioning and now the investigation is closed. The phone call I wasn't aware of either."

She fell silent and guilt washed over me. With a final sniff, I wadded up the tissue. "Sorry for the outburst. I'm not usually such a watering can."

"No worries."

A knock sounded on the door. A policewoman in uniform armed with a glass of water entered the room.

Grateful, I drank.

The sergeant waited until I had swallowed the fresh fluid. "About the rose petals. Yes, it sounds rather outlandish. Let me guess, the door to your room was open and anybody might have entered."

"Probably."

Sergeant Sarah pursed her lips. "Okay, let me talk to my DI. But this is all very inconclusive. And investigations cost public money. My gut tells me there might well be more than what we're seeing now. But I can't reopen the case based on a hunch. Isn't there anything else you remember?"

I shook my head.

Sarah's impeccable nails drummed on the scratched table. It was gray like the walls. Gray like my mood.

"Ms. Coldron, one more thing. Given that we originally dealt with a suspicious death, we ran a few routine checks on you and your cousin."

"I was miles away, in a classroom full of witnesses." Somehow, I had kept a bunch of teenagers interested in dead Romantic poets. The lesson had been fun. Correcting the essays less so. The phone call came straight afterward.

"Correct. Your cousin was at the pub. The landlord of the Whacky Bramble has alibied her. They were preparing the bar for lunch. In case you wondered."

She was very perceptive, though for the life of me I couldn't visualize Daisy skulking in the landing with the monkey wrench, or worse, the bouquet of death. Despite everything, she had loved her mother.

I finished my water and Sergeant Sarah rose. "I'll give you my card. If you notice anything untoward, you can also tell Hunter." An unexpected grin followed her statement. "Don't make him do something he might regret later. He wants to join the CID, but he must learn to walk before he can run."

She appeared to be a good judge of people, appeared keen to help, and I was grateful for it. I trusted her. A more seasoned officer might file me under gaga and arrange for a nice padded cell. Still, a weight lifted off my shoulders when I escaped from the cop shop into the hesitant spring sunshine.

Sorry, Aunt Eve, things went a bit pear-shaped.

I pushed the remote on my car key. When heavy footsteps approached from behind, I shot around and beheld the ubiquitous Constable Hunter, still in uniform.

He stepped aside. "Oh sorry, didn't you notice me?"

Teachers are supposed to have eyes in the backs of their head, but I hadn't been on the job long enough. "Not until now."

"Ah, in that case, my apologies. I, um..." Alan's jaw was working, but no words came out.

It had been a dreadful day, and I wanted to put my feet up. "Is there a problem?"

"Eh, yes. I'm in a bit of a pickle."

"You lost your truncheon?"

His cheerful smile crinkled the corners of his eyes. "No,

my car won't start. I've got an appointment at the pub at five o'clock. Security measures because of these burglaries, see?"

"How about the AA?"

Hunter pulled a face. "Haven't turned up yet. They probably noted the address, enjoyed a good giggle over us incompetent coppers and put me at the back of the queue. I've got a jump lead, but my colleague won't have time for another half hour. I wondered if I might catch a ride—never mind, sorry for asking."

I might not be on my best behavior, but there was no reason to take out my crappy mood on the poor constable.

"No, I'm sorry. Hop on in, then."

My good deed reaped instant rewards when he navigated me to a quicker route back into the countryside.

"How are things going?" Alan asked once I had overtaken a fleet of tractors. The stink of manure and diesel fumes filled the car, and we opened the windows simultaneously.

"Phew. It's an accident now," I said.

"Seems to be, yes. You might not agree. I wouldn't either," Alan said with his calm voice. "If there's a culprit, there's a reason. If there's a reason, the death of your relative is not so meaningless."

The sudden bout of thoughtful insight was too much. I could only nod. My eyes were tearing up again. Wordlessly, Alan unfolded a tissue and fluttered it at me.

"Thanks." I grabbed it, figuring the cop shop must order them by the ton.

With a sniff, I dabbed at my eyes, hoping Alan the bobby wouldn't arrest me for driving under the influence of grief. He didn't even look at me and busied himself with wiping first his left hand, then his right hand. I took a mental note to clean the inside of my car at the next opportunity. The steering wheel kept sticking to my hands.

"Try to remember what happened in the past few weeks." Alan wadded his issue and shoved it into his trouser pocket. "Even if it strikes you as irrelevant. There might be something we overlooked. The police aren't perfect, you know."

In the distance, the standing stones popped into view along with the thatched roof of the pub. Blast, somehow Alan had directed me to the Swindon road. When I left earlier, I had detoured via Beckhampton. As the stones grew in the distance, my insides twisted into a knot, and I decided I needed help. On my own, I would get nowhere. Sergeant Sarah might be an intelligent and sympathetic woman, but she wasn't around. The constable was.

"Something bothered my aunt. Severely."

"She didn't tell you what?"

"No. Your sergeant doesn't believe this will make much of a difference."

"Hm."

I sensed his gaze on me as I signaled and turned into the pub's car park.

"It's a shame I've got the meeting now," Alan said, with genuine regret in his voice.

The car stopped, and I kept the motor rattling along. "Can't be helped."

"Let's talk tomorrow. I don't know what crazy hours I'll be on during the next days, but we'll work something out. I'm a police officer. We'll uncover whatever is going on. Will you be okay in the meantime?"

Define okay. "Sure."

With a nod and bright smile, he clambered from the sagging passenger seat and disappeared into the pub.

Alan's enthusiasm was contagious, and while my mood didn't exactly soar, it at least lifted from the dungeons to the ground floor. He gave me hope when I needed it most—and the courage to do something else I should have done ages ago.

I turned off the engine and got out of the car. It was early evening and the road was busy, so I took a while before I managed to cross to the other side. My heart was fluttering in my chest, a trapped moth.

Don't do it. Don't do it.

I strode across the empty expanse of grass, passing a stone shaped like a horse head, and ignored the others lined up behind as if waiting for me, daring me to go on. The stone I was after sat right next to the road, half-hidden behind a giant butterfly bush, its shriveled flower pods drooping with water like unshed tears.

I had Google-mapped the place many times, but never before visited. At first, I kept my gaze on the grass. At the last moment, I looked up.

A solid wall of black seemed to stare back at me, soot from the burning all the passing years hadn't washed away. Our car, a sturdy Volvo, had careened across the road, tumbling over before it smashed into solid rock and went up in flames. I never learned what my parents were doing down here. We were living in Windermere at the time, where I had been staying with a friend. Windermere was where they'd been buried before my aunt whisked me away.

Facing the monster meant I would suffer from nightmares, but the visit was overdue, and my evasion tactics had gotten me nowhere.

"Excuse me?"

I swung around and faced a tweed-clad man. Ramrod straight, his reddish mustache flecked with gray, he stood on the grass and regarded me with concern. He dragged a brownish dog on a leash, one of those rat-like creatures with bulging eyes that broke out in a volley of shrill yaps.

"Buster be quiet. Are you Eve's niece? Gloria Mornings described you quite well."

Worry nipped at my insides, but all he did was thrust out his hand. "My condolences. I'm Colonel Elmsworth. Eve was a great person."

"Indeed." I shook a set of sinewy fingers.

He stared at the stone. "Looks rather sinister."

"Well, I'm sure you're familiar with the local history."

"Actually, no. I moved here last autumn. Arrived shortly after Gloria did."

The dog was straining on his leash. With an apologetic look, the offer to call on him anytime and a friendly goodbye, the Colonel departed. He left me alone on the darkening henge with only the wind for a companion, whispering of buried dreams.

I was shivering with cold but couldn't move. The stone that killed my parents held me, their daughter, in its thrall.

A sudden, bright light blinded me, and I shook out of the trance. Cars were rushing along the Swindon road, their headlights switching on. My teeth were chattering. I stumbled away from the henge, dashed through a gap in the traffic amid the hooting of horns, threw myself into my car and drove to the Witch's Retreat like a demented firecracker.

Once I had arrived, fortunately in one piece, I unlocked the front door, remembering to remove the spare key from the hanging basket. Then I picked up the six condolence letters lying on the mat. Inside, I heard the clicking of claws, a plaintive yowl, and a fart.

"Hello, Tiddles."

I placed the envelopes on the reception counter and hoisted the smelly animal onto my shoulder to nuzzle her furry cheek. She was warm and alive, and her purring presence helped evict the specters of my past. I nudged the swing doors aside with my hip before detaching Tiddles' claws and lowering her to the kitchen floor. First, I filled the bowl of my feline companion. Next, I checked the flora on the sill. No movement on most of them, but the one on the right had unfurled a leaf and was sprouting a second bud. If we had done nothing else, the Simpkins sisters and I between us had saved one of auntie's plants.

"Come on, you buggers." I poured more water on the lot. "You can do it." Fortunately, there was nobody but Tiddles to watch me deliver a pep talk to a row of desiccated plants.

Canned baked beans on burned toast—the gunge in the casserole dish reeked of industrial seasoning so I poured it away—helped to restore parts of my dubious sanity, but once I had admitted the latest salesman, I was too tired to do anything but retire to my room with a geriatric lump of fur for a bedfellow. Tiddles at least was happy, hogging the lower part of the duvet and leaving my ankles uncovered. None of the paperback romances that came with the room appeared even remotely attractive, and I was too wound up to read. I switched off the light and let the thoughts chase each other through my head.

Financially, I would be secure, but I would have to give up my teaching job. Should I, could I, accept those terms? By doing so, I might shift further into the crosshairs. Not that I believed in the Tarot, but the notion of a shadowy opponent spinning an evil plot fit right in with the rose petal incident.

The images in my head switched. I would have Daisy hanging around my neck like a millstone for the rest of my life.

What had happened up there in the attic, among the chairs, nightstands, and linen sheets? What made me convinced I had seen something important that didn't register at the time? My thoughts blurred and flapped across to the henge where a drunken bastard had destroyed a family.

The film playing in my head became more bizarre: dark shadows circling the roof, a jingle-jangle tune mixed in with the screeching bang of metal slamming against rock, my aunt tumbling through the skies amid a flurry of rose petals. I woke up with a start and cold legs.

"Bloody beast," I mumbled, attempting to pull the cat-heavy covers over my feet.

Then I heard it. My rude awakening wasn't caused by either nightmares or nighttime chill.

The ceiling over me creaked. Somebody was in the attic.

8

BURGLAR ALARM

With a curse, I shot from my bed. Fury flooded my veins and burned away the dregs of yesterday's frustrations. Some bastard in Avebury was playing deadly games. First, with my aunt. Now, with me. It was high time I worked out who was behind whatever was going on in this place.

A whack on the button atop the alarm clock made it glow the hour back at me. Five past two in the morning. I fumbled around in the dark for my cardigan and trousers. The Witch's Retreat was built in the early nineteenth century and, despite the recent renovations, I didn't trust the ceiling—light might seep through cracks in the plasterwork and alert the intruder. My shoes were wherever I had kicked them yesterday evening. I would have to go barefoot.

From upstairs came another creak. I cracked open the door to my room. The corridor lay empty, filled only by the moonlight filtering through the window. I tiptoed along the soft carpet to the curtain on the other side, which was no longer blocked by the police barrier. Either the sergeant had told Alan to take it down, or he had acted on his own initiative.

From above came more squeaks, a whole series of them. I pushed the fabric aside with a swish that intruded the nighttime quiet. The next moment, I realized I had forgotten the key.

"Damn."

I bit my knuckles. If I talked to myself, I might as well announce my presence by blowing a trumpet. Apropos blow, I noticed a breeze in my face, unsurprising given the door was leaned to, not closed. A split-second later, I remembered. In my panic yesterday morning, I had forgotten to lock up.

An experimental push on the panel and the door swung into a secretive gloom smelling of dust and old flowers.

One by one, shapes materialized from the darkness. The unused sofa. The maw of the trapdoor, with rays of moonshine seeping through the opening, their reflections glinting on the aluminum ladder sitting below.

My wrath flickered to ashes while I recalled countless heroines, caught between the bent covers of paperbacks or encased in the gilded tomes of literature, who ventured into a dark place and never returned.

With a parched mouth, I forced myself to catch any sound not part of the night's stillness. A cloud must have sailed across the moon; the light dimmed, and the landing disappeared into shadow, but not into silence. I heard scuffing so subdued it was almost not there.

The landing had become a trap. I needed to get out but didn't dare move. Instead, I strained my ears until they hurt.

From the attic came a muffled snick followed by a faint, cool breeze that slithered under my makeshift attire and drew goosebumps from my skin. Apart from the roaring in my head, all was calm again.

Another soft sound wormed its way into my brain, a different one this time. It originated from the corridor, not from above.

Something brushing over the carpet.

I took a step backward and collided with the old sofa. Pain shot up my ankle, and I fought down a scream.

I heard a whooshing noise in response, followed by a disgusting odor—and purring. A warm body rubbed against my bruised shin, and I swallowed a shriek.

"Tiddles, what are you doing here?" I whispered. More purring.

I pricked my ears, but the darkness above yielded no further sounds. The formidable alliance of the cat, sofa, and myself must have driven the intruder away, unless he was hiding on this floor, somewhere close. Behind said settee, for example.

Mustering the shreds of my courage, I groped along the wall until my fingers hit the nub of the switch. Was I ready for this?

A quick push and light flooded the landing.

Apart from grandma's clunky heirloom, and a bedraggled cat, the surrounding space was empty. Blessed be electricity; it was one of the better inventions of humankind. The light emboldening me, I called at the dark opening above me.

"Hello, the attic?"

Thankfully, I got no response. What would I have done, had there been one? Still, somebody had been up there, of that I was sure. How did they get out?

No matter what might be going on, nothing would get me into the blasted roof space in the small hours. Not wanting to disturb Alan, I returned to bed, making sure my room was locked. I even shoved a chair under the handle. Despite these safety measures, sleep wouldn't come. When the fuzzy gray of the new dawn lightened my room, I rose bleary-eyed and soaked under the hot shower until the skin on my fingers had gone all wrinkly, eco-conscience be damned. The moment I emerged from among the vanilla-scented steam, the orange glow of the streetlights turned off and the lid slammed on the wheelie bin in the front yard. The noises of civilization, the sounds of people. People meant safety, and Alan might be awake by now.

I slipped into jeans, a maroon T-shirt, and my green fleece. Having made sure my damp hair was halfway under control, I traipsed down the stairs and along the silent corridor to Number Three. A light knock brought no results. A more determined double rap didn't change things. The room was quiet. Either the man was asleep or on an early shift.

I turned around and faced Number Four. No signs of life from Chris either.

Perhaps the attic could wait?

My former fury rekindled. No, it couldn't.

Armed with a torch from the drawer in my nightstand, I climbed the ladder into a roof space filled with the sound of rain washing over the shingles. It was another beautiful day for waterfowl and intrepid attic explorations.

Upstairs, I flipped on the lights and put the torch in the pocket of my jacket. The place looked unchanged—no, wrong. The footsteps left behind by the police officers and the tracks made by my trainers were smudged in places as if somebody had walked around in stocking feet.

I rotated but observed no further dissimilarities, until a faint breeze flowed over my cheek. The breeze brought along the essence of spring: moist, fresh earth, a scent best described as green. The logical explanation would be an open window, but the two visible in the roof above were shut, which was good, given the lusty shower drumming down on them.

The one set in the opposite wall was a different case entirely.

Every time a gust hit, it trembled in its frame. When I fingered the handle, the locks jiggled. They weren't engaged and, with the help of the torch, I discovered a minuscule gap through which the air flowed. I pulled on the handle—and the window flew open, missing my nose by inches.

My breath halfway under control, I found dots of a whitish, rubbery substance all over the inside of the frame. Silicone was my best bet. It dried fast and would keep the window closed without it being locked, more so as the frame was slightly warped.

Sergeant Sarah's cohorts, preoccupied with fingerprints, trapdoors, and ladders, might well have overlooked this crafty arrangement. So, had I during my first visit, even if I had noticed the draft.

I stuck my head out of the window, drew a lungful of soggy air and scanned the view of the garden not blocked by the low-sloping roof of the shed. Its ridge was almost on a level with the attic window. On the right, I beheld metal treads leading to the gutter. They were probably meant for the chimney sweep. With the collapsible fire escape ladder hanging from the lowest tread, a fit and determined person would get up and down from the attic in no time.

Now I faced another problem. To close or not to close the window? If I didn't, whoever used this secret entrance would carry on. If I shut it, my anonymous foe would know I was on his tracks. On the other hand, that person most likely already did—what I had heard this morning must have been the sounds of a hasty flight when I puttered about, a flight so rapid, the intruder forgot the ladder.

"To heck with you," I mumbled and shut out the draft together with the tangy spring air.

I gave myself a mental pat on the back for unveiling part of the mystery. Still, my find didn't explain the problem with the trapdoor. I returned to the opening to peer at the now clean floorboards of the landing below and the wooden pole lying to one side, which featured a hook at the top.

A spark of inspiration struck, and I climbed down, grabbed the tool, and scrambled upstairs again. After two or three failed attempts, I pulled up the ladder. All I needed to do was to slot the hook through the inside handle and heave the trapdoor toward me until the door nestled in its frame.

Eureka. One closed trapdoor.

Closed, yes. Bolted, no. The trapdoor had been bolted when the cavalry arrived.

Botheration.

I used the pole to push the trapdoor back open, carefully lowered the ladder and sat down in the opening, my legs dangling.

The scenario with the secret entrance screamed burglar. Sergeant Sarah had mentioned them. If it hadn't been for the blasted bolt, I would've assumed they were the culprits.

No, that didn't work either. One needed to be on the inside at least once to rig the window. Still, with both the front door or the back door standing open most of the time, and convenient keys on display in flowerpots, I couldn't rule out enterprising criminals.

My head went into a spin. If not the burglars, who else could have been up here?

Daisy?

Unless she was searching for hidden treasure, she would

never think of interrupting her beauty sleep to creep around under the rafters or scramble up roofs. But whatever was bothering her might act as a game-changer. Nor could I rule out the possibility she might be operating on behalf of the people to whom she owed money. Another sisterly chat was called for.

Alan was a policeman, which counted at least one point in his favor. Initially, I had thought him clueless, but he had shown remarkable insight. From that perspective, Alan had hidden depths, and he was certainly fit.

So was Chris. He had been with my aunt when she died and something about him struck me as odd.

A niggly voice told me neither of them was staying at the Witch's Retreat by chance. My aunt might well have invited Chris, but what about Alan? I would have to be very careful here. I also needed to quiz the other guests. Some, like the Burns family and the Ragworts, I hadn't even met. The salesman in Number One I discarded. The poor chap had only arrived yesterday evening.

For a moment, I thought I heard the tinkling again, the lost music from the carousel. My head whipped around.

I notice nothing out of the ordinary, but somehow the atmosphere in the attic had shifted, appeared less green, and had become menacing, like a black cloud pressing on me. Well, it was raining again.

My gaze fell on the lower part of the door to Daisy's room. The time had come to have a little sniff.

Back down in the landing, I jiggled her doorknob. But the door was locked. No problem, I had lots of keys. I jangled my way through them but none of them fit. Perhaps I should be less surprised given this was my set. Sergeant Sarah still held on to auntie's. With nothing left for me to do, I shoved the keys back in my pocket. My stomach chose that moment to growl a reminder that I had risen before the crack of dawn and been climbing up and down the damn ladder like a rampant rodent. Before I could even contemplate further sleuthing, sustenance was needed.

Downstairs, two people occupied the breakfast room. One table had already been vacated. An empty teacup, a folded napkin, and crumbs indicated my hunch had been right and Alan had left for the early shift.

Next to the bricked-up fireplace sat a middle-aged man with a greasy comb-over, an equally oily smile and a flurry of brochures: The latest salesman, who I had never properly looked at when I checked him in. I acknowledged two minus points in the landlady department.

"Care to join me, Miss?" My new guest caught my eye and beamed a toothy smile. He waggled a brochure at me. "I would like to show you something."

A quick look at the pamphlet revealed special offers for triple glazing. That was the last thing I needed now. Security locks would've been a different story.

"Excuse me," Chris spoke from behind. "There's something I need to discuss with Ms. Coldron."

He pushed aside his bowl of cornflakes and, with a hushing of black leather trousers, he slipped into the corridor. I bounced the salesman an apologetic smile before following Chris.

"Thanks for rescuing me," I said.

"I wish I could." The smile playing around his thin lips didn't quite reach his eyes.

A hollowness spread throughout my stomach. "You have a special way of cheering people up."

The lips flatlined. "I apologize. Unfortunately, this is no laughing matter. I tried to get hold of you all day yesterday. Seems like you were out a lot."

"Yes."

Was it worth dropping a bomb and see what floated to the surface? "Out long enough for somebody to dump rose petals in my room."

His face stilled. His long lashes fluttered once. "Like the ones your aunt was lying on? You need to be careful." His voice was level, all emotion drained away.

"Because somebody is trying to scare me out of my wits? Or do you mean because my aunt is dead?"

Chris said nothing.

Nor did I. The silence between us hung heavy with meaning.

We cracked at the same time.

"It's not—" Chris said.

"What were you—" I said.

We fell silent once more.

This time, Chris was first to recover. "Oh damnation, this is all so difficult." He banged his fist on the wall before he swung back to face me. "I know I sound like a male version of the Delphi Oracle, but what can I do?"

"Tell me what's on your mind, for example."

His face turned grim. "You don't want to know. And yes, I know it sounds even more idiotic."

"It does. But I appreciate your concern."

He heaved a sigh that sounded like it came from a bottomless well. "Sure. All included in the service. I've botched this, haven't I? Perhaps you had better stay away for a while until the cops have sussed things out. Failing that, I suggest you talk to Mr. Ragwort. Let him take care." He checked his watch and rolled his eyes. "Oh blast, I'm late again. I'll be back."

With that, Chris swung around and dashed up the stairs two steps at a time.

Whatever he might have done for Aunt Eve, it had nothing to do with her bits and bytes. Quietly seething inside, I made my way to the kitchen. Only one Simpkins sister was in sight.

"Where's Cecily?" I asked, fiddling with the kettle.

"She's poorly. Migraine. Gets it every so often. One day it'll be the end of her," Alma said in a lugubrious tone.

"Can you cope?" I asked. The B&B was not full, so the workload couldn't be all that bad.

Alma sucked her teeth while cracking eggs into a pan.

That boded ill.

"The missus gave a hand last time Cec had the head," she said in a hopeful tone.

My instincts told me to dodge the unspoken invitation. The interrupted night was already taking its toll: my bones hurt, my eyes felt sanded, and I couldn't stomach whatever needed "doing" in this place. Still, the niggly voice of wisdom told me not to alienate the Simpkins sisters. The two of them might be short of cash, but they had their pride. Plus, the ladies kept this place afloat.

"Well, I'm no good at cooking. Could I help with the dishes?" I compromised.

Alma's face wrinkled into a smile, telling me I had made the right noise. "There's the dishwasher for that. But if you could start on the rooms, it would help. If you could make the beds, dust, and hoover, it would be great. Never you mind the bathrooms. I'll do them."

She fidgeted with the towel, and I sensed there was more coming.

"Number One will be leaving soon. I've prepared the bill, like Mrs. Coldron used to do, seeing you're new. But you'll have to check it. Make sure I've done things right. It's on the reception desk."

"Great, thank you for taking care. I wouldn't know where to start." I better get my act together. For a short while at least, I would have to play the landlady.

And then you're going to sack Alma and Cecily, my inner voice taunted.

Alma's eyes lit up, but before she had time to say anything, the front door slammed shut.

"That would be Mr. Lentulus. Always in a rush, that one." But her smile was indulgent.

Outside, a car started up and spurted away. Once the pebbles had settled down, an idea sprang up in my mind. Cecily's illness and Chris's and Alan's absence gave me the perfect excuse for searching the rooms of the two gentlemen.

9

SCARY LITERATURE

The vacuum cleaner snagged the cloth of the tea table loaded with tourist pamphlets, the jolt nearly tearing my arm from its socket. With a growl, I jerked at the hose, and the machine swung free to trundle after me. Not only was the hoover making a racket, but it also weighed a ton and was tricky to maneuver. Still, I had to admit the thing was efficient. I pressed the nozzle onto the carpet, and with a lusty roar the machine slurped up the dust and crumbs littering the floor.

Not a bad pastime.

I ran the nozzle under the heaters. Very satisfying, since it stopped me from mulling too much over the dratted attic, Chris's idiotic behavior or the petal incident. I vacuumed my way to the back, turned off the cleaner and unplugged it. On my right lay the door to Number Three, the room Alan stayed in. Opposite, on the garden side of the house, waited Number Four, Chris's room.

Number Two, a few meters back on my right, anticipated the return of the Ragworts. So, did I. Perhaps, Alma would know where to find them. Numbers Five and Six on the left still were crammed full of the Burns's clutter and I decided collecting debts gave me a good reason for calling at the farm. Upstairs awaited Aunt Eve's bedroom, yet another chore on a fast-growing list.

One step at a time. I pulled out auntie's keyring and faced Alan's room, then Chris's. The choice was easy. I rapped on Chris's door and when I got no response unlocked it and entered, dragging the hoover behind me.

Now that I stood inside the man's room, I felt silly. What was I doing, invading somebody's private space? Cleaning was the obvious response, but housekeeping duties were a pretense.

I glanced around a room littered by male clutter. If I vacuumed in here, the machine would suck up stray socks, crumpled papers or—well, yes, a pair of stretch trunks. I was a respectable schoolteacher; I should frown upon the disarray and leave. What I did was pick up the pieces of debris with two fingers and deposit them on the nearest chair, upholstered in apricot velour, after having hoovered its surface.

The color scheme of this room was a charming, but feminine, mix of peaches and creams, complemented by white wicker furniture. Number Four also sported a comfortable-looking settee and a glass-topped coffee table, both swamped with papers, books, and computer paraphernalia.

Despite the clutter, I rather liked the place. It was a rental, yes, but Number Four appeared almost cozy, a true temporary home. The memory of a soft scent, an exotic mixture of linen and incense permeating the atmosphere, I liked even more.

"Down, girl," I said to myself and opened the window on a stiff breeze.

After that, cleaning became easier. If the occasional handwritten note found its way into my hand, it was by coincidence.

Trust me.

Not that I stumbled upon anything relevant: the squiggles didn't resemble auntie's elegant penmanship in the slightest. The few words I deciphered gave me the impression Chris might be interested in genealogical research. He did mention he was a historian by design.

I stacked a pile of notes next to two space-age laptops and a cashmere pullover with a prestigious label—yet another item of clothing shed willy-nilly onto the floorboards. The careless treatment of expensive items made me wonder what his background might be. My family had never been short of a few pounds, but both my mother and my aunt had taught me to look after my belongings. That Chris didn't told me he was used to money. The oversized aluminum suitcase sitting on the trestle table in the farthest corner must have also set him back quite a bit.

Unfortunately, it was locked.

I noticed a book distinctly at odds with all the modern gear. Bound in smooth leather, it displayed gilded letters on the spine while leafy engravings decorated the front like an age-old tattoo. The binding and paper were artificially distressed; the whole thing was an obvious fake but still beautiful. Wondering why somebody would have bothered, I picked the book up and opened it to the marbled front page.

I recoiled. Not beautiful after all. Evil incarnate, more likely.

Unlike Chris, I was no studied historian, but given auntie's obsession with all things Wiccan and witchy, I knew enough to be disgusted.

Before me lay a copy of the *Malleus Maleficarum*. The Hammer of Witches. It mimicked the first edition published in 1487.

The *Malleus* was one of the most disastrous treatises of world literature. Printed at the dawn of the so-called age of reason, it set out to prove witches existed, and by applying certain procedures, such as torture, ensure they could be outed.

The *Malleus* became the dark bible of the witch hunters, causing the deaths of hundreds of thousands of innocent men, women, children, and even animals.

I might not be Miss Super Sleuth, but to me, it was obvious Chris's thesis must have explored yet another grim period in human history.

When a sudden brightness exploded into my eyes, I blinked. April was up to its usual tricks and the sun had come out. Even with the window shut, I heard birds chirping.

I placed the fake *Malleus* back where I had found it and headed for the bathroom to scrub invisible soot and very real dust from my hands. As a clue, the tome was a bit of an anticlimax, since it didn't tell me anything of interest. No sooner had the thought entered my head than I registered the canvas bag shoved under the sink.

I kneeled and fumbled with the zipper.

I spotted coiled ropes of striped nylon. Beneath them nestled a fancy set of crampons that looked like they might come in handy during the next ice age. Or, failing that, one could use them to clamber up slick surfaces, such as roof tiles. Another rope lay to one side, this one with three vicious-looking hooks on top. A quick surf on my smartphone taught me the purpose of the thing: When lassoed, at least one hook would always land with the pointy bit down. Two strong flashlights, assorted carabiners, an ax, and a crowbar completed the collection. My mind was racing, searching for explanations. Either Chris was a hobby mountaineer who crowbarred his way up the rock face, or he made his money by breaking and entering.

—

Confusion, regret, and anger propelled me to the door. As I was about to twist the knob, I heard a small noise outside the room.

He's back.

There was no place to hide. I would have to act my way out. At least, my trusty hoover waited at my side, the perfect alibi.

While breathless seconds ticked by, I stood utterly still, with my ear pressed to the door panel. Blood rushed through my veins, while behind me I sensed the rank presence of the sinister tome, watching me, polluting the air in the room with its evil. In the bathroom lay the tools of Chris's nefarious trade. The atmosphere grew denser and denser until standing still became impossible.

I ripped the door open, rushed into the corridor—and nearly bowled over Alma, who carried a duster and a bucket with some foamy liquid slopping inside.

She shrieked the same moment I jumped backward.

"Sorry," I said, my heartbeat somewhere in the stratosphere.

"It's all right. I tried to work out which room you were in, things being so quiet. Thank you for helping."

She was about to enter Number Four when I remembered the Ragworts.

"Hah," Alma said. "They're probably signing the contract for their new house this very moment. Friend of mine saw them with the estate agent. I reckon they'll be back latest by tomorrow. Now, you go and do your things. I'll take over from here."

Even if it meant I would have to snoop—pardon, clean—in Alan's room another time, I was glad for the respite. I needed some breathing space to sift through the chaos crowding my brain. Back in my humble Number Seven, I dropped onto my freshly made bed and crossed my arms behind my head, staring at the ceiling.

But I couldn't lie still. Invisible ants seemed to swarm over the duvet, making me twitch and shift on my bed.

Who or what was Chris really? Should I inform the police about the gear I had found in his room? By themselves, tools and climbing equipment proved nothing. If he was a bona fide hobby mountaineer, I would end up with egg on my face and a pissed-off customer on my hands. What if he had been my nightly visitor? I ditched the idea. Why would he clamber up rope ladders when he could take the stairs? Unless he had been on a training session for the next heist.

The more I thought about it, the fake *Malleus* in the Witch's Retreat struck me as bizarre. What might I find in Alan's room? In Daisy's? Or auntie's, once I dredged up the courage?

The mental roller coaster took a while to slow down, and when it did exhaustion from my sleepless night smothered my frantic thoughts. One after the other, they became dream fragments. Eventually, the babble in my mind hushed.

I napped.

I woke up to the clap of a thunderbolt. At least, that was how it sounded to my still groggy brain. The sounds of spurting gravel and a vehicle driving away made me suspect

Farmer Marty instead.

A quick check of the alarm clock revealed I had dozed for more than an hour. The rest had refreshed me somewhat, but now I suffered from a woozy head and a fuzzy taste on my tongue. I got up and flipped on the kettle sitting on my in-room tea trolley. Outside, the sun still shone. Trust me to slumber through the one sunny day of the week. Worse even, I was wasting time I didn't have. I had been given a week's leave and an ultimatum from auntie. I had better crank my backside into gear.

Steam rose from the mug and wafted toward the blasted attic. As an avid reader of mystery fiction, I knew all the tropes. I had never imagined they would one day become real. There could be only one logical explanation why the roof space was so popular: my aunt must have hidden something up there or people believed she did. Now, I needed to find out what it was, who wanted it and why. Easy peasy. No matter what might have been bothering my aunt, it must have preoccupied her so much, she ignored a painful infection. Not that I was fully sold on that theory.

The tea was still too hot to drink, so I left Number Seven and strolled to the corridor window facing the garden. Along its walls, rows and rows of daffodils mirrored the sunshine with their cheerful flowers and lush green foliage. The birches framing the place on three sides now sported a lime-green fuzz, and above it all sailed puffball clouds over skies so blue, they looked painted.

An impulse struck, and I downed my tea, burned my tongue and descended the stairs to the French doors in the conservatory. They were locked. This time a key fit, and once I had crossed the light tiles of the terrace, I was outside on the lawn. A squelchy lawn, I noted the same moment I remembered I wasn't wearing shoes.

With a sigh, I removed my now soggy socks and inspected my new environment.

"Garden shed" were not the right words for the brick annex to the house that stuck out at an angle from the middle of the main building, like a too-short stem on a T.

Once I walked past the back of the annex, the scenery

changed.

The plaster crumbling from the walls of this part of the house appeared gray rather than cream and was streaked with rust stains from leaky pipes. The pipes had been replaced, but they left evidence behind. From the walls, my gaze dropped to the ground, which was covered in gravel and lined by scruffy rhododendrons on the side facing the house. Clusters of daffodils added a bright splash of color against the dark foliage. On the far side, a narrow passage along the garden fence allowed vehicle access from the front. To my right, two steps led up to the back entrance. When I pushed the handle, the door swung inward. Alma had done it again; the back door was unlocked.

After rectifying her oversight, I looked up and saw two rows of latticed sash windows running across the width of the first floor that had to belong to Numbers Four and Five. Further up, under the roof, gleamed the windows of auntie's bedroom.

I caught a ripe whiff of refuse coming from behind me and turned in disgust. The wooden doors to the annex stood open. It housed two large commercial dustbins and a hoard of gardening and building clutter. Chalky bags of what had to be cement left behind from the renovations leaned against one side next to stacks of ratty bricks. This part of the Witch's Retreat reminded me of a poor relation, neglected and desolate.

There was one item to tick off my list. I stepped over to the side where the annex protruded from the central section of the house, its red roof tiles soaring toward the blue spring skies. Somehow, I had expected it, but my heart still jumped in my chest. The fire escape ladder had disappeared.

Without shoes, I couldn't brave either the gravel or the slippery ground inside the shed. I peeped in from the entrance. No ladder.

Had Alma removed it? Not impossible, but not likely either.

Perhaps there was a reasonable explanation for this ladder business like there would be a logical explanation for crowbars in people's luggage and rose petals scattered over my beds.

I shook myself like a soggy dog and traipsed back to the other side of the garden, the pretty one the guests enjoyed. From among the luscious grass, a white wrought-iron bench and table invited me to think things over. I accepted the offer and sat down on a metal seat that was dry but still chilly to the touch. Or rather my bum. The sun shone, a balmy breeze tousled my hair, and a pair of bright yellow butterflies tested their camouflage among the flowers, lifting my spirits with their carefree flutter. My sluggish brain awoke as well, yawned and checked in for action.

I dug for my phone and the business card Sergeant Sarah had given me.

"Swindon CID, Sergeant Widdlethorpe speaking?"

"Myrtle Coldron here. Sorry to bother you, but I think my attic has turned into Paddington Station."

"Come again?"

"Sorry. Somebody was up there this morning. I discovered an open window, glued shut with what I think is silicone. More than once, I would say. And a collapsible fire escape ladder dangling from the roof, which has disappeared now. I still need to have a word with my housekeepers. Perhaps the ladder is part of the services. Anything seems possible in this place."

The crowbar and Chris's climbing gear jumped from the back of my mind to the tip of my tongue, but I swallowed in time before the words escaped. Like the sergeant, I lacked evidence. Plus, the guy smelled nice.

A hiss of indrawn breath tickled my ear. "No way. It's got to be those darn burglars. Blast, I'm not even sure we checked the window. Somebody seems to be rather familiar with that place of yours. Was anything stolen?"

"There's so much clutter, it's hard to tell."

"Okay, if I were you, I would make sure the all entrances to the house are closed at all times. Do the guests have keys?"

"Two, yes. One for the front door and one for their room. Otherwise, the Simpkins sisters are in the habit of leaving back doors open. Also, they keep burying spare keys in flowerpots. Some regulars arrive quite late and check themselves in."

She snorted. "Quite normal for a small village. It makes me wonder why your unknown athlete even bothered with the acrobatics. Ask your housekeepers about the ladder, just on the off chance. Let me know what they said."

"Will do. Tell me, could the visitor and the funny window arrangement be connected? To what happened to auntie, I mean?"

"No idea, but I wouldn't like you to run a risk. Can't you stay somewhere else?"

"If I move, I'll never find out what is going on."

A growl reached my ear. "Don't you play Miss Marple. I'll try the DI, tell him we might have overlooked something. Not sure he will bite. He gave me an earful yesterday."

"I've got to be killed in my bed before your boss makes a move, right?"

Sarah sniggered. "If I thought you were in mortal danger, I'd drag you out of the place kicking and screaming. Okay, I'll take your statement on file. Promise me one thing—if you get attacked or threatened in any form, please call."

For a moment, we both were quiet.

"Ms. Coldron? Are you still there? I've asked Constable Hunter to keep an eye on you whenever he's around. He's our burglary liaison officer and he tells people how to protect themselves. Mention the ladder to him, he can have a look. Anyway, keep me in the loop, will you?"

"Yes. And thank you." Her words didn't make me strike Alan off my list, but he slipped down a notch. Sergeant Sarah might not be the Constable's biggest fan, but she trusted him.

And I trusted her.

10

A NIGHT OUT

My face sought the sun. Balmy spring breezes caressed my cheeks until a shadow fell across my closed eyes. When I blinked at the sky, I found it almost covered by a fluffy blanket of gray that was busy swallowing the rest of the blue. I took it to be a sign from the heavens I should stop lounging around and whipped out my phone once more.

I expected voicemail, but Daisy responded on the first ring as if she had been waiting for somebody to call. "Yes?"

Breezy and breathless, her voice reminded me of Marilyn Monroe.

"Myrtle here. Listen, cuz, we need to talk. Would you have time this afternoon? Actually, this evening might be even better. I could take you out for dinner?"

Daisy remained silent. I could nearly hear the cogs in her brain whirring and the click when the levers slotted into place. "You went to see the solicitor?"

"Yes. That's why I want to talk to you. But not over the phone."

"Mh. Suppose not. Alright, let's meet. Dinner's not a bad idea, but I suggest we stay here at the Whacky Bramble. I've got an appointment later this evening."

"You're not working?"

"No, given it's Thursday. Once in a while, I have a day off." Now, she sounded a lot less like Marilyn and more like Sharon Stone in one of her scarier roles.

"As is your right," I said mildly. "The pub works well for me. I need to be back at the Witch's Retreat by eight at the latest." The comment smacked of Cinderella, so I added, "I've got another guest coming."

Alma had left me a message.

"Ah, okay. The Bramble it is, then. Greg will do you a discount since you're family." I accepted the peace offering, agreed to meet at six o'clock and rang off.

Now what? Do battle with the Burnses? Fret over the Ragworts? I lacked the energy for either. Instead, I decided to check out the clothing situation. When placed next to my cousin I would always score second, but there was no need to put myself at an even bigger disadvantage by showing up in frumpy gear.

Unfortunately, frumpy gear was all I had packed.

I rummaged around and finally, at the bottom of the suitcase, I hit pay dirt. I put on a pair of new red chinos and a halfway decent T-shirt—black, which suited my mood. The trousers nipped my waistline. Either I had grabbed the wrong size in the shop, or my recent diet was to blame.

I clipped on the gold loops, my last-ever present from my parents, and applied eyeliner and mascara. When I looked in the mirror, the Hollywood eyes clashed with my waxy complexion. I should have washed it all off, but it was getting late. Sure, I could take the car, but walking still felt safer. No time to put on another face; this one would have to do.

I grabbed the old Barbour and headed for the fields, trundling along the same path I had taken yesterday morning. The late afternoon sun poured a golden glow over pastures and hedges, furry with the first green of spring. Soon the blossoms would erupt and draw a frothy veil over the landscape, celebrating the eternal surf of the seasons, an endless flow of hope, fulfillment, and sorrow. For my aunt, however, the tide had gone out.

The sob escaped before I could stop it. My eyes teared up, but I stopped myself from wiping them. It would be a hoot and a half if I arrived at the pub with panda eyes. The thought made me giggle, and I was glad to be alone. A crow perched on an elm tree but the bird didn't seem to mind my silly mood and cleaned its feathers instead.

"Hello, there." A deep male voice hailed me from behind. Hysteric yapping ensued.

I whirled around. Behind me on the flattened grass stood the tweedy form of Colonel Elmsworth. This time he was accompanied not only by Buster, the canine rat but also by a female with horse teeth, wearing a Barbour. Hers was in a much better shape than mine.

"Oh, good afternoon, Colonel," I said. "Hello, Buster."

The dog wasn't fooled and bared its teeth at me, a growl issuing from its bonsai chest.

His master stroked the bristles of his mustache and beamed. "May I introduce Emma? Mrs. Bingham, I mean."

Ah, she of the casserole dish.

"How thoughtful of you to bring the dish," I gushed. "I really appreciate the effort." That was true even if I hadn't enjoyed the cooking.

Mrs. Bingham stretched out a hand that might have belonged to a man, it was that large. Her grip was firm and dry. "Glad you liked it. We'll all be there for you if you need us. Will you take over then? With Dottie—Mrs. Wytchett, I mean—in hospital, things are not moving along as they should. We've already missed the equinox."

Elmsworth pulled a face. "Emma, take it easy. We don't even know if anything will happen. Eve's been gone such a short time. The poor girl must have her hands full."

Equinox? More of the Wiccan bollocks, for sure. A girl I was not, but I took Elmsworth's comment in the spirit it was meant. "Eh, yes. Give me a while to work things out, will you? I'll let you know if I need anything. It's kind of you to offer."

I smiled, considering myself lucky to escape with another handshake, and pressed on, the squat pencil stub of a church tower in view.

While I marched along, accompanied by the oblivious burble of the river Kennet, the tip of a standing stone blipped in my peripheral vision. I could take the route through the village like I did yesterday morning or cross the stream to approach the pub from the side that harbored the larger part of the henge. The second option was shorter. With the light of the setting sun in my eyes and the reproachful bong from the church tower in my ear, I advanced on the henge.

From a distance, the standing stones looked like mismatched sculptures: one tall and pointy like Lot's wife, another rounded like a super-sized golf ball, and another the horse head that hid my parent's marker. Behind them peeped the mossy thatch cap and Tudor façade of the Whacky Bramble. As I made my way, the lights flickered on in the pub, winking like a beacon. On my right, the stone where my parents died sprang into view. Somebody had draped a chain of dandelions over one side as if a child had tried to make the bad go away. Touched despite myself, I stopped to scan the pastures harboring the motley collection of ancient rocks. A ring no longer existed—there were too many gaps. I beheld a pair of ramblers, striding toward the pub, their rucksacks bouncing with every step, a Wiccan in a long skirt, her ear pressed to a tall rock covered in lichen—and a lonely Druid, his arms in a fluttery white robe outstretched to the heavens. Thousands of years old, these boulders still were revered by many.

Not by me.

I turned my back on the henge, zipped across the road and entered the bar. There, I spotted my cousin lecturing a young man covered in acne spots on the use of the beer pump. Savory smells wafted into my nose, promising culinary comfort already enjoyed by other guests, like the elderly couple holding hands at a recessed table and a large group of males on a post-work jolly seated at the back. Daisy gave me a welcoming smile before she pressed a black menu into my hand.

"Gimme a mo, and I'll be with you. I've reserved a table for us over there."

She pointed at a tall and narrow casement window covered

in a crisscross pattern of lead, the windowpanes reflecting the lights like facets on a diamond. I took off my Barbour and chucked it on the seat before wriggling into a high-backed pew built of dark wood and covered in cushions featuring a wide variety of pinks and purples. The tablecloth picked up the theme, and so did the tea lights dancing in deep purple bowls decorated with fake blackberries.

I flipped open the menu and had a hard time stopping myself from drooling.

Daisy appeared, a vision in a glittery white tunic worn over leggings made of a caramel-colored velvety material. Her hair was artfully piled on her head and the makeup perfect. Not bad for a grieving daughter. I slapped my mental wrists and gave her a friendly grin. "Hullo, Daise. I had a look at the menu already. Sounds delicious."

She nodded. "Greg is holding down the fort for a friend of his, but I reckon he's by far the better cook. Try the dressed crab. It's to die for." She slapped her hands over her mouth, her Spaniel eyes flooding with sudden moisture.

My heart went out to her. Daisy had her own way of coping. Keeping up appearances was a crucial part of her strategy. I reached across and pressed her clammy little hand. "She won't be forgotten. Never, ever. Not while we're around." Daisy's smile looked so lost it was painful to behold. She fumbled in her golden clutch for a linen handkerchief and daintily blew her nose. Then she rose.

"Right. Steak and chips are great, too. With creamed peas and grilled tomatoes. You'll like that. I'll have a gin and tonic. You?"

"Yes, please. To all of it." Who cared about waistbands these days? For some strange reason, I thought of the unfinished bottle of champers I had shared with Chris. By now it would have gone flat. What a waste.

Outside, dusk was settling in, and the headlights of the passing cars drew brilliant starbursts from the windowpanes.

Daisy returned with a tray on which she had placed our drinks, together with a basket of bread and packaged butter. Next to it lay the cutlery rolled up in burgundy napkins.

"Tell me, what did the solicitor say?" she asked, once she

was seated again.

"You won't like it, but we'll work something out. Listen, can this wait until after dinner?"

Her sudden pout told me it could not.

Still trying to work out how to break the news, I welcomed a reprieve in the form of a giant with piercings, a nameplate reading "Greg," and teeth gleaming white in his ebony face. He produced our crabs with swift efficiency. "Do you want the mains right up, or wait a bit?" he asked, his words dripping with a honey-sweet American accent. Georgia? The Carolinas? Somewhere like that.

On another day or with a different dinner partner I would've asked for a break, but the moist pink crab served on rocket with a drizzle of olive oil looked promising. With too long of a pause, hostilities might ensue that would stop me from enjoying my food. "Right up is fine for me. Daise?"

She poked at the wedge of lime bobbing on the bubbles of her gin and tonic. "I guess so."

The giant slunk off, cat-footed, and I raised my glass. "To mother."

Daisy chinked her glass against mine, and I let the tart sweetness of the drink roll past my palate. The crab was even better, but I only got two forkfuls before Daisy struck again.

"About that solicitor…"

I wouldn't get a moment's peace and quiet before Daisy knew the details. Not afterward either, but that was a different matter.

Once I had braced myself for the fireworks, I set down my cutlery and told her.

11

NOT A MOMENT OF PEACE

The callous glare of a full moon invaded my room, transforming walls into translucent screens between this world and the beyond. Perhaps mixing the gin and tonic with two glasses of red wine hadn't been such a wise move. Between fretting in my bed, stumbling into the bathroom to guzzle buckets of tap water and trying—unsuccessfully—to pull the chintz curtain into the path of the encroaching rays, sleep slipped away. Instead, an endless loop of last evening scrolled over the inside of my eyelids.

True to form, my cousin had morphed from a fluffy kitten into a mature panther in less than a second flat. "I knew mum would do something like that. How dare she?"

The question was rhetorical, so I tuned her out and concentrated instead on the salty richness of my crab. Daisy had my fullest sympathy. Confronted with such a will, I too would have hit the roof. Between my cousin's berserker act and my delicious starter, it took a moment before the outlandish behavior of the tea lights registered. They flickered and sputtered, thinning into forked tongues of whitish flame one moment, contracting into an orange glow the next. Sparks flew from the wicks, and a blue haze spread over the table, reeking of woodfire and berries. Pressure behind my eardrums built up to a shrill whistle until something popped.

"Have you got nothing to say?" Daisy's comment shattered my trance. She started on her crab. The lights steadied.

"Uh, I couldn't get a word in edgewise." I placed my cutlery on the plate before facing first the now peaceful flames and then my cousin. "Daisy, it might come as a surprise, but I agree with you. The will is a handful. But you know mum. Knew, I mean. I suspect she wanted to help you. My problem is, I don't understand what prompted her. Care to explain?"

She didn't answer. The giant materialized again, giving Daisy's half-full plate an admonishing look. "Girl, you need to eat."

"Yeah, sure. I'm finished, though."

He disappeared with the dishes.

"Daisy—"

"It's none of your business."

I counted to three before I responded. "I'm afraid mum has made it my business. Don't tell me it's the usual problem with having too much month left at the end of the money, for I won't believe that."

My cousin sipped from her drink. Then she tapped her fingers, painted in orange, against her cheeks. When she spoke, her voice was strangely serene. "No. An investment scheme." Her eyes lit up. "The return is brilliant. Forests. It's right down your street. How about if we use some of the inheritance to buy more shares?"

"I think not," I said, using the kindest tone in my repertoire. "Let's see if I understand things correctly. There was this great opportunity, you bought in, and now they need more cash to keep the scheme going? In the meantime, you don't have enough to pay your bills?"

She deflated. "No. I mean, yes."

The "great opportunities" changed in nature, but Daisy had been falling for getting-rich-quickly schemes ever since she became of age. Nothing new there, at least nothing that would have forced auntie to make an impromptu will.

"Did you invest a lot?"

"Well...fifty. Thousand, I mean. But I borrowed at a great rate. Trouble is, no matter what I fork out, they always want more. And they're getting a bit nasty."

Oh, my gosh.

"Eh, yes. I suspect they would."

"Don't give me that look. Mum's loaded, but all she ever did when I got into trouble was lecture me. Even if she coughed up in the end," Daisy breathed with girlish hurt in her voice. "I want to be independent."

Then why did you leave school without an exam and keep mucking about with odd jobs?

"I understand why you did what you did. But something seems to have upset Aunt Eve. I mean, more than usual. Otherwise, she wouldn't have made the will."

"Mum hated the idea, because of it being linked to Ignatius Industries. But I had no clue at the time, right?" The restaurant was heaving, otherwise, her shrill voice would have caused more people than the elderly man at the next table to frown at us, his chunky glasses reflecting the tea lights.

"Sorry." Daisy took another sip.

Bob Ignatius was the archetypal successful entrepreneur: business ideas by the dozen, all turned to gold. At least it said so in the stories spun by the media. To the best of my knowledge, fraudulent investment schemes had never formed part of the man's portfolio. While recent upheavals on the stock markets might have put a spanner in the works, he still seemed to be filthy rich. Ignatius struck me as the type of person Aunt Eve would have hated out of principle. But there were plenty of his ilk around, so why would she get het up over this one?

My cousin toyed with the bling on her necklace, a mulish expression on her face.

Greg appeared again, bearing my steak and a crispy tomato and tofu pie for Daisy plus two glasses.

"Here's some lovely Californian wine to go with your dinner," he said, a smile splitting his kind face. "On the house."

We chorused our thanks.

Daisy strangled her napkin. "He's such a sweetie. Let's talk about this another time, shall we? Maybe by then, I will have a solution. But I'll need some cash to bridge the gap." Her eyes glittered with a fake brightness. That she was in over her head was clear. But until she told me who was after her, there was little I could do.

"Daise, until probate is granted all I've got is my salary. I'd need to talk to auntie's finance guy—"

"Can you, please? The next rate is due and I...well, without Greg, I would be lost," she said, averting her eyes. She stabbed her pie instead.

I swallowed a piece of steak so tender it almost melted in my mouth. but the juices went bitter on my tongue. It was all about her troubles, as usual. I, too, was lost. "I'll try my best. Daisy, just what shall I do?"

"You're asking me? That's rich. You and mum were as thick as thieves. You're the one she trusted to sort things out, so why don't you? I'm nothing but a stopgap." The delicate china-doll face froze on stubborn lines. A familiar expression: Daisy was about to clam up permanently.

We fell silent, cocooned in our misery among the raucous guests and the alcoholic fumes. Not for long though, since too many questions were clamoring for attention. I went for the men. Men were right down Daisy's street.

"What do you think of the two long-term guests? Chris and Alan, I mean." It took an effort to keep my voice neutral.

Almost all her pie had gone, and she frowned at her phone. "Need to make a move soon. What about them? I have no idea what mum saw in the weirdo. Chris, I mean. It was unnatural. Seriously. The other one?" A mean gleam stole into her eyes. "He's a loser if you ask me. Walked the London beat, tried to join Scotland Yard, twice, and failed. Well, it's what Chris told mum. Not sure I believe him. Mum did. Don't know why."

My head was spinning. "You're telling me he was her lover?"

Daisy scowled. "Myr, sometimes your sense of humor is warped."

As I had feared, she fell silent and fiddled with her smartphone until I had swallowed the last of my chips. Then she jumped up. "It was great talking to you, but I gotta go. Let me know when you have the dosh, right?" She sketched a wave before she sauntered off, the crowd parting for her in admiration.

Of course, she didn't settle the bill.

From there onward, things got rather fuzzy. I probably shouldn't have downed the second glass of red wine on my ownsome-lonesome, but like so many things it had sounded like a good idea at the time. After a taxi had taken me back to the B&B, the clock on the kitchen wall showed seven twenty-five. Once the latest sales guy was safely installed in Number One, I could call it a day. The broken night and the stressful dinner had sneaked up on me. My muscles hurt, my eyelids drooped with fatigue, and my ever-present guilt had come knocking.

I had invaded Daisy's and Eve's lives. Not by choice, but I had shoved Daisy off the single-child throne. At least that was the way she saw it.

On the windowsill, something rustled, interrupting my thoughts. Did we have mice? Tiddles needed to take her job more seriously. With only the single lamp on over the sink, the kitchen was steeped in twilight, so I turned on the main lights.

Nothing.

I stepped closer to the row of plant pots. No mice. No life either. Most of the primulas were dead with one exception: On the very right, the one flower that had come back to life showed more leaves and little pinkish buds. It also had doubled in size.

Why just one of them?

The doorbell gonged in reply.

Mr. Fforde, "Two effs for double efficiency" boomed his welcome at my face. I recoiled. His dinner had included beer and onions, neither of which sweetened his breath. He kept talking while filling out the registration form, hopping from efficient names—his—to even more efficient knives—his wares.

"Sheffield Steel, madam. The best, simply the best." My guest fumbled for something in his briefcase.

I gave him a bland smile and turned to fish for the key to Number One. A heartbeat later, a shadow loomed over the panel, moving, growing, raising a fist. A fist grabbing a knife.

Heat flushed my veins. With a shriek, I whirled around.

His eyes widening with surprise, Mr. Fforde stepped backward, the bread knife still clasped in his right hand. The briefcase lay open on the counter, a fleece wrapper displaying a whole array of sharp objects. His eyes nearly popping from his face, my guest lowered the cutlery and tilted his head. "Are you all right?"

I was. Sort of. Just a bit short of breath. "You scared me," I said, pointing at the knife.

Mr. Fforde regarded the object he was still wielding, then me. An uneasy smile surfaced on his face. "Oh, I wanted to show you our special offer. Mrs. Coldron appreciated the quality of our products. I thought you might be interested?"

Auntie had been too kind.

Mr. Fforde must have realized he would not close any deals tonight since the knife slid back into the protective cloth and the briefcase shut with a snap. With sweaty hands, I handed over the key. Fortunately, Mr. Fforde knew his way around. After a wordy apology, he climbed the stairs to his room.

I had followed Mr. Fforde's example and sought rest. The events of the day ran through my head, tumbling over each other and vying for attention. First was the attic, which thankfully lay quiet tonight. Then Mr. Fforde, who I filed under moronic but harmless. Next, I worried about the gear in Chris's room. I really should have told Sergeant Sarah.

Daisy's vengeful spirit rose, pushing aside all thoughts of Chris. How far would she go to get her money? Could she be involved in her mother's accident? If she had wrapped the Southern giant around her little finger, he might have cooked up a juicy alibi for her.

That sounded like a plot from one of the abs-studded historical romances stacked on the nightstand. But the thought kept burrowing in my mind. Wriggling. Niggling.

With a groan, I switched on the light and scribbled a reminder on the notepad placed next to the telephone. "Daisy alibi? Check."

I switched off the light. The loop started afresh.

I pulled the pillow over my head, but my head wouldn't quiet.

With the new dawn, clouds shifted across the moon, and I fell asleep, waking less than two hours later. The leaden weariness of insomnia fogging my brain was joined by a headache hammering away. Never again, I swore, not knowing whether I meant the mixed drinks or my investigations.

A headache I could treat with a painkiller. The investigations were another story. I had no proof we were dealing with murder, and my sleuthing suffered from a sorry cast of suspects, no solid motives, and a lack of real clues. Yet a deep-set niggle kept telling me something was rotten in the village of Avebury. To solve the puzzle, I needed to be fit, so I snuggled back into my bed where I soon drifted back to sleep.

—

When I woke up a few hours later, I felt more human. My headache was gone. So was, presumably, my breakfast. I would have to go shopping, eat something before tackling Mr. and Mrs. Burns, followed by a hunt for the Ragworts. My eyes fell on the note on the nightstand, and my mind started spinning again.

Daisy. And then there was Greg. He seemed a decent sort, but then I had only met the guy yesterday evening. A glance at my watch showed it might well be too late for breakfast, but also too early for the pub to be open. I placed my note in the drawer. Greg and Daisy would have to wait.

A quick shower later, I drove toward the outskirts of Swindon. The supermarket Alma recommended was easier to find than the vanished ladder, which—according to a now migraine-free Cecily—had never belonged to the house. I devoured two croissants and a double latte in the bakery, stocked up on fruit, granola bars, and canned soups, and returned to the village in much better shape, this time via the Swindon road. Back at the Witch's Retreat, I flung three days' worth of dirty laundry in the washing machine, unseparated.

Those clothes were old, and there was no danger of colors running. A quick phone call to the solicitor followed. Sneldon informed me the coroner was about to release the body. An appointment had been made with the undertaker. Probate was underway. I had three days left. It was time to shift gears.

12

CLUELESS

Wytchett Farm lay off Long Street, which connected the newer part of Avebury with the historical village center. The whole layout reminded me of an onion, where medieval and Tudor buildings formed the core, with the slate roofs and turd brown bricks of the latest housing development making up the outer layer. These modern buildings, most of them set in terraces of at least three, were bog-ugly. The Witch's Retreat, in its Georgian splendor, preened itself among them, the red roof visible from far away. Wondering how my aunt ever got permission to use such garish tiles, I turned right at the corner of Nightingale Lane into Long Street. There was no footpath, only muddy potholes, and the sparrows crowding the electric cables observed my erratic progress, chittering with merriment.

Precipitation set in and shut them up.

I smelled the farm before I could see it. The wet weather had done nothing to wash away the pungent odor of cattle manure and the sharp sting of chicken droppings. The stench intensified when I approached the oblong shed built of cracked red bricks and covered in a crescent-shaped corrugated iron that had seen better days.

Across a small yard lay two more buildings, farming

paraphernalia scattered in front, none of them new, but all well cared for. Farmer Marty's battered white van sat parked opposite an open shed from which issued the clucking and fluttering of many birds.

Alma, the fount of local information, had told me Wytchett Farm specialized in free-range chickens and Friesian milk cattle.

I hollered twice across the steel gate, where I received no response other than an agitated flurry of wings and a lowing in *basso profundo* from the cowshed. There was nothing to be gained here. I retraced my steps around the puddles and wandered into the spacious front yard of a weathered historical building whose row of tiny mansard windows in the roof reminded me of the fake eyes on a lamprey eel.

Raindrops plopped from the hood of my old Barbour onto my nose, trickling down my face.

At least my trip was not in vain. To judge from the Wellingtons in various sizes and states of muddiness lining the steps to the entrance, the family was at home. I searched for a doorbell and, finding none, banged the ornamental knocker. Quick steps rushed to the door. It gaped inward to reveal an elfin young woman peeping at me, maroon strands curling around and in front of her pallid face.

"Have you found them?" she asked.

"Uh, found who?"

"My little pumpkins, Robbie and Johnnie. They're mad about the animals and keep sneaking into the stables. It's no problem with the chickens, but the cows bother me."

"I've come from the stables. Sorry, Mrs. Burns, I didn't see your sons. You are Mrs. Burns, aren't you?"

The woman nodded and wiped her forehead, leaving a yellowish smear behind.

"I'm Myrtle Coldron from the Witch's Retreat. Frightfully sorry to intrude on you like this, but I have a question regarding the bill for your family's lodgings."

For a moment she looked bewildered. "Oh, sorry. Where are my manners? I'm Jenna. Do come in." Jenna stuck out her hand, which I shook gingerly. Their stickiness had a marmalade feel to it, even if the aromas that accompanied her every movement belonged to the Indian subcontinent.

After following the mother of the twins along a narrow corridor, I found myself in a cluttered kitchen, dominated by an old-fashioned iron Aga oven with turquoise doors, the source of the exotic smells.

"I'm preparing apple chutney," Jenna explained. "Marty has plenty of frozen fruit I can use. I sell the jars on the market. I also brew country wine. Gives us extra cash, which helps now Jeff has lost his job again." She bit her lip, but the words were out. "Would you like a cup of tea?" she asked. I accepted, promising myself I would not force a cash-strapped young mother to pay her debts. She needed the money when I did not. Fresh peppermint tea landed in front of me, served farm-style in an earthenware mug. Jenna dropped onto the opposite chair, and from up close I noticed the fine lines of worry spreading from her dark eyes. Her shoulders sagged under an invisible burden she was too frail to carry.

What I suspected to be the origins of her troubles came trampling into the kitchen on a puff of cigarette smoke, causing Jenna to jump up and topple over her seat.

"They've disappeared again," she wailed.

"Where's my tea?" was the unsympathetic response.

Jenna handed him her mug, shooting me a warning glance. She needn't have bothered. My inner bully alarm was ringing. With his bushy eyebrows, flat nose and a distinct lack of neck, Jeff Burns even looked the part. My shoulders tight like steel girders, I rose from my seat, stretching to my full height, which gave me a slight advantage over my adversary. "Mr. Burns, I'm Myrtle Coldron, from the Witch's Retreat."

That was as far as I got. Burns slammed his mug on the table so hard it cracked, causing the tea to flood the surface. His face flushed red. "You're not trying to give me more trouble about the bill, are you? Are you?"

"Jeff, please," his wife said, rubbing her eyes. "I thought things had been sorted?"

Burns ignored her. "You dare to threaten me in my home?"

Unless I was mistaken, this was his brother-in-law's home, but he didn't strike me as the person to appreciate such details. Nor had I threatened him—yet. "I'm not sure what you are on about, Mr. Burns, but the fact is you have been occupying Numbers Five and Six for the last eight days when your booking was for four days. I need to understand what your plans are. And, yes, I would require payment. The bill's still open."

Somewhere, in the recesses of my mind, I knew my chances of learning something about my aunt's troubles on this visit were vanishing fast, but I wouldn't let the tosser get the better of me.

The outside door slammed shut, and I heard footsteps. Jenna rushed out of the kitchen, abandoning me to my fate. I checked for weapons and found one of the apple-smeared pots within reach.

Burns snorted, his feet planted wide. "If you're looking for cash, you've come to the wrong place. Otherwise, you are welcome to clear the damn rooms and send my stuff across. But make sure you break nothing, or I sue you. How do you like that, eh?"

My mouth was as dry as the applesauce caked on the Aga, but I was determined to hold my ground. "I'll do nothing of the sort. You better pay your debts. Otherwise, you'll hear from my solicitor—and the police."

His jaw seemed to be grinding his molars to a fine powder. I took a step closer to the pot.

"You'll regret this," he bellowed. "I'll ruin that murder house of yours!"

My fingers hovered over the pot handle, ready to grab and swing, when Farmer Marty entered, followed by his sister. His ruddy cheeks were aflame, and his eyes glittered. But his wrath was not directed at me.

"Jeff, stop this nonsense. Stop it right now."

Burns opened his mouth but was not given a chance to speak.

"I said stop it. Leave us."

With a growl, Burns stomped away. A door slammed somewhere in the house; then all fell blessedly quiet.

Farmer Marty heaved a sigh. "I apologize for my brother-in-law's behavior. Life's rather rough for Jeff right now. When I found out he hadn't bothered to settle, I told Cecily I would take care of the bill. Didn't she mention it?"

It might have been wiser to check with the Simpkins sisters before calling at the farm, but then I had been motivated by mysteries, not the cash flow.

In any case, it felt equally wrong to take a hard-working farmer's money. "Look, if you can get your stuff shifted by tomorrow, I'll charge for the four days your relatives had originally booked but nothing more. Just don't tell that tosser," I said.

Marty looked relieved. "Thank you, Ms. Coldron, that's mighty kind of you. You're like your aunt. She was a great person. I'll make it up to you, I promise."

"I have to apologize," his sister said. "Since his employer kicked him out, Jeff thinks the world is after him. Never mind, I'm sure you have other things on your mind. Your aunt was such a wonderful person and what did I do? Run away." Tears glittered in her eyes.

"Never you mind. But why the hurry if I may ask?"

Marty and his sister swapped glances, but it was she who responded. "Jeff and your aunt didn't get on so well. I figured he'd be voicing off if we stayed, making the police draw the wrong conclusions. Here, under Marty's roof, he's more subdued. Well, sort of." A wry smile pulled up the corners of her mouth.

I decided to leave them in peace for the moment. It was an opening; I could not ask for more. When I returned home, a glass of apple chutney weighed down the pocket of my cracked Barbour.

Call it intuition or call it a whim: I didn't continue on the street but headed for the group of birches that bordered on auntie's land, wondering whether there might be a back entrance to the garden.

There was and it was easily found. The wooden gate stood wide open, and a collapsible fire escape ladder lay in the unkempt grass, a ladder last seen yesterday morning from the attic window. I couldn't imagine a burglar leaving the tools of his trade hanging around. Unless that particular burglar was renting a room and was short of space.

"Don't mess with my mind, whoever you are," I mumbled to myself, and dragged the blasted ladder into the bushes on the other side of the fence, locking the gate behind me.

What this place needed apart from a security expert was a gardener to trim last year's creepers and prune the rhododendron that had run wild. Twigs tore at my hair and water soaked my neck as I dug my way through the undergrowth until I emerged on the unrenovated side of the building. A quick check skyward confirmed the attic window was still closed and so were the ones belonging to auntie's bedroom...

Something else was there, something that did not belong. Shadowy movement flitted past the windowpanes of auntie's bedroom.

Another intruder.

Chris was my first thought. Daisy, my next. I even thought of Alan.

Then I stopped thinking and shot toward the back entrance, cursing when I found it barred. I fiddled with the keyring and then stormed inside, up the stairs and onto the top landing. As feared, the door to auntie's bedroom gaped open.

I edged closer to the door and listened. "Who's there?" My voice boomed through the opening to the attic until it got lost among the rafters.

No response.

Heat scorched my veins. Fury propelling me forward, I barged into my aunt's bedroom, slamming the door against the wall.

The place was empty of trespassers but in a state of chaos. The bathroom door stood ajar, emitting light and the steady hum of the extractor fan.

"Whoever you are, this is not funny anymore." My voice cracked.

Still no response.

I tiptoed to the bathroom. A rushing sounded in my ear as I shoved the door open wide.

The bathroom was empty too, missing even a shower curtain somebody could have been hiding behind.

My pounding heart slowed, and anger gave way to uneasiness.

"Hello?"

As if in response, the ceiling of the bedroom creaked once. The intruder must have fled to the attic.

From outside came a clatter and a metallic rattle. Somebody was descending the aluminum stepladder.

A minute ago, my anger would have gotten the better of me and I would have barged outside, ready to rock. Now, doubt had settled in and kept me rooted to the terracotta tiles of the bathroom. What could be worse than a stroppy cousin or the resident burglar?

A killer.

I slipped back into the bedroom but stopped, not wanting to be seen.

From outside came another clank, followed by a thump. The intruder had reached the landing.

Right now, one of Jenna's cast-iron pots would have made a useful weapon.

I recalled the words of the sports teacher at my school. "Weapons can be turned against you. Trust me, you don't want to get close to an aggressor." The sports teacher had also said to the huffing, red-faced ladies struggling through his self-defense course, "Kick them in the gonads. Poke them in the eyes."

That assumed whoever was out there had gonads to be kicked. Plus, I would be standing on one leg, which was never a good idea. The poking in the eye part, however, deserved merit.

"Make a lot of noise," our teacher had added.

That I could do.

But my mouth remained shut and my legs were rooted to the floor.

A dark shape shifted past the entrance to the bedroom, making for the corridor.

The villain was about to escape, and I would never know what had happened to my aunt.

My inner barrel overflowed. I could no longer stand still. "I see you," I yelled, and threw myself at the entrance.

A dark arm blurred down.

Something heavy whooshed past my nose.

I threw myself backward the same moment the object slammed into the side of the door. It sent splinters flying, one of which hit my cheek. I stood in the bedroom with funny little wheezing noises coming from my mouth, my heart going like a sewing machine, and something warm trickling down my cheek.

Blood.

From the corridor came the sound of running feet. They got fainter as they thumped downstairs until the front door closed with a bang.

For quite a while, I listened to the screaming inside. When it finally quieted, I allowed my fearful gaze to rove over the door frame. It showed a ragged, fist-sized dent. If whatever had damaged the wood had hit my head, I would now be dead.

My hand touched the trickle on my cheek, which was already drying.

I had been more than lucky.

A violent shiver shook my spine. It made my teeth chatter.

No accident, no accident, they clacked.

Somehow, I found the courage to enter the landing.

My gaze fell on a flurry of petals. Yellow this time, they lay sprinkled under the aluminum ladder where my aunt had lain. Somewhere up in the attic jangled the broken toy, its music at discord with the choir once more keening in my head.

That was it. I needed to get out of here.

Somehow, I made it down the stairs and into the sitting room. There I sat, curled up in auntie's armchair, too frozen for tears.

I heard birdsong in the hedge, the neighbors greeting each other in the streets, and Tiddles' claws on the floorboards.

Her feather-light body clambered onto my lap, sharing warmth and a fart, unchilling my soul.

13

SNIPPETS OF THE PAST

With Tiddles purring over my heart, I stepped to the sitting room window facing the car park. Chris's car was gone. Alan's clapped-out Panda I hadn't seen all day. The next guest, another salesman, wouldn't arrive until this evening. One lonely vehicle waited outside; mine. I could leave everything behind. I could drive back to Southampton and sort out things out from the safety of the school. But then my anonymous enemy would have won.

No way.

The cat suffered a kiss between her pointy ears before I lowered her onto the seat of the armchair. Tiddles sighed and curled up in a ball, the bones of her spine a string of lumps under her fur.

My feline companion taken care of, I called Sergeant Sarah. I landed on voicemail and left a message, telling her about the second intruder and the gear in Chris's room. Task completed and hands empty, the hushed silence that had befallen the Witch's Retreat in the aftermath of the attack weighed heavy on my chest. It reminded me of the quiet that had greeted me upon my arrival. Back then, however, I hadn't been alone.

All those never-ending minutes I took to climb back

upstairs and tiptoe past the petals, I listened for sounds that should not be there, for movement that didn't belong.

Nothing. Not a single creak.

Finally, safe in auntie's bedroom, embraced by the sweet ghost of her scent, a sigh of relief exploded from my chest. This afternoon, I had been first too busy and then too shocked to notice her perfume, but now a soothing scent of flowers, citrus fruit, and talcum powder wrapped itself around me.

The comfort was needed, for this time the chaos in the room registered in all its glory. Either the police or the unknown aggressor must have ransacked the place. The bedspread had been ripped open, drawers were overflowing and the lamp on the nightstand lay on its side. Auntie's poor plants had been swiped off the windowsill onto the floor, where they piled in a broken heap next to the upturned hamper. Two broken bowls of potpourri, their contents littering the floor, completed the disaster zone.

I could only hope the boxes with the clippings and photo albums had survived. Whenever something caught my aunt's interest, out came the scissors, and the booty ended up in the containers. Apart from the attic and the office, which I had already searched, they were one of the two places I could think of where she might have hidden a message or something worth killing or stealing. If the boxes were gone, I would never forgive myself.

You should have checked earlier.

I whirled around and went almost dizzy with relief. There, squatting on top of the open wardrobe, sat the precious cartons with their red and white stripes. Something, however, was off. Three cartons squatted on top of the wardrobe—one more than expected.

The cherry-red stripes on two of the boxes sitting in front of me looked faded. Those would be the ones I knew about. If she left me a note, it would be in there. I knelt on the fluffy rug, opened the first box and hit on the scrapbook I used to mull over, first with my parents, then with my aunt.

When I flicked through the stiff pages of the album, the translucent paper between the pages crackled its reassurance, releasing a faint smell of mothballs.

Here I was, a baby in many poses, most of them decidedly unflattering. Photos of my parents and my aunt entered the photographic arena until they were joined by my cousin, looking cute and sullen, even back then.

The snapshots of my early childhood were followed by holidays on French beaches and rambles in the Lake District. I was ten at the time and hated hiking with a passion. All of my early life waited in that box: photos taken at school, birthday parties, our move from London to Windermere—reminders of a protected childhood, smiled upon by my father, who was my teaching role model, and my mother. A whole series of images showed mum in her small craft shop, smiling, surrounded by rolls and rolls of gauzy fabrics, beads, buttons, and lace—a child's treasure trove. We had spats; they wanted me to do things, I gave them lip. An intact middle-class family. A miracle.

Everything imploded shortly after my fourteenth birthday. The evidence of that horrible afternoon also lurked in the box, underneath the happier memories. Usually, I dug no deeper.

I gingerly picked up several yellowing newspaper articles announcing another juicy disaster that became yesterday's news in an instant. The end of my world meant nothing on a grander scale. "Couple dies in mysterious hit-and-run accident" on the front page, the theme changed to "Police close roadside accident case"—a notice at the back of the local rag a few days later. Finally, there was the funeral announcement: "James Wicken (37) and Emily Coldron (35), survived by their daughter Myrtle, mourned by Eve and Daisy Coldron."

It was ironic their deaths, or rather the subsequent adoption by my aunt, should have stopped the mobbing at school. My new classmates no longer called me a bastard like the old lot used to do. How wrong they had been. My mother had never cared much for the traditions of the Coldron family, but she kept her name after her marriage and even saddled me with a plant label. When prodded for reasons, she claimed that "some things are important, others are not." But when I wheedled for explanations, she clammed up.

A teardrop splashed on the brittle paper of the ad. I hastened to wipe the moisture first from the clipping and then from my eyes. The sad bunch of snippets was all that remained. Their grave didn't count. I hadn't visited in years. Instead, I cradled them in my memories.

The album I placed on the floor with the clippings piled on top. The other scrapbook, Daisy's heirloom, I leafed through and found no secrets. When I grabbed the box to return the albums, a weight shifted inside. I fished in the depths of the cardboard container and retrieved a faded file. On its spine, I read "Farnsworth Detective Agency and Security Detail. Client: Eve Coldron."

True to herself, auntie took nothing for granted. Instead, she paid a detective agency to find the truth. While she shared the overall outcome, she refused to tell me the details. One could say my aunt didn't play her cards close to her chest, she kept them inside her bra.

I opened the file and recoiled at the images of a crumpled and scorched wreck, smashed against the sooty rock. My parent's Volvo had careened across the road, rolled over, and then crashed through the fence that separated the street from the henge until it hit the standing stone. Shortly afterward, it exploded into flames, the remains of which marked the rock forever, a reminder of their passing.

The report spelled out the details with terrible precision. Grateful my aunt had spared me at a time when I wouldn't have been able to cope, I forced myself to read on.

No ash particles coated mum and dad's lungs. They must have died upon impact and never noticed when the car burned. Curiously enough, the report was written by an eyewitness. A Farnsworth detective had been following the Volvo from "the assignment at the Avebury churchyard"; he observed the accident and recalled their last minutes.

A dark limousine had come from behind. Accelerating through the s-curve that led through the village, he screeched past the detective's car before ramming the Volvo. When my father braked and tried to evade him, the murderous madman slammed into the sturdy vehicle once more, sending it into a tumble and against the standing stone. His evil work done, he sped away, leaving it up to the private dick to try and save my parent's lives. But the Volvo burst into flames before he could reach them.

Despite those observations made by the Farnsworth detective, the ruling was "drink-driver." Case closed.

The detective disagreed and called it "malicious intent." But he had no proof to back up his claim. After scouting all over Britain, he found the damaged vehicle in a scrapyard. It had been sold for cash and the identification number filed away.

I wondered why the detectives might have been around in the first place and leafed through the report with sweaty hands. With every page I turned, the story became more bizarre. Far from being hired after the fact, the agency had been contracted a few days before Aunt Eve and my parents met in Avebury. Their job was to escort my aunt in an armored car from the churchyard to Swindon. It didn't say where to, and I suspected the information had been removed, presumably by my aunt. The Farnsworth pros didn't escort Aunt Eve alone. With her traveled an old headstone belonging to the Coldron family. I even found a letter from the local vicar, allowing her to remove the marker. Auntie and the headstone made it safely to their destination. My parents did not.

My hands sank onto my lap, and I stared at the room with unseeing eyes.

Aunt Eve had told me she felt responsible for mum and dad's death, but never explained why. The report held the grim truth. My parents must have died for one of auntie's mystic shenanigans. For whatever reason, somebody must have been after the headstone and, when he couldn't get at it because of the bodyguards, took out his wrath on my parents. My throat aching with silent sobs, I got up and grabbed the fresh bottle of spring water resting on auntie's nightstand. I gulped down the liquid, drops of it splashing onto my grubby blouse.

Then I jumped onto auntie's messed-up bed. I pummeled the duvet and howled my rage at the room.

It took my inner voice a while to make itself heard.

Are you finished now? Do you feel better?

I didn't. My head was dizzy with exhaustion.

There are two more boxes for you to search.

Once more, I lowered myself on the rug to tackle the second box. Again, its contents were familiar. This was my aunt's life.

She had been a correspondent for the BBC, traveling all over the world—to India, Iran, the States, Australia, China—there was hardly a place on Earth she hadn't visited, at some point with lover and baby in tow. Aunt Eve wrote features about those faraway places, usually in a less than flattering fashion. After the tragedy, she ditched her career—along with Daisy's father—to take care of me. From what I understood, the separation had been in the cards for quite a while, at least for auntie. Not for my cousin. Daisy missed her father, who soon forgot about her, and she longed for the exotic countries her family visited.

Auntie became a freelance journalist. While she contented herself with staying in the UK, she didn't drop her crusade and wrote scorching pieces on fraud and greed while raising both Daisy and me.

I wondered whether Daisy would have been better off with her dad. The next moment, I wadded the thought. The guy had never cared enough to send more than the obligatory Christmas card and eventually not even that. All those memories left a bitter taste on my tongue, so I dug deeper into the box.

Last year's clippings showed auntie living her new life in Avebury. I sifted through a flurry of paper cuttings in different shapes and sizes showing strangers as they shook hands with my aunt or were clinking glasses with her. Other than Gloria and the Colonel, I recognized two of the faces: Jenna Burns and Marty Wytchett. The photo was taken at the pub, and they were half-hidden by an older man with tortoiseshell spectacles and his fit-looking wife, all of them raising a toast to my aunt. The caption under the article identified them to be "Damian and Rosie Ragwort at the reopening of the Whacky Bramble pub."

He struck me as being familiar, but I couldn't place her.

A photo and another yellowed clipping slipped from the

pile and fluttered to the floor. I picked up both items and sensed moths swarming my stomach. The picture showed a gravestone, apparently ancient since the writing was all but obliterated though the name was legible enough. "Coldron." The moths fluttered harder. The churchyard shot to the top of my priority list, then sank again. There would be nothing left. I reached for the clipping instead.

A man was found dead in a ditch close to Marlborough. He had been shot once in the chest, at close range. A closer glance sent the moths into a frenzy. The article dated the discovery of the corpse to three days after the death of my parents, and my aunt had added a single word in the margin in a red felt pen, now discolored and faded.

"Him."

I pressed my hands on my diaphragm, following the rising and falling of my breath, and concentrated on calming the moths. I needed them quiet to investigate the content of the mystery box. A blue folder containing a family tree lay on top of the printouts crammed inside the carton: copies of birth and death certificates, more family trees, and sheets with long rows with names. Auntie must have added genealogy to her hobbies. Though, in a wild way, it made sense. Headstones and tracing one's ancestors went well together. She might well have hired Chris to help her.

The next shocker I found by accident.

The tourist brochure seemed out of context until I came to its center spread, which showed a map of Avebury's outer circle of standing stones and displayed two inner ones I hadn't even known to exist. Not that I cared overly much. There were still plenty of relics to keep the tourists happy.

Black dots marked the stones still standing and red dots the ones that got lost throughout the ages. The two smaller circles within the outer ring had especially suffered—not more than a handful of rocks were left of the southernmost one. The center of the concentric dashes that denoted the vanished northern circle had been marked with a red cross, and on the right, a line streaked toward the margin. In her elegant handwriting auntie had written, "When I die, let them scatter my ashes here."

Blimey, had I found her message? I decided it sounded too defeatist. There had to be more, and I picked up the family tree in the folder.

The yellowed document lay stiffly in my hand as if I were dealing with parchment, not paper.

Could I be barking down the wrong hole and this conundrum revolve around auntie's foray into genealogy? That would mean even the headstone caper that claimed my parents might be unrelated to the drama unfolding in the present.

No matter what might be going on, the family tree was no doubt valuable, so I got up to wash my hands before I picked it up once more.

14

RESTLESS PIECES

The Asher family, extinct since 1602. That was now the second document in this house referring back to the time of the witch hunts. I wasn't stupid. I could smell a rat—or a clue—when I found one. I wondered what time the mysterious headstone might have dated back to, but the amateur photo was fuzzy, and it was impossible to decipher the faded squiggles on the stone.

A quick check in the box revealed nothing else of interest. Clutter or not, I would have to plow through the shelf in the sitting room before my enemy did. I glanced at the family tree. A safer place was needed to store the old document.

The boxes were heavy, but I shoved them right to the back of the wardrobe. I kept the Asher family tree in its folder and my photo album. Having locked the door to auntie's room, I then wriggled the doorknob of Daisy's place—which was still locked—and strode downstairs.

I didn't get very far. One floor down, a male voice exploded into my eardrum. "Myrtle."

"Cripes."

Chris's sudden appearance sent a jab into my solar plexus, my hands snapped up, and the album and folder tumbled down the stairs, spilling their contents.

We both stared at the mess on the steps, then at each other. "Stop doing that," I shrieked.

"Doing what?" Chris asked, with a bland look.

He bent down, grabbed the album and cleared the debris without so much as a glance at my baby photos. My ears had burned for nothing. But once Chris hit upon the yellowed piece of parchment, he started before scanning the content.

"Do you mind?" I reached across and snatched the Asher family tree from his hands.

"Sorry," he said. "I've been trying to get a hold of you, and it never works out."

Thoughts zoomed through my mind. The man could be a common criminal. He might have been my aunt's IT support, her lover or a hired genealogist. Or he could be something a lot more sinister. A furtive glance at his hands showed them clenching and unclenching, didn't reveal whether one of them might match the gloved fist of the assailant.

"You've found me. Rather abruptly, I dare say."

"That's not what I meant. Do you realize it's a historical document you've got there?"

"Yes. That's why it was in a folder."

"I love old texts," Chris said wistfully.

"Now, there's a surprise."

"This needs proper protection, or it will get damaged."

"Yes, especially if I drop things when somebody jumps me on the stairs."

"My apologies, I didn't mean to upset you. Are you well? You look a bit pale."

"What is it you want?" I asked, forcing myself not to look into his night-black eyes. Perhaps they were deep brown; it was hard to tell in the half-light of the staircase. Why had it gone so dark?

"I wanted to warn you."

"You what?"

He stood there in the gloom. It was as if his presence pressed on the air molecules, forcing them to thicken. Fragrant incense wafted from Chris in waves that swirled around me in a hypnotic haze, and the pressure in my chest grew until my breath came in hiccupy, little gasps. I took a step backward.

He raised his hands, a frown slanting his eyebrows. "Don't—"

Downstairs, the doorbell rang.

Once the echo of the gong had faded away, the light came back on. It was only a thick cloud traversing the sun. With all the adrenaline slopping around inside me, my olfactory senses were acting up.

"Gotta go, that must be my latest salesman."

"Myrtle, please. I'm not joking. Have you talked to Mr. Ragwort?"

"I don't know where he is."

"Me neither, that's the whole problem. Okay, let's try a different tack. Meet me at the henge. Tonight at seven."

"I can't make it tonight." No way would I even think of going somewhere with the weirdo until I knew where I stood with him.

"Ah, crap. Sorry. Well, okay. Tomorrow at seven. At the horsehead stone. Oh, wait a minute, I'll give you something for your document."

Chris shot back into the corridor before I could refuse. He returned with a cotton cloth and gloves and placed them on top of the album and folder I was cradling in my left arm.

"Chris—"

"Here, use this to wrap it up. Use the gloves when you handle the parchment. Please do me a favor. If anything is amiss, give me a shout. Here's my card." He pressed a rectangle in my other hand, closed my fingers over it and gave them a short squeeze.

"Chris—"

He whirled around and stormed down the corridor and into his room. My inner eye projected a dark cape fluttering after him. The door slammed shut. I slipped the crumpled card into my pocket.

The doorbell gonged again, more insistently, so I descended, placed the whole shebang on the counter, and welcomed Randy Johnston, Senior Sales Executive for Cyclone Technology Vacuums. What a grand title for a polite, fidgety young man with a prominent Adam's apple.

His presence was reassuring; it provided a welcome

distraction from the bleakness besieging my mind. That must have been the reason why I asked my question with more interest than I might have otherwise shown. "What's cyclone technology when it's at home? A house-proud hurricane?"

Twenty minutes and many glossy brochures later, I managed to send Johnston on his way with his keys. If nothing else, the interlude helped me to regain a wonky balance, and I escaped to the sitting room.

I checked my phone. There was no response from Sarah, so I left another message. Failing that, I could give Alan an earful if he ever turned up.

The light was fading. If I were to clear the shelf any time before Doomsday, I needed help. I would ask the Simpkins sisters tomorrow.

Feeding myself posed a challenge until I spotted the menu of "Mukherjee's Mobile Mahal" lying among the papers on auntie's desk. I ordered dinner and locked up the Asher family tree and my album in the filing cabinet. Then I hit the Internet. It appeared that the Ashers had been wealthy farmers, living south of Avebury until the witch hunters put the ax to them on top of a few others while they were at it.

I unearthed one nugget of gold when I happened upon the name of the chief witch hunter: Robert Enrique Ignatius. I leaned back in the swivel chair and stared at the ceiling.

Coincidence? Unlikely. Like his ancestor, the modern Ignatius was nothing but pond scum, using his riches to meddle in politics. Nor was liberalism his forte. Supremacist, racist, fascist...find a noun, any noun, with a negative connotation ending in *ist*, and it fit the guy like snakeskin. They had to be related.

"My, my, Mr. Ignatius, it appears we've been burning the witches a few centuries past," I said to the monitor, wondering whether my aunt had known of the connection. She must have. She had been a terrific journalist, and the information was not precisely hush-hush.

I tried to figure out how my latest discovery fit the overall puzzle, but soon my head hurt, and the letters on the screen kept wobbling in and out of focus. I switched off the computer.

After finishing my dinner, I yawned my way through the

weather report—a dry day ahead with temperatures in the low teens—before I went back to my room. Late evening curry is not all that conducive to a good night's rest, but after today I was exhausted enough to zonk out in seconds, waking up twice because I was thirsty. All was calm in the attic and auntie's room. Even the cat's snores were less noticeable than usual. That, unfortunately, couldn't be said about her farts.

I had opened the window to let in some air, and when I woke again to a sunny but crisp morning, my breath billowed out in white. No cat was in sight, but I spotted a suspicious lump under the duvet. When I padded to the sideboard for some underwear, the icy floorboards chilled my feet and outside frost powdered the shingles. Would it ever get warm this year?

A quick rummage through my shoddy wardrobe warned me warm weather would have to arrive tomorrow or I would be out of clothes. My trusty, but by now grubby, green fleece would serve another day. So would the jeans, but by tomorrow they would be overdue for a wash. Perhaps it was time to go for retail therapy in the Swindon outlets. The thought alone boosted my mood. I deserved a treat for persevering. If Sergeant Sarah still hadn't made contact by lunchtime, I would visit her in person.

Downstairs, breakfast was almost over, but this time I beat the bacon curfew. Alan had already left, and Randy Johnston and Chris were rustling their way through their respective newspapers. I could have sworn Chris was watching me through his *Guardian,* his gaze tickling a spot between my shoulder blades. I ignored the itch and entered the kitchen from the conservatory.

"Morning." I greeted the ladies busy clearing the clutter.

Instead of responding, Cecily opened the cupboard under the sink and got out a pan. "How about some French toast today?"

My waistline screamed no, but my mouth said, "Yes, please" before the brain could take over.

Alma smiled at me. "Marty said he'd come in the afternoon with a few friends to sort out those rooms. Did you hurt yourself?" She pointed at my cheek.

I fingered the nick, which was small and had already scabbed over, and ignored the queasiness in my stomach. "Battle scars," I said. "Tell me, what's it with the bloke? Jenna's husband, I mean. Is he mental? Why does she put up with him?"

Alma pulled powder blue gloves over her fingers and started scrubbing the wooden cutting boards. "He used to work as a Health and Safety Inspector up north. He hasn't found his feet down here."

Alma was a local girl. "Up north" most likely started at the top end of the Bristol Channel.

"Marty never liked him," Cecily volunteered. "From what I know, Jenna wanted to get out of here, met him—he's a lot older—so that was that."

"Why did they move back in the first place?" I asked.

"He lost his job, and Jenna missed Avebury. Her family has been here forever. Shame her mother died so young, but Dottie looked after Marty and Jenna very well. Brought them up to be decent people."

Dottie. Another name I had heard recently, but I had no idea where. "Dottie Wytchett?"

"Yes, that's her. Poor thing's getting on a bit. Has been popping in and out of hospital recently. Otherwise, she surely would have called. Does a delicious casserole dish."

"She wasn't by any chance helping my aunt with tracing some ancestors?"

Joyous sizzling came from Cecily's pan when she said, "But of course. A funny hobby, if you ask me. I mean, if you want to explore your own family, fine. But that? She was always on the lookout for those folks, ringing them up or visiting and persuading them to come here." Using her wooden spatula, she turned the toast; it was already browning nicely on one side. Four rashers of bacon joined the bread, curling along the edges in an instant.

"What folks?" I asked.

"Oh, I don't know, really. No idea where she got the names

from. Every time she found a dessi...a dissi...I don't know the word, but she was mightily pleased."

"Descendant," I said.

Cecily waved the spatula at me, splattering fat over Alma's freshly cleaned kitchen top. "Dissident. That's it exactly."

Not quite, at least I hoped not.

"Ah, one question. Would you have some time today to help me clear the shelf in the living room? I'll make it worth your while."

Cecily and Alma looked at each other. "Been wanting to do this for ages," Alma said. "Mrs. Coldron didn't let us."

Excitement poked me in the ribs.

"Today won't work," Cecily said. "We've got something on. But how about tomorrow?"

Excitement stopped poking. Could I risk waiting another day? If I started now, I might finish in the afternoon. But there was the appointment with the undertaker, which weighed almost as heavy on my mind as the blasted shelf. I couldn't do both. Once I started clearing the books, even the dumbest villain would know something was afoot. Nor could I rely on nobody noticing what I was up to. No, this job needed to be done in one session.

And I craved my treat.

Was this a reasonable way of solving my problems? No, it wasn't, but somebody had tried to kill me yesterday, dammit.

"Fine, tomorrow it is."

I had to survive the visit to the undertaker. Then I could go shopping with a clean conscience.

Half an hour later I was on my way.

For a Saturday morning, the traffic was surprisingly light. The navigation app in the ripped seat pocket blared: "Drive straight on for another four miles."

Four miles—and over four days since I arrived here. Despite my aunt's death remaining shrouded in mystery, possible motives were taking shape. My hunch had been spot-on: The attacker must be looking for something my aunt had hidden in the Witch's Retreat, either on the shelf my aunt didn't want to see cleaned or in the attic. I hoped the hidden object wouldn't turn out to be a headstone.

That doesn't fit onto the shelf, silly.

It might have been bricked up in the wall during the renovations.

Why would my aunt have hunted down the scions of those oddly named families? Why call them all to Avebury? How did the Ragworts fit into the mix?

The whole affair was like holding an invisible tiger by the tail. Any moment, the beast might materialize, show its fangs and snort its rank breath into my face.

"At the roundabout, take the second exit," the navigation app said.

A blue van shot across my path from the left, and the driver fingered a rude greeting.

Bloody idiots, the lot of them.

The jury was still out my other suspect, Daisy. Somehow, I had never made it to the pub. No problemo, it was easy to fix the oversight on the way home.

"Take the next right."

I set the blinker, turned, and bounced off the curb. Red hot anger flashed through me. The person who had designed those narrow streets ought to be shot.

Then there was Chris. Did auntie find out about his secret trysts with the crowbar and he killed her for her knowledge? But how? Even if that were the case, he should have run for the hills ages ago instead of pestering me.

With an ear-splitting roar, a monstrous vehicle materialized in my path.

My stomach flash-froze, and I yanked at the steering wheel.

With screeching tires, my car shot around the obstacle and straight through the crossing. Hooting and wild flashing followed. I could have sworn the street tilted and straightened out again.

I raced on, my foot glued to the pedal.

A petrol station popped up on my right.

I jerked the steering wheel around once more, still way too fast, and careened past the pumps. The car bounced to a shuddering halt in front of the little shop. A moment later, a face appeared behind the glass panels, the mouth a big round O.

There I sat, shaking in my seat, a lump where my stomach had been, my breath searing my windpipe.

"Turn around if possible," the navigation app said.

I wobbled into the shop and bought myself an iced tea and a bar of chocolate. Back in my old Ford, I polished off the drink and devoured the chocolate while the images of my near-accident kept replaying in my head. I must have been inches away from getting rammed by that lorry.

I needed to stop spinning wild theories while driving. Otherwise, I would be the next one lying cold in a coffin.

15

ANTIDOTE

Miller's Funeral Service operated from West Swindon, a safe distance from the psychedelic roundabout that made the town notorious. During the drive, I checked every side street. I braked when the lights turned yellow, stuck to the speed limit and still arrived on time. I must have been racing like a wild thing during the first part of my trip.

"You have reached your destination," said the navigation app.

"Are you so sure?" I asked, looking around. I crept past a row of whitewashed Georgian buildings complete with bay windows, porches, brass knockers, and similar adornments. Lawyers had hung their shingles here, so had chartered accountants and even a midwife. I didn't see a funeral home, at least nothing that resembled the image nurtured by reading every single Stephanie Plum adventure. A flashy affair with neon lights and large windows showcasing the latest trend in coffins would've caused me to stomp on the brake pedal.

Miller's was nothing like that. Therefore, I nearly missed it.

What I took at first to be a black and gold pub sign featured the undertaker's name without stating the business. An arrow under the board advertised customer parking in the rear. The only other client had arrived by hearse and was being transported inside by two gentlemen in dark suits. The metal door they pushed through couldn't be the main access, so I parked the car and returned to the front where the ebony veneer of the entrance gleamed from the pebbly plasterwork.

My smartphone chose that moment to warble the theme from the Harry Potter movies into air reeking faintly of chemicals.

That would be the sergeant. I would have to rehash yesterday's attack.

The lid flew off my memory box and back came the images in all their gore. My fingers turned slippery, and it took me a while to retrieve the phone that kept mocking me with its tinkling.

"Hello, Myrtle Coldron here?"

The response was a faint crackling and hissing.

"Hello-oh."

More hissing. Was it breathing or static?

The connection broke.

Strange, but these things happened. My phone had a life of its own and kept ringing people while it tumbled among the junk I hauled around. Somebody else seemed to be suffering from the same problem.

My phone safely returned to the leather backpack, I entered a room that struck me with its stark efficiency. No subtle violin concertos played in the background and there were no plush carpets, only a modern office with fake beech wood desks surrounded by white, unadorned walls. Bronze chandeliers hanging from the ceiling were the one concession to interior design. There was no clutter. Everything appeared neat and professional.

Just like Aunt Eve.

Those damn tears constricted my throat when reality hit home. This was it. This was the end of the line. Even if I solved the mystery, she would not be coming back. We were preparing for her burial.

"Madam are you all right?" said a smooth voice, the tone concerned. A gray-haired man in a charcoal suit and silver tie walked up and laid a hand on my arm. This simple touch made me want to bawl out loud. I dug my fingernails into my palms instead, embracing the pain. "Sorry, I'm not myself lately."

"That's unfortunately not unusual in this type of situation. Welcome to Miller and Daughters, I'm Mr. Miller. Ms. Coldron, I presume? If you would follow me, please."

The funeral director led me into a cubicle separated from the central office by a large wooden folding door, which he pulled shut. I found myself in another no-nonsense room. This time, however, somebody had tried to brighten things. The walls were adorned with pictures of a birch copse in spring, autumn, and winter. Not summer, though. Mr. Miller dealt with the twilight side of life and did so expertly. Calmly, he took me through what he called the arrangements. Auntie wanted no ceremony, only a simple gathering of her friends at the henge.

Mr. Miller steepled his fingers over his silvery tie. What I had taken for blurry black dots were in reality minute feathers. "Mrs. Coldron wanted to be cremated," he said. "She has, however, left no clear instructions on the disposal of her ashes. Any suggestions?"

I pulled open the zip of my rucksack and dug out the tourism pamphlet I had—at the last moment—remembered to bring. It fell open on the center spread, and I pointed at the cross and the comment. "Can this be done at all?"

Miller's index finger tapped the brochure. "If you're thinking of an official ceremony, which is not what your aunt wanted, it will take a while. If not, I can hardly advise you to go there and act on her wish."

Miller stared at me intensely as if saying, "Go right ahead."

"Isn't this a bit strange?"

He pursed his pale lips. "Strange? People pay money to have their ashes scattered from a mountain or into the sea. Why not in the old henge? Was Mrs. Coldron a pagan?"

"In her spare time," I said. "The idea strikes me as—untidy."

Mr. Miller hesitated before he spoke. "She made all these arrangements fairly recently," he said. "It gave me the impression there was something on her mind. To be quite honest, I didn't expect to have her with us yet. Such a healthy and vigorous person."

The man would make a great confessor. His voice flowed like balm over my jittery nerves, and it was hard not to share my bagful of troubles there and then. Instead, having discussed more unsavory details and dates, we rose.

"Well." Miller's hand was already on the doorknob. "No need to decide on the spot. You can always bring her home and deal with things later."

I stared at him. "You mean keep the urn?"

Mr. Miller smiled his professional smile, which economized on the display of teeth. "It's quite common. Maybe she has left further instructions that supersede the ones you have here?" He pointed at the pamphlet. "Then you can be certain you're not doing something you might regret later. You wouldn't be comfortable with it, believe me. Shall we go ahead then?"

I assumed Mr. Miller meant the cremation. I swallowed once and nodded. The funeral home would contact me when it was all over. We shook hands, and I left, his words still echoing in my mind.

Keep the ashes? I could ask Daisy, but I still was unsure where I stood with her. The thought hurt, so I shelved in for the moment.

Back in my car, I headed for the outlet center. My visit to the funeral directors had been oddly therapeutic, and when I parked, this time in a vast open space where canned music brayed from the loudspeakers, I mentally thanked Mr. Miller for his moral support. Sympathy was part of his business, being a practical tool of his trade, but he had helped me a lot.

A few more boosts like that, and I should feel *compos mentis* again.

I went shopping.

The outlet center was heaving, and I had to push my way through the lunchtime crowd. Where should I start? Work my way out from the inner layer at Veronica's Desire or vice versa at Chic For Less?

Once more, my phone threw Harry Potter at me. Like last time, there was no voice, only crackling and hissing. This time, I decided it didn't sound like static. It sounded like somebody's rapid breathing.

"Tosser." I disconnected. If I needed any proof somebody was after me, here it was. Unfortunately, he had hidden his caller ID, which meant I had no log.

Relax, my inner voice shushed, helpful for once. *Tell Sarah when you meet her later.*

I sucked in courage together with a lot of soggy spring air and joined the fray.

Trousers came first since those were easy. A pair of decent jeans, a pair of beige slacks. I had my eyes set on some emerald ones, but the shop assistant talked me out of them. Shop assistants often tried to talk me out of wearing bright colors. They said they didn't go with my pale face, the freckles or "that strawberry blonde." Usually, I stood my ground, but this saleswoman went the whole hog and pulled me in front of a body-length mirror, pointing out the merits of neutral colors until I caved in. I had to admit it made buying T-shirts easier. Orange, red or olive—they all would go well with those new trousers.

"The green is okay, but I would be careful with the other two," said a familiar voice.

I turned around and faced Sergeant Sarah. Despite carrying two large carrier bags, she appeared unruffled and quietly elegant in the black-and-white striped blazer she wore over a white blouse.

"Have you considered buying a jacket?" Sarah asked. She tried her best to hide it, but there had been the briefest wrinkling of her nose when she examined my beloved fleece peeping out from under my disreputable Barbour. Fair enough; it did whiff of cat and fried breakfast.

"That comes later," I explained. Guilty as charged for looking dowdy.

Sarah frowned. "I suggest you try matching things from the outset. I've seen something that might suit you." With that she turned around, leaving me no choice but to follow the fashion police. She plowed her way through the mall crowd easily, even without blue lights flashing. To give Sarah her due, when we emerged hours later I was loaded down with bags and their contents made me happier with myself. I would never have gone for what Sarah called "spring colors," but they suited me. The long blazer in a gold-specked creamy chenille was my favorite. It fit my annoying bust while camouflaging my even more annoying hips.

"I owe you a coffee," I said, when I panted out of the last shop, glowing with happiness. "And a cake. Or whatever it is you take," I added. With her figure, Sarah probably thrived on undressed lettuce leaves.

"I'll take both, but you don't have to," she said.

Aha, no lettuce then. My kind of girl. She was wrong though—I needed to. Here was another young woman, competent, likeable and making her way in a tough profession. I figured she must be harboring similar sympathies. Otherwise, she wouldn't have spent the last two hours helping me with my purchases, sometimes giggling like a teenager at the clothes I found suitable and she did not.

By the time the coffee, water, and cakes arrived we were swapping anecdotes of our respective professions—superiors in positions they didn't deserve, colleagues from hell—typical girl's talk. Yet our conversation wasn't altogether ordinary. There was an elephant squeezed in with us in that busy café, and I decided I would be the one to name it. Sarah was too tactful.

"I've just come from the funeral directors," I said. "Do I assume correctly there has been no further development with that non-investigation of yours?"

Sarah stirred the rest of her coffee and sighed. "I'm afraid so, yes. The DI flips when he hears the word 'B&B.'"

That reminded me of something. "You lot did go through my aunt's boxes, the ones she kept in the bedroom, right?"

"We did indeed. But there was nothing relevant in there." She scrutinized the inside of her cup. "Nothing relevant to the case."

I winced. She must have seen the report on the headstone caper that cost my parents' their lives.

Sarah reached across and grabbed my arm. "I was hoping

to stop you from rummaging around up there, that's why I kept the keys."

"Happens I had a spare set."

Sarah's grin faded away. "I knew the moment I got your messages. My apologies, whenever I wanted to return your call and your aunt's keys, these burglaries interfered. Speaking of burglaries, what exactly did you find in Mr. Lentulus's room? Ah, did you enquire about that ladder?"

"Well, according to the Simpkins sisters, the thing doesn't belong to the house. I found it hidden in the garden, by the way, just before the attack. As to Lentulus, think crowbar. Ropes. Stuff like that."

Her eyes widened and her mouth twitched. "I won't ask you what you were doing in the man's room in the first place. You think he might be part of our gang of burglars?"

"Eh, yes. I can see you don't agree. He told me he's a historian by design and works in IT, but I had my doubts."

"He's a database specialist and a professional hacker," Sarah said.

"Isn't that illegal?"

"Not necessarily. Mr. Lentulus advises companies on how to block holes in their firewalls. Attacks them, and when the walls come tumbling down, shows them how to make them stronger."

"From what I saw in his room, hackers must earn a boatload of money."

"Hah, I wonder why that guy bothers to work at all. Oops." She covered her mouth with her hand.

"Why wouldn't he?"

Sarah shook her head, seemingly reading her future in the dregs of her now-empty coffee cup. "Can't tell you."

I narrowed my eyes. I had experienced the woman in her official capacity, her body language stiff and forbidding. Now, she was leaning forward as if waiting for me to contradict her. It was worth a try.

"Come on, that's not fair. It can't be a police secret, otherwise, you wouldn't have let rip like that."

A deep sigh. A spoon tapping on the saucer. "You're a disgustingly shrewd observer. It wasn't even related to the investigation."

"Sarah..."

"Okay, okay. I'll tell you. Please don't blab. Otherwise, I'm in real trouble. We found the connection by accident, and it's got nothing to do with your aunt's demise."

"Out with it. What connection?"

"He doesn't need to burgle. He's loaded. That's because he's Bob Ignatius's nephew. On the maternal side, hence the different name."

16

GOING AROUND IN CIRCLES

Ping, ping. The spoon chinked on Sarah's saucer. Even in the crowded café, the sharp sound rang out and heads turned toward us. The babble lulled before it swelled once more.

"Urgh." My mind went to the fake Malleus and I wiped my hands on the greasy napkin. Had my aunt known who she let into her house?

"Yup. Give Mr. Lentulus his due, he's trying to make a living without drawing on the family fleshpots. But enough of that. I need to know what happened yesterday." Sarah fumbled in her ruby red leather purse and fished out a notepad. Pen poised, she gave me an intense look, the policewoman back in control.

At first, telling was hard. That arm whooshing down, the hole that suddenly appeared in the doorframe, the splinters flying—the horror returned with a vengeance and the sediment of yesterday's panic coated my tongue. But we got there eventually. I reached for my glass of water and found it empty.

"We'll order some more," Sarah said. She stowed her notepad away, an unreadable expression on her face. "Why didn't you contact Hunter? He's got most of the weekend off for once, but he wanted to leave you a message or email on where to reach him."

"Hang on, I'll check my spam filter." Sure enough, there it was. Sent from his private email account, he listed his private phone number, which was way beyond the call of duty. My treacherous fingers crept into my pocket and touched the little card Chris had given me. I withdrew them hastily.

"Okay, I'll talk to the DI. You might have spooked the alleged attacker and he, that's assuming it's a he, overreacted. Let me finish," she hastened to add when she saw my expression. "If you ask me, it's obvious there's something rather fishy going on. I believe we should have another look. Let me see what I can do. Can I convince you to move out in the meantime?"

I shook my head.

She sighed. "Didn't think you would. You're too stubborn for your own good."

"What would you do in my place?"

Her lips pursed. "Touché. But whatever else happens, keep me in the loop. Or the constable if I don't respond immediately. Now, let's order something stronger than water."

Amen to that.

She signaled for the waitress, a young woman who I guessed hailed from Sub-Saharan Africa. The nameplate over her gray and burgundy-striped smock read "Teena." She wove her way around the tables, the beads in her ebony braids clacking.

"Would you serve sparkly here?" Sarah asked.

"With pleasure." Teena clacked her beads and dashed off.

Once she had brought our order, we clinked glasses to our new friendship. I promised once more—both to Sarah and to myself—that I would be more cautious in the future. Cross my heart and hope not to die.

An hour later I rolled—carefully—out of Swindon in much better shape than when I arrived. Some twenty miles on, the golden light of a spring afternoon softened the outlines of the lost rocks, almost as if it wanted to heal the scars left behind by the passing of time.

The car stayed in the pub's client parking. I would eat at the pub after I had another word with my cousin. The meeting with Chris needed canceling, and I fumbled for his card. My fingers closed around the little rectangle, but something stopped me from pulling it out. Instead, I strolled northward through the circle, my shadow lengthening at my side, gliding over the lush green grass, curly leaves of cowslip and fresh daisies. There were few stones in this part of the ancient monument, so it was hard to get my bearings. I shrugged off my backpack and removed the tourism brochure. According to auntie's map, this had to be the right spot, but the soggy ground under my grotty trainers could be a cow pasture, minus the cows, anywhere in rural England.

Instead, the diluted remnants of sheep droppings caked the grass. From the banks that embraced the empty circle a murder of crows took off in a rushing of wings. Their departure signaled the sparrows and finches to start their sunset chorus in the bushes. My aunt's future resting place made for a scene of bucolic calm, a scene distinctly at odds with the worry sweeping through me.

My mobile phone shrilled into the clammy air and the uneasiness mushroomed into dread. "Yes?"

Static. The same buzzing and breathing I had encountered twice before. Nope, this was no accident.

This time, dread got pushed aside by a hot stab of fury. "Listen, you wanker, whoever you are, stop this. I've called the cops." I stabbed the disconnect button in barren wrath. Had I mentioned the calls to Sarah? No, I hadn't. Typical.

The chill wind found its way down my neck, and the hairs rose in response. I could have sworn the stones had shifted, had crept closer while I wasn't looking. The cold spread through my body, so I moved, heading for a whole cluster of the old rocks. Without the brochure, I wouldn't have known there once had been three circles, two smaller ones within the confines of a more significant ring on the outside.

"What the builders had in mind was a body of a snake passing through a circle. It's a traditional alchemical symbol,"

Chris said. My heart leaped at my throat and I slipped on something that hopefully was a damp leaf and nothing worse. No way could it be seven o'clock already.

I swallowed. "Hello, and good afternoon to you, too."

"Your brochure isn't very accurate," Chris responded, digging his hands into the pockets of his cornflower blue walking jacket—an expensive brand, of course.

"Well, my aunt wrote it and she tended to be quite thorough with the facts. She wants to be buried here." I bit my tongue, but the words were already out.

He regarded me through long lashes wasted on a man. "You mean within the stone circle? Or right here?"

I gave him a blank stare.

"The northern part would be much more suitable. There's supposed to be a hotspot there. May I?" Without waiting for my response, Chris snatched the brochure from my hands and scrutinized auntie's comment. With a nod, he handed back the pamphlet. "Makes sense. If one believes in those things." He strolled across to the nearest standing stone and leaned against it, his arms dangling at his sides, his long legs crossed at the ankles. He had the Latin-lover good looks I swooned over in my favorite movies.

"Hotspot?" I asked. My cheeks would have qualified, but I couldn't imagine that was what he meant.

"The prime meridian ley line runs straight through the circle. At certain points, the power is supposed to be extra strong. Some people claim they can feel it."

"Do you?"

Chris laughed as the wind tousled his dark hair. "Not me, no. Sorry, I'm a factual guy. What about you?" His gaze became intense, pinning me to the spot. "Do you feel anything when you're close to the stones? Or, more generally, since you arrived in Avebury?"

I regarded the sodden ground at my feet and the flattened daisies. Nothing hot about this place. Apart from a certain young man leaning against a piece of rock, that is.

The wind sprang up again and crept up my arms, a millipede made of air.

"I'm a factual girl."

His face grim, Chris pushed himself off the stone and ambled toward the outer bank. I followed him like a lamb before I realized what I was doing. He stopped at another boulder, but in the grip of a nameless frustration, I walked on. This time, he trailed after me.

I whirled around. "What's your problem? Why this cloak and dagger routine?"

The sun disappeared behind a bank of clouds, backlighting their edges with a fiery rim. Again, the wind rose, stirring the twigs of the nearby trees, carrying with it a moist bouquet of squashed grass and garlicky aromas from the pub.

"Myrtle, this is not about mysteries. This is about you. If you don't..." He shook his head and turned away from me. His fingers, long and slim, almost lovingly traced the surface of a standing stone, its flat top dripping with a blood-red fungus. While I waited for words that never came, I grew cold again. And more frustrated. Every human being has a breaking point. With anonymous aggressors coming after me, auntie's bizarre demise, the frustrating will and the general atmosphere of sticky confusion and slow-burning menace, my patience overstretched and ripped.

"Either tell me what your true purpose is or leave."

There was a strange glitter in his eyes when he regarded me. "I can't tell you. You've got to work it out for yourself. Yes, I will go. I'm doing more harm than good. You have my card. Call me if you need me. I'll come as fast as I can. Oh, and be careful around Alan."

Why did I suddenly feel so hollow inside? "That's two things."

His smile was without humor. "Look, Alan is both lazy and ambitious. He'll do anything to be accepted into the CID. Getting this case reopened and solving it would do nicely, believe me."

"I wouldn't mind if he did."

"You might not like his methods."

When Chris left, he took the sun with him.

The aromatic warmth of the Whacky Bramble draped itself around me when I entered, but it did nothing for my black mood. I hung up my coat and shook hands with Greg, the gentle giant, cringing at my nasty thoughts about him. Soft piano music drifted from the speakers. The pub was almost empty. Occupying the same table near the window sat the elderly couple from two days ago. A little voice niggled at the back of my brain telling me I had come across them somewhere other than the pub.

"Table for one?" Greg asked.

I tuned out the loneliness howling inside. "Yes, please. Unless my cousin is around?"

He guided me to the same pews where Daisy and I had dined. Once more, flames danced in their deep purple bowls and the gaudy pillows beckoned, only they didn't suit my mood. I wasn't hungry either. What was I doing here?

"She took another day off, ma'am. She works too much as it is and we've got a helper now. You didn't catch up with her yesterday, then?" Greg asked. He handed me the menu. "She went across to fetch something from her room. At least that's what she planned. With her, I'm never sure where I stand. She's such a butterfly," he said wistfully.

Butterfly? I wondered whether Daisy had indeed shown up and, instead of talking, had lashed out at me in auntie's room. She worked out. She might be stronger than I could imagine, but was she strong enough to power a hard object into the doorframe? The chill crept deeper into my bones. If my scenario was correct, then my cousin must have hated me with a vengeance. Whatever little appetite might have brought me here had gone out of the window with Greg's words. To be polite, I ordered a chicken salad and, once the Saturday evening crowd had arrived and the pub was heaving, I had it wrapped up and left.

I pushed the invading thoughts aside for the return journey, but the moment I opened the door to the Witch's Retreat, the evil mill started spinning again in my head, faster than before. Chris's car was gone and the key to the room hung on the board. He pre-paid by the week, that much I knew. How I wished there had been a bill to settle.

It was inconsequent of me, yes. But who cared.

Not that Chris was my biggest worry. Daisy deserved the honor. She had been here yesterday and never shown herself. Or maybe she had. At best, she harbored a secret. Perhaps she even knew why my aunt spirited away the headstone and where it was hidden. At worst, she might be trying to drive me mad or away from the B&B. With me no longer lodging in Number Seven and being a general nosy nuisance, she would be free to explore the attic.

The knots in my stomach twisted and tightened.

That was assuming she was after the headstone or whatever else was hidden here. Things could be even worse. With me out of the way, Daisy would inherit everything.

The mill spun faster.

The American giant appeared to be ever such a kind man. At the same time, he was smitten. Still, it couldn't have been Greg on the ladder. He would have made a lot more noise.

Somehow, I had ended up in the kitchen, fidgety like a jellyfish stuck on a live wire. The place was tidy as always. Yet, it looked different. When I faced the window, I saw why. One of the Simpkins sisters had emptied the pots of the dead flowers, cleaned them and neatly stacked them on top of each other. In proud possession of the windowsill sat the surviving rogue primula, covered in a riot of pink and yellow blooms. More buds were poking out from underneath the curly green leaves.

"You're a miracle, you know," I said to the plant. I checked, but it had enough water. I took a mental note to go online and find out what sort of primula it was. Apart from the clashing colors and the size, it looked perfectly ordinary. Yet, when I first met Chris, the flower had been all dried up.

Chris was gone and it was my fault.

I slammed the lid on my traitorous thoughts.

Shortly before exiting the kitchen, I noticed the same faint rustle as before. I whirled around. No movement. No mice. No cat either.

"It's about you," Chris had said.

"About you... About you..." The echo of words that I thought were unspoken whispered from the corners of the empty kitchen.

Was I now going mad?

I fled to the reception where I found a plate bearing a lopsided pound cake dotted with raisins on the counter. Underneath it sat a pile of condolence letters and a note from Alma.

The Ragworts have returned to Number Two. We've got two Druids in Number Five and a professor in Number Six. The prof I can shift to Number One if he wants to stay on. There's no space for the Druids after tomorrow, the Germans are coming. Herr and Frau Schlüsselblum with their son and daughter. They need big rooms. Need to discuss.

P.S. Cake is from Linda at the Crystal Dawn.

Either the booking challenges spelled out in Alma's blocky handwriting or the piece of cake I broke off and munched yanked me out of my blue funk. Whatever it was, it also triggered an errant brainwave. I knew where I had seen the couple I had encountered first on Thursday, then again tonight, sitting by the pub's window—in auntie's clippings.

I had found the Ragworts.

Or rather, they had found me.

17

POISON

Despite—or because of—yesterday's upheavals, I slept like the dead until the dawn chorus chirped, tweeted and crowed its way into my subconscious, waking me up. The pearly light of the morning seeped through a crack in the curtains, and Tiddles lay in her usual place at my feet, twitching and whimpering in the throes of a kitty dream. Still wondering why the *concerto al fresco* had disturbed me today when it hadn't before, I made for the bathroom and relieved a pressing need. The air in Number Seven was fresh, but not quite as freezing as yesterday. That was typical. Now I had kitted myself out with new gear, spring had finally arrived. At least, nobody had tried to remove the Asher family tree from the filing cabinet. Everything was still in place when I checked last night. Either that or my new clothes neatly stacked on the off-white sideboard, buoyed my mood.

I felt at peace with myself for about ten seconds. Then I heard surreptitious footsteps outside in the corridor. Brushing across the carpet. Stopping in front of my door.

Number Seven was the only guest room on the top floor. Other than Daisy, me or the Simpkins sisters, nobody should need to come up here. The Simpkins sisters didn't sneak. Daisy might, though.

Then there was silence. Had I imagined things?

Tiddles' head shot up, and she murped at me sleepily. The cat's pointy ears twitched, but her hearing wasn't the most reliable at the best of times. I strained to listen but got only white noise that rapidly filled with the drumming of my heart.

Time stretched on an elastic band while I crept to the door and pressed my ear against the panel. Between the roaring in my head and the triumphant crowing of a rooster outside, it was impossible to make out any alien sounds.

Sucking in air, I counted to three, turned the key, ripped open the door and shouted, "Who's there?" into the empty air of the corridor.

No intruder. Not a speck marred the deep-sea blue of the carpet.

You're dreaming.

When a breeze tousled my hair, I looked up. The window facing the garden stood open and admitted the persistent crowing of the over-energetic cockerel. The Simpkins sisters' obsession with leaving things open was fast becoming a royal pain in the patootie.

I checked the landing and found both the trapdoor and the entrance to my aunt's room shut. Daisy's door was still locked. I decided enough was enough. Unless Sarah returned my aunt's keys sharpish, I would get a professional locksmith on site—if necessary, at gunpoint.

My pulse had dropped from life-threatening levels to something merely unhealthy, and I climbed back into bed. My feet were numb with cold, so I tucked them under the duvet. A soft weight moved along on top of the covers. Tiddles was searching for company.

"Come here, old stinky pelt," I mumbled. The cat snuggled in the crook of my arm, her fur feathery silk under my hands. She sighed once and fell asleep again in an instant. Tiddles' purring warmth was reassuring. Before long, I joined her and dozed off.

A slightly more civilized hour saw me on my way down the stairs to the conservatory. Two gentlemen in flowing white robes beamed at me over their breakfast when I bade them good morning. They swallowed their fried mushrooms and blessed my path.

That was kind of them. If my path on this Earth were to continue, I needed all the help I could get. With a spring in my step, I passed Alan's table, sporting the number three on top of a cauldron. It sat untouched. His car waited in the car park out front, and I deduced he must be enjoying a lie-in. Well, it was Sunday, after all.

The Ragworts sat at the table in front of the old fireplace, struggling through their full English. I gave them a friendly greeting but didn't make any further overtures since I wanted to observe them first. Checking out the cereal buffet on the sideboard gave me the perfect alibi for inspecting the newcomers.

In their mid-sixties or thereabouts, they were kitted out with practical hiking gear, their waterproof coats dangling over the one free chair at their table. Both looked lean, the woman unhealthily so. Her clothes flapped on her gaunt frame as if bought in stouter times. Pain had stamped lines into her narrow face, and her baby-fine white hair was cropped short; I wondered whether it might have fallen out and was growing back.

Auntie's pictures had shown her in much better health. It was likely the reason I hadn't recognized her before.

Her husband appeared unchanged, apart from his hair, which was streaked with gray. He gazed at his wife through his tortoiseshell spectacles, an anxious expression on a face as smooth as hers was haggard.

They pushed back their chairs, and the woman struggled out of her seat.

I dashed across the room to their table. "May I help you?"

"You're a darling. Once I get moving, all will be fine."

"You're Eve's niece, aren't you?" her husband asked.

I turned around and faced his bespectacled face. Violet owl eyes blinked, magnified by the lenses.

"May I express my condolences at the passing of your aunt? Such a wonderful person."

I shook his dry, stick-like fingers and mumbled something noncommittal.

Mrs. Ragwort smiled at me. "This must be a tough time

for you. I hear you're a teacher, not a landlady. Oh, where are my manners? I'm Rosie. I used to be a teacher myself, you know. Damian here was a librarian. Very brave of you for taking this place on."

"Well, thank you, but I've got help. Cecily and Alma are real gems." After another dose of small talk, I might be able to ask the questions that really weighed on my mind, such as: "What the heck is going on here?"

Rosie's face lit up, haunted by the ghost of her youth. "They are, they are. You're fortunate. Still, losing Eve was such a shock. She did so much for us, brought us all together." A surprising passion trembled in her thin voice. Reddish blotches discolored her hollow cheeks, and her eyes had taken on a feverish shine.

Her husband patted her hand once more. "Hush, the doctor said not to get excited."

I was ready to launch my first question when Damian spoke again. "We've bought a property here in Avebury, isn't that nice? We'd like to stay on at your place for a while, if we may, during the renovations."

"I'd be honored. Actually, you mentioned something interesting about my aunt bringing you all together. Perhaps—"

Rosie checked her wristwatch and clucked anxiously.

Damian nodded. "Frightfully sorry, we've got to meet with the builder. Let's talk later, all right?"

He shook my hands once more with enthusiasm, Rosie smiled her waning smile, and slowly the couple shuffled toward the exit, Damian matching his stride to his wife's hesitant steps. I wondered why they needed the hiking gear when she was apparently not capable of much exercise. Perhaps they wanted to support the illusion. Maybe they wanted to believe they still were the people they had been before illness and old age imposed their indignities.

They spoke to each other, ever so softly, and it had to be a freak of the currents in this house that I caught some of their muted exchange.

"I don't believe she's aware, dear," said Rosie.

"No," said Damian. "Nothing we can do about it."

The door shut behind them. I wanted to scream and kick

the furniture, but it would have startled the druids. What wasn't I aware of?

Still seething and cursing British politeness under my breath, I shoved open the door to the kitchen, my hands full with depleted fruit bowls.

"Morning, ladies."

"Morning," Alma said. "You found my message?"

"Yes. And the cake. We can have it later, once we're done with the shelf. You're still game?"

"Oh, yes," Cecily said.

"Number Two is empty," I said. "Mr. Lentulus is gone."

Alma dunked her dishes, and Cecily kept polishing cutlery. "Means we have space for the argy-bargy prof," she said eventually.

It didn't take me more than a couple of seconds to work out what she meant.

"Archaeology? Yes, we do," I said.

Crockery clattered in the otherwise silent kitchen until Cecily opened the door under the sink and deposited a clean pan inside. "Well, I've thrown out those dead plants. They didn't look right, their leaves all shriveled up. Made me sad to no end. Should I have kept them?"

"No, it's okay. They won't ever come back."

Her tired face lit up with relief while for some odd reason my mood dropped to the antipodes. I grabbed a bowl of cornflakes and some tea before beating a retreat to the conservatory.

Alan's table remained empty.

My appetite had vanished, so I nibbled at my breakfast before I pushed back the bowl and retreated to my room. On my way up the stairs, I took a mental note to ring my—or rather Aunt Eve's—financial advisor tomorrow. The sooner I found a way of keeping my ladies employed, the better, and without me running the show. Daisy's pecuniary plight could wait a bit until I knew where I stood with her but inquiring what might be possible wouldn't hurt.

I also needed to cajole the headmistress into giving me another reprieve, if necessary unpaid. No way could I continue with my teaching duties while bogged down with this mess.

When I entered the top floor corridor, my eyes fell on a piece of paper blown under one of the coffee tables. I must have forgotten to close the window. My oversight corrected, I kneeled and picked up the sheet that I suspected belonged in one of my aunt's cardboard boxes.

A quick glimpse and my stomach petrified into a leaden lump. That piece of paper had never been part of auntie's collection. The note was covered in letters crudely cut from newspapers and magazines, glued onto the paper kidnap-fashion to form a short but disastrously clear message:

Bitch. Where are they? My patience is running out. You have forty-eight hours to find them. If you don't, you will regret it. Your aunt is dead. Need I say more?

I hadn't imagined the footsteps this morning. Somebody had been up there and delivered this letter, which then got blown away by the breeze. It still found me. How I wished it hadn't.

I raced down the stairs, the sheet of paper in my hand, and banged on the door to Alan's room. No response. Why did he have to be asleep when I needed him? I fumbled for my smartphone to call Sarah. Hang on, he might be at breakfast.

I bolted back into the conservatory, and there he was, just sitting down at his table.

I slammed the disgusting note next to his plate. "Read this," I shouted. Fortunately, Alan was the last guest left in the room.

He studied the letter. "Oh, bugger," he said and whipped out his mobile.

Alan blurted into the speaker, apparently calling in reinforcements. I sank onto the nearest chair, dazed.

Alan wrapped the napkin around his hands and picked up the note. "This is evidence. HQ will have to check it for fingerprints."

"You'll find mine on there," I said.

"Yes," he said with a frown. "I wished you hadn't touched it. Can't be helped. Can I get you something?" he asked a tick belatedly. "You're rather pale."

"Tea," I said. The panacea for all woes, but I needed it. My throat had dried up, and my head was spinning. This couldn't be happening.

Alan grabbed a fresh cup from the neighboring table and poured the dregs from his pot. I drank greedily, holding onto the cup with both hands, my teeth chattering on its rim. Warmth spread from my stomach and diluted the shock. The bitter brew made me come to my senses, and the terror slowly dissipated.

"I spoke to Sergeant Widdlethorpe yesterday. She said to let her know when something else happens. I would imagine this letter qualifies." My voice sounded croaky. I was babbling but I couldn't help it. "There's the business with the petals. Twice. Plus, I disturbed another intruder the other day. And somebody's been calling me without ever saying a word." I blurted out the words in one breath.

Alan was scanning the note once more. "I called in the troops, never you worry. Do you have any idea what the writer of this little missive wants? It makes me wonder if your aunt hid something."

He frowned at me from under his fringe. "Think," he urged.

Nothing was further from my mind than thinking.

Cecily turned up and deposited a piping hot pot of tea on the table. Grateful for her kindness, I poured myself a fresh cup. Alma's head poked through the door to the kitchen, and she regarded me with a world of woe showing in her eyes. "I knew Mrs. Coldron's death was the doing of an evil person," she said.

"No evidence for that," Alan said. "Interesting vocabulary in this note, though." He pointed at the first word of the message, which had been cut out whole from an article in a glossy magazine. The word was beautifully penned, adorned by whorls, gilded leaves with little figures crawling all over the design, but it was hard to decipher.

"What do you make of this?" Alan flapped his hand at the message. His hands were large and generous with light blond hairs feathering the knuckles. They were nice and at odds with his callousness.

I figured he must be keen on using my troubles to boost his career as Chris had said. Alan reminded me of a high-speed train thundering down the track with me sucked along in the slipstream. If it brought the desired results, I had no problem coming along for the ride.

"I didn't know they called women bitches in the middle ages," I said.

Alan frowned. "Believe me, they didn't. I did my thesis on manuscript culture in Europe. I would know. Plus, the cutting must be a photo of an illustrated bible or something. The monks copied those texts in the scriptorium. Unlikely they would use such language."

Cecily moved closer, her shadow falling over the sheet. She would have tapped it, had Alan not grabbed her hand. "Careful, fingerprints," he said. He was overdoing it, but there you go.

She backed away, her eyes still fixed on the note. "But that's not what it says. It's not the right word."

"What word?" Alan rubbed the palm of his hand with this thumb.

"Bitch?" I asked. The tea had done its job, and my anger was resurfacing.

Cecily clucked her tongue. "That word, yes. No, I mean. It says something else. That's what I mean."

Alma crept next to her sister and read the note. She nodded. "Yes. Not that nasty word."

"What are you lot on about?" Alan repeated his question, his gaze shifting from the paper to the sisters and back again.

"Tell me," I said.

The Simpkins sisters spoke in unison, like a Greek chorus. "Witch."

18

WHICH WITCH

Witch. Lurking among the elaborate scrollwork of the magazine cutting, the word reminded me of those trick images camouflaging figures, faces, and objects: hidden one moment, all too visible the next. Some bastard had called me a witch. Where I needed guidance from my aunt—a note, a letter—anything, all I got was a whacky message.

Did it scare my socks off?

Oh, yes.

"I would need a plastic bag for the letter. Can you get me one from the kitchen?" Alan said to Alma. His voice penetrated the confused sludge clogging my mind.

"Now I've ruined your weekend," I said.

Alan, standing on the other side of his table, drummed the backrest of the chair with his fingers. "Never you mind. It's more important to work out what might be behind the threat." His gaze bounced off me and landed again on the message from the glue artist, where it stayed. I wondered whether I might have overlooked something and stepped closer.

"Don't!" Alan grabbed his napkin and used it to carry his precious note to the French windows. Fogged up with condensation and covered in a rash of raindrops, they didn't let through enough of the light he needed to examine the threatening message, assuming that was his goal. The guy really ought to work on his family liaison skills. The way he acted made me wonder whether he might view me as a culprit and not a victim.

Alma returned, Cecily trailing behind, with the bag Alan had requested. He wrapped the napkin around his fingers and used it to deposit his evidence in the plastic pouch.

"Do me a favor and check the wastepaper baskets," he said to the Simpkins sisters.

"What for?" Cecily asked.

"Well, the letters are cut out from newsprint and magazines. It's unlikely somebody would throw away the leftovers here, but I want to be sure."

The ladies strode off, two bloodhounds on the scent.

When Alan faced me—or rather a point somewhere over my left shoulder—his brows were drawn into a line almost as straight as his fringe. "Is one of these salespeople still around?"

"Mr. Johnston left yesterday."

Alan deposited the bag on the table, whipped out a notebook from the depth of his pants and addressed the French windows. "He'll have to be contacted."

No way would young Randy write threatening notes. He had arrived on the scene well after my aunt's death. But Alan was thorough and thorough was fine with me, though why the blasted message would have brought back the awkwardness from our first encounter was beyond me. The way he kept staring at the fogged panes, wringing his hands, made me wonder whether he wanted me to leave the room.

I decided to take the bull by the horns. "Is there a problem?"

Alan swung around, this time meeting my gaze. "What do you mean?"

"You're acting a bit odd."

He forced a smile. "Sorry. I'm not the world's greatest people person. It's such a great opportunity. Eh, I mean, something really is off in this place, don't you think?"

Again, he gave me the full wattage of his baby blues. Not for long, though.

"Yes, fascinating, isn't it?"

Alan seemed oblivious to sarcasm. "Don't you have any idea what this person might want? See, I rang the DI, not the Sarge. He's the one we need to convince. The note on its own won't wash. What we need is evidence."

The Asher family tree came to mind. However, it was an it, not a "them." I decided to hold on to it a little longer. From what Sarah had told me, the DI would not budge even if a bomb went off in the Witch's Retreat. His blasted budgets were all he cared about. But Alan was right—without the boss, we would get nowhere.

"Do you think your DI will come out on a Sunday?" I asked Alan.

"He told me he wanted to meet you. Should arrive soon. He doesn't live far from here."

"Well then, how about if we wait for him in the sitting room?"

Alan licked his lips. "Uh, yes. Okay. That's very kind of you."

When we entered the corridor, I heard banging outside and the voices of the Simpkins sisters, probably engaged in a dive into the paper wheelie bin. Another voice, most likely belonging to Mrs. Mornings, was quizzing them about their exploits. Oh, great. The news that Eve's niece had received an ultimatum would spread through the village like wildfire.

Did I care? I told myself I didn't.

In the sitting room, I sank into auntie's armchair, while Alan perched on the far edge of the beige settee, the plastic bag hidden by his capable hands. "The DI should be here any minute now," he volunteered.

He reminded me of Gollum, slavering over the ring. Unable to sit still, I jumped up and paced the sitting room, circumnavigating the moth-eaten Turkish carpet. With every stride, I sensed Alan's gaze on me grow heavier until I could bear it no longer and whirled around. He wasn't even looking my way but seemed to have found something fascinating to observe in a window that framed sullen clouds scudding across the heavens. I stepped closer to the crammed shelf and let my fingers roam over the backs of the nearest books when a knock sounded on the door.

The Simpkinses entered, ready to report to base.

"We checked all the wastepaper bins," Alma said.

"Plus, the one outside," Cecily said. "I took a quick peep at the rest of the rubbish, but it got emptied yesterday."

Their faces told me they had found nothing. "I understand. It was worth the try," I said.

Alan, who had risen, gave the Simpkins sisters his friendliest smile. Why them and not me? "Thanks for your efforts. At least we know where we stand."

"I've had another idea," I said and rapped on the shelf for emphasis. The recipe book dropped from its slot, right into my hand. Odd, I could swear it had been wedged between two other tomes.

I must have used more force than I thought.

I faced the other three. "Aunt Eve kept collecting all sorts of snippets and printouts. If something caught her fancy, she would keep it. See here." With trembling fingers, I opened the precious recipe book, and two clippings dropped to the floor. One was for carrot muffins, American-style. The one for Austrian *Vanillekipferl* had gone greasy with use, and when I picked up the two recipes, I breathed in the rancid sweetness of almonds.

"Well, I suppose you get my drift." I pointed my thumb at the shelf behind me. "I'm convinced this is one of two places where she could have hidden something."

"The other one being the attic, right?" Alan asked.

"Or her memory boxes, but both the police and I have sifted through those," I said.

"Yup," said Alan. "I understand nothing in those boxes is of real interest."

I took that to mean the Asher family tree didn't qualify. But the police had been searching for evidence, not hidden objects.

"She wouldn't have a safe or something up there?" he asked.

"Mrs. Coldron wanted to have one installed," Cecily said. "But every single specialist she called was booked out for months."

Her comment reminded me of the locksmith, who somehow had slipped from my to-do list. My next thought was a lot less pleasant. The notion of a safe implied auntie had indeed been looking for a place to hide "them." The chilly spider legs of fear feathered down my neck. It was unfortunate that other than a headstone I had no clue what I should be looking for. Two headstones, perhaps?

Nope. Too big for a safe.

"Perhaps she used one of these hollow books? Not very effective, the first place every burglar searches but there you go," Alan said.

I stared at the shelf. With graves crowding my mind, that idea had never occurred to me.

"Well, one way to find out," Alan said. His blue eyes shone; he seemed to have recovered from whatever had been souring his mood earlier. He snapped his fingers. "There's something else. Should we ring your cousin, tell her what's going on, in case your aunt told her something?"

Auntie might well have done that. Somehow, I doubted Daisy would let me in on her secrets. I checked my watch. Nine in the morning. "It's too early to ring my cousin. Alan, your boss doesn't seem to be in a hurry. How about if we clear the shelf in the meantime?"

"Sounds good." He reached over his shoulders and pulled the dark blue police sweatshirt over his head. It meant he wanted to join the search, which was good.

Alma shot out of the door.

"Where's she going?" I asked her sister.

"She'll be getting rags, a bucket of water, that sort of thing."

"Hang on, I wasn't planning a spring-cleaning session. I'm trying to find something," I said.

Cecily shook her head, determination showing on her face. "We've wanted to do in this room for a long time. No time like the present."

A T-shirted Alan, displaying an impressive set of muscles on a fine-toned body, gave us an impatient jerk of the head. "Let's get cracking. How about if you two take the books from the shelves and stack them on the floor and I go through them?"

His approach was an efficient way of going about things. It also meant the Simpkins sisters and I would do most of the work. Alan was supposed to be the expert on searches, so I pushed up the sleeves of my new long-sleeved shirt in a soft indigo batik print. Trust me to embark on a cleaning session—or a hunt for clues, depending on perspective—when wearing my new gear.

The joint efforts of two housekeepers, one police constable, and a grammar school teacher yielded one packet of ginger snaps and two rolls of digestive biscuits hidden behind the reading matter, two of the items well past their sell-by date. We also discovered an incredible pile of paranormal romance in paperback and a wide range of more respectable publications from Shakespearean plays to an old telephone directory of Swindon and environs. We were aflutter with clippings, but not one of them gave anybody the slightest inkling they could be useful.

The Simpkins sisters were in their element. They had lovingly dusted every single book, cleaned the boards, and rearranged everything in alphabetical order. Unfortunately, the shelf had yielded neither hidden treasures nor messages from auntie. Alan even checked the wall, but the measurements all added up, and nothing had been plastered over. He echoed my frustration when he sank onto the settee, crunching one of the fresher ginger snaps. I could almost see the thunderclouds gathering above his head.

"Frigging waste of time if you ask me," he said through a mouthful of crumbles. "I was hoping we would find something for the DI." He checked his watch. "Blimey, what's keeping the man?"

"We got the whole shelf sorted in less than two hours," Cecily protested, opening the front window and pouring an evil-looking liquid onto the gravel as a police car rolled past the window and parked.

"Oh, lookee there. I think your boss has finally deigned to

show up," Alma said.

Alan stood. "Let me get him." He shot from the sitting room like a cork popped from a bottle of bubbly.

"Bit too full of himself, that one," Alma spoke under her breath while Alan's broad back left the sitting room.

"Come on, the constable did muck in," Cecily objected. Alma shrugged, and the sisters went to prepare a round of tea for everyone. The moment they left the room, the phone at the reception desk rang.

The Simpkinses tromped down the corridor to catch the call, and suddenly I was alone in the sitting room with a squeaky-clean shelf. I heard footsteps coming closer and two male voices. One was higher in pitch, almost whining, which I identified as belonging to Alan. The other one sounded gruff, so I braced myself for impact.

A stout older man entered. A few inches shorter than I, he was sporting a sharply clipped graying mustache that framed an unsuitably babyish mouth. A sparse goatee sprouted from the receding chin, almost like an afterthought. His hair looked full at first sight, but a closer look revealed the pink scalp underneath the carefully groomed waves. I wondered how much time the man spent in front of the mirror each morning. He had to be color blind; his suit jacket in fuzzy oranges and browns hurt my eyes. Alan followed behind, ramrod stiff and shaking his head at me, though what message he wanted to convey I couldn't figure out.

"Detective Inspector Diloff." My visitor introduced himself without extending his hand. Instead, he pointed at the settee, asked "May I?" and sat down. Alan placed himself in front of the window as if he wanted to keep both of us at arm's length.

"I came myself. Wanted to get a feel for this place," Diloff said. "The constable tells me there's been an incident. A threatening note, to be exact?"

"Have you seen it?" I asked.

"I have now," Diloff drawled. Colorless eyes bulging like marbles were daring me to respond.

"Sir, may I say something?" Alan came to the rescue.

"No, constable, you may not. I would prefer to hear Ms. Coldron's version of the events."

"I appreciate your coming on a Sunday."

He barked a laugh. "Don't thank me yet. I keep hearing about this place. About you. I wanted to meet the person behind all these—incidents. You seem to have bamboozled Sergeant Widdlethorpe into believing there's villainy afoot. Well, then. Go ahead. Convince me."

Heat flushed my cheeks. This man wasn't my friend. Still, once I was describing the petal attacks, the vanishing ladder, my encounter with the intruder, the calls, and, lastly, the note, I got more and more convinced that the sheer amount of "incidents," as he called them, should be enough evidence to re-examine the case.

As it turned out, I was wrong.

19

POLICE PROCEEDINGS

"It's all circumstantial." Diloff brushed aside my worries with a fleshy paw. "Regarding your observations about the burglar, I'll ask Sergeant Widdlethorpe to take them on file. But burglars tend to be nonviolent unless provoked. Which you did."

I opened my mouth.

He gave me another imperious wave of his hand. "I'm not finished yet. Your note interests me. You say you found it under the table in the corridor when you returned from downstairs, but not when you set out? Despite having heard footsteps before?"

"Yes," I said. "The drafts must have blown it away. I only spotted it when climbing the stairs."

"I see. Any idea who this missive might be from?"

"I have no clue," I said.

The bulging eyes rolled, giving him the air of a petulant toddler. "Let me rephrase that. Do you have any enemies?"

"Not before I came here."

DI Diloff poked a chubby finger in my direction. "Do you want us to help you or not? If you do, how about sharing a name? Or two?"

I caught myself crossing my arms in front of my chest

and was annoyed with my defensiveness. It was Diloff's job to coax responses out of witnesses, and all he did was piss me off. Sarah had been a lot smarter with her questions, had shown a human side, where Diloff was nothing but a pompous ass. Still, I would have to play along if he were to be of any use to my cause.

"My cousin is acting up. She needs money and is not happy about the will."

"She's got an alibi."

"Yes, but I'm not sure how much it's worth. I think she and the landlord are an item."

"Anybody else?"

"Jeff Burns. Now resident at Wytchett Farm. Got stroppy when I asked him to pay his bill. The hangups started right after my little exchange with the guy. I think he's capable of more. Not his wife and brother-in-law, though. They're fine."

"That's for me to decide, Ms. Coldron," Diloff said. "Anything else?"

Pompous ass didn't describe him by far.

"Well, I'm not sure what Mr. Lentulus is up to. He's left, though."

Alan mumbled something that sounded suspiciously like "good riddance."

Anger stabbed into my chest and threatened to rip off my bland expression.

"He was cleared of all suspicions. Unless you have new evidence, he's out of it," Diloff said, stroking his goatee.

I nearly asked if Ignatius had been greasing palms on his nephew's behalf but swallowed the comment. Instead, I rose, showing the interrogation was over. "There's no point in continuing our little chat. For the record, I don't think Burns is behind the letter. He's all about direct threats and blustering. This letter is too complex for him."

A condescending little smile played around Diloff's mouth. "We shall see." The inspector didn't budge from the settee. He tapped his nose, feigning inspiration.

"What about you? Are you a complex person, Ms. Coldron?"

"What are you implying?" I had a fair idea, but I wanted

to hear it from him.

Diloff said nothing while that faint smile still hovered around his rosebud lips.

"Mr. Diloff, you are telling me I made up this letter myself, correct?"

Diloff tutted. "Detective Inspector, Ms. Coldron. Sadly, it appears your aunt brought her unfortunate demise on herself. We have excellent health care in this country. She should have availed herself of it. My understanding is you didn't like the truth. Having your letter turn up at this point is, shall we say, convenient? But I will keep an open mind. Should there be any other occurrences that convince me of third-party involvement, I will act, believe me."

"Basically, I need to get offed before you open the case again?"

Diloff curled his upper lip with disdain. "You are exaggerating, Ms. Coldron. Rest assured, I would intervene if I thought you were in any form of danger."

"In this case, you might as well leave, Mr. Diloff, since I have nothing else to say to you. Oh, pardon me, I meant Detective Inspector. But first, I want the note back."

My unwelcome visitor finally moved his behind from my settee. "I'll keep it as evidence for the time being. I would also suggest you refrain from bothering my officers. We're busy with real cases. Our budgets are stretched. Very stretched." He shook his head, an expression of fathomless woe on his pudgy face.

Don't expect me to feel sorry for you, tosser.

Alan escorted the DI outside, like a track-suited butler dismissing an unwanted caller. When I could hear them no longer a scream exploded from my lungs, and I hit the coffee table with both fists. Why did these things keep happening? Was there a big red mark on my head, saying "Thunderbolts here?"

I sagged into my trusty armchair, feeling lost and alone. A clicking of claws coming from the den told me I had company after all. Tiddles had spent the afternoon in her beloved knitting basket, but now that things were quiet again, she came out of hiding.

The cat sat in front of me, her ears turned my way like furry receivers.

"I didn't handle things very well, did I?"

Tiddles plonked herself on the floor and started licking her nether region. She farted, and I flapped away the stink.

"Quite honestly, it doesn't matter. Diloff didn't come to listen. He wanted to lecture. If he thinks he's going to stop me, he can think twice."

Tiddles gave me a greenish stare, one leg at almost a right angle, pointed at the ceiling, her spine curled in the feline version of a yoga exercise.

"Well, as long as that moron is in charge, we can basically forget the cops. I really don't want to get Sarah into trouble. As to Alan, well, let's assume he's on my side. Or, better said, we might have common goals."

Tiddles spread her claws and nibbled the space between them.

"In any case, I'm stuck with him. And the attic. Something is up there. Has to be."

From outside the window came voices, raised in anger. I jumped up from the chair and slunk toward the curtain, making sure not to move it. A few more days in the village and I would turn into a curtain-twitcher with the rest of the neighborhood.

"Exactly what I expected," Diloff said next to the window. "The woman is hysterical. Very attractive, I give her that. Nice face. Nice curves. But pushy, used to having her way."

"Sir—"

"She's construed all these incidents, that much is clear. They're too outlandish to be real. Rose petals, hah! I've seen a lot in my long career. Trust me, I'm familiar with the type."

"Sir—"

A car door creaked open. "And you had better focus on your exams. If you want to join the CID, you'll need to put your nose to the grindstone, son. Take a bit of advice from an old battle horse."

"With all respect, sir—"

"Well, it's up to you how you spend your weekend. But don't moan about being tired. I'd say there's a one in ten chance she's not faking it. If you want to bet your money on that, be my guest. See you tomorrow, bright-eyed and bushy-tailed."

"Yessir!" Alan said, sounding defeated.

The car door slammed, and an engine revved, followed by tires crackling over the gravel.

"You twatwaffle," Alain said once the DI had gone.

I slipped back to my armchair, mirth bubbling inside. Poor Alan. Though he had acted mainly for his benefit, not mine. My gaze fell on Aunt Eve's recipe book. It lay next to the pile of clippings Alma had removed from its interior, the one for the apple pie resting on top. I reached for the book and, almost by themselves, my fingers flipped through the dog-eared pages, finding more recipes, first from my grandmother, then from my aunt. I wondered about the origins of the book. It looked and felt old, its pages stiff and smooth like the Asher family tree. The front cover told me nothing, but on the inside back cover it read "Petunia Coldron, 1804" in a flowery script. Actually, I would have thought the book to be older than that.

I flicked through more of the stained pages, some of them glued together with noxious substances. My ancestor must have started the book at the back, for it was her script that covered the last twenty pages. The middle part appeared to be empty.

I wondered where Alan might have got to. Gone to lick his wounds, most likely.

Could the anonymous menace covet the recipe book? Unlikely. Even if the collection of old cookery tips dated back to the Napoleonic Wars, it was too scuffed to be valuable. Plus, the recipe book had never been hidden. Wondering about the veritable flood of old manuscripts I had come across, I found the start of Petunia's entries and read.

In the Year of the Lord, 1804. I will record our lore, lest it be lost. Beware and use the knowledge with caution. With nobody left to guide our hands, we might well cause harm where we wish to heal. Remember, it is never evil we serve.

That was a rather overblown way of telling people how to pickle cucumbers.

Once I had become accustomed to the curly handwriting, reading became easier, and I didn't take long to work out that Petunia's instructions were not of a domestic nature. She had to have been a herbalist of some sort—the plant listings for each "potion" were a clear pointer. None of her concoctions sounded remotely healthy, with digitalis, oleander, and ragwort thrown into the mix. Had she but used her brews on the French emperor, the European continent would have been spared a lot of grief.

The entries got weirder as I read on. At some point, Petunia even considered binding somebody's shadow by invoking Nature's spirit seven times as a rational way of keeping relationships going. Intrigued despite myself, I thumbed my way through the text. One passage caught my eye. It was hard to miss, given it was claiming prime real estate in the middle of one page.

Dead plants can be revyved, if they perished very recently, through touch and by sharing your skylles. Beware, never try this with anything in the animal kingdom. We no longer have the power, and you myght die trying.

Apart from being rather heavy on the "y," the comment was inane. Cats might have nine lives, but nobody had come back from the dead yet.

What about the primula, though?

Well, duh, the plant had been desiccated, not dead. Still, an uneasiness pooled at the bottom of the stomach. From there it spread, like a cold tide flooding my body. Could magic be real? Could I be...?

No, stop this. Stop it right now.

I snapped the book shut. Planet Earth was round, and gravity existed. The Hogwarts Express rolled only in fiction.

Heavy footsteps sounded in the corridor. I scanned the coffee table and snatched a *People* magazine to cover Petunia's legacy. My ancestor might have been a bit batty, but she had been family, and it would be rude of me to let her end up as evidence in another transparent plastic bag.

"Sorry for that," said a flustered Alan when he re-entered the room. His cheeks were flushed, and frown lines entrenched under a wet fringe. He emitted the scent of apple soap. He must have spent quality time under a cold shower. "Let me guess, you noticed? I was trying to tell Diloff the window wasn't closed, but..."

I made sure to calm my voice. "No harm done. Your boss might be convinced he has my measure, but it works both ways. Can't be helped. Where are Alma and Cecily?"

"They were late for their cleaning job or something. They've left," Alan said. "What now?" he asked with a speculative glance. A drop from his wet fringe landed on his nose, and he swiped it away.

"The attic, I dare say. Are you game?"

His mien brightened. "Sure. Unless we should check the office first?"

"I already did. There's nothing but papers." They included a historical document in the filing cabinet, but it was none of his business.

"Okay, then. Go ahead, I'll fetch a torch and a better tape measure."

He held the door open for me. It appeared we were friends once more. This would be my third trip to the attic. Either it would be a case of third time lucky or I would be out of places to search. What would happen then was anybody's guess.

20

ATTIC RELOADED

Alan arrived a good ten minutes after me, and he took ages to drag himself up the aluminum ladder. When his head peeped through the rectangular access hole, he looked rather pale around the gills.

I dropped the yellowed thermal underwear I had been rifling through. "Anything the matter?" The mushroom smell of mold reached my nose, making me sneeze.

"Cheers." Alan dragged himself into the attic. "I don't like heights. They give me vertigo."

I placed the ski-boots I had shaken upside down back on their mat. "Ah. I would imagine it makes your job a tad difficult."

"Yes," Alan said, his expression glum. I waited, but he didn't explain. Instead, he picked his way toward the back wall and had a go at it with his tape measure. My hands resting on the cracked plastic of the boots, I watched him work. Alan fixed the tape with a nail on one side and then ran it along the wall. To me, the plasterwork looked straight enough, unlikely to hide a secret space, but one never knew. Grateful for his help, I threw myself at the trunks full of bog-ugly crockery and Daisy's painting paraphernalia, the sole items as yet unchecked. No surprises hid among the junk, so I rose with a groan and stretched my back.

Where to go from here?

A slow pirouette brought the chair into view, its stuffing bleeding in dirty clouds onto the floor. I had examined the thing already and so had the police. Between us, we might have missed something. I grabbed the backrest and turned the piece of furniture on its head, exposing springs and dirty padding. My fingers touched wooly fill and found the chalky remains of the fingerprinting powder. Then my fingertips hit on some thickish wire. I let them trace a rounded coil. They slipped over the smooth metal until they hit a sharp tip. *Ouch.* A broken piece of spring.

I sagged onto my haunches. My thoughts jumped from chairs to sofas.

"Alan?" I hollered at the side wall he was busy measuring.

"Yes?" He pushed his fringe aside, leaving behind a sooty smear. The tape measure zipped back into its metal case with a snap. It must have hit his fingers, for he dropped it with a curse.

"Is it worth checking the settee in the landing?"

Alan shook out his hands with a sour expression on his face. He lifted the fingers toward his mouth as if he wanted to suck on them but thought better of it. "Nice try. I checked the bloody thing before I came up. Zilch, nada."

Yet another dead end.

The duty shower was drumming down on the roof and shadows closed in on all sides. I dragged myself off the floor and brushed off my hands. At a loss about what to do next, I stepped closer to the two fake baroque nightstands I had already searched twice, stumbled over a piece of brick and stubbed my toe.

"Oh, to hell with it."

One kick and the obstacle shot into the pile of clay bricks stacked against the chimney, next to untidy rows of old magazines.

The dim light of the rainy afternoon in cahoots with the dodgy glow thrown by the overhead lamp made the chimney stand out like a rock, life's castoffs blown up against the grayish plaster. Dust motes swirled, shifted by tiny eddies of air, tickling my cheeks. I was transported back to the scene from the waking dream that haunted me after my first visit to the attic. My subconscious—the voice I had pushed aside and forgotten about while life as I knew it skidded downhill in a landslide—was telling me I was missing something.

For a moment I thought I heard the carousel. But no, it was only Alan, climbing over boxes containing the toys and my cousin's ballet costumes, tape measure in his hand.

Measurements. Something about them nagged at the back of my mind. The nightstands abandoned, I crept closer to the chimney. Two smokestacks, used to service the fireplaces in the Witch's Retreat, were now bricked up. The smaller one on the other side stood free of clutter. This one was different.

"Come on, you bugger, give," I whispered. A chimney, magazines stored around its bottom, and a heap of rubble. Something was wrong with the picture.

The answer lay at my feet, so to speak. One of the paper piles protruded farther into the room than the others, as if something behind it was pushing it out.

I kneeled, pulled the papers away from the chimney and found an uneven wall. Free of the plaster covering the rest, the reddish stones had been bricked up by an inexpert hand, with dried cement leaking through the cracks. The brickwork was stuck on the outside rather than filling a hole in the chimney.

"Alan?" I shouted. "I need you here. Bring a hammer with you."

"What?" Rattling and swearing accompanied his approach, as he stumbled over a ski boot, which caused the old broom to clatter onto the floor.

I stepped aside to give him a full view of my discovery.

"Now, that's what I call nifty. Well done." He kneeled and ran his hands over the brickwork and whistled through his teeth. "A false wall. I'll have a word with our SOCO chap. He should have spotted this. About the hammer, hang on, I have an idea."

He rushed back to the garden side of the attic and returned with an old poker and a rusty ash shovel. "If this doesn't work, I'll try the tool shed."

Alan grabbed the poker with both hands and rammed it

into the wall. Chunks of brick sprayed in all directions. He repeated the attack, his muscles bunching on his forearms. His firm hands thrust the poker through the mortar until the false wall crumbled. Another couple of pushes and Alan broke through a cavity close to the floor. My handyman dropped his tool, went down on his knees and peered inside.

"So?" I was jittery with expectation, but there was no rushing this guy.

Alan grunted and pointed his flashlight at the hole. "Can't see much, but there's something inside."

He slammed the poker into the wall a few more times and enlarged the cavity. Next, he hacked away at the broken bricks with the ash shovel until the gap was big enough for him to put his hand through to pull out a plastic-wrapped USB stick covered in a reddish residue.

"Hah." Alan removed the plastic and presented the stick on his extended hand.

Finally, a message from my aunt.

I snatched the little rectangle from his palm. Alan pulled away his hand as if stung.

Where were my manners?

"Oops, sorry," I said. "You can't imagine how relieved I am we've found this. Let's check it out on auntie's computer downstairs. Oh, wait a moment." My wrists were slimmer than his. I encountered no problems when squeezing my hand through the hole and probing the rough, crumbly edges of the small cache while Alan looked on in silence.

"It's empty. Let's go."

With the stick in my jeans pocket and a spring in my step, I clambered back down the ladder.

Alan followed a lot more slowly. "Go ahead, this will take a while," he hollered from above.

I was booting up the computer with sweaty fingers when he turned up and stopped at the arch that separated the den from the sitting room.

"Tell me," he said.

"It's not password protected, that's for sure. Ah, here we go. Only one directory."

And one file labeled "Greetings." An electric shock zapped

through me. I had been right. The dusty little device contained the message from my aunt I had been hunting for. I swiveled around on my chair and faced Alan. "Can you please leave me for a moment? I suspect this might be personal."

His nostrils widened. "What makes you so sure?"

"We didn't have time to talk. She would have left a message for me. I know her. Knew her."

For a moment, it was touch and go. He reminded me of a cat about to pounce on a mouse, not a copper keen on a piece of evidence. "You realize this stick can make all the difference to the investigation?"

My fingers itched to hit the enter key, but I didn't want him to read what might well be my aunt's last message.

"Yes. Please, Alan. We can decide what we do with this afterward. But this is between her and me."

His posture slackened slightly. "All right. But be quick about it." He strode away from me, kicking the carpet when he passed under the archway.

I pivoted back to face the screen, double-clicked, and the file released its secret. When my gaze raced across the text, the gelid feeling in my stomach returned. This wasn't what I had bargained for.

Congratulations—You bastards were looking in the right place, which is why I moved them and left this note instead. Disappointed? I hope you are. You won't find them. Ever. I'll protect them with my life. If I can't, the others will. Leave us alone. Haven't you caused enough havoc already?

Eve Coldron.

The file was created on the twenty-sixth of March, the day after she went to make her will. If I needed any proof "they" existed, here it was. They had even been in the godforsaken attic. With tears blurring my vision, I slumped in my seat. It was all my fault. I had allowed us to drift apart. I had deserted Aunt Eve when she needed me most. It served me right that I didn't know where "they" were. Or what "they" might be.

I had less than two days to find out. The headmistress

would kill me.

She might not be the only one.

A shadow fell over the computer. Alan, for once standing close. "Are you finished?"

I waved at the screen. "Be my guest."

"What on Earth is that supposed to mean?" he said, annoyance clogging his voice. He stabbed at the screen as if it would change the note to something more useful. All he did was smear the glass.

"Not what I expected and not what we were looking for either."

Alan was quiet, and I tilted my head to look up at a male forehead scrunched up in concentration. "You know, I think you're being a tad pessimistic here. It's the first real proof that there's more to the death of your aunt. The DI might scoff at the note from this morning, but this he can't argue away."

"He'll say I bricked the thing up myself."

Alan regarded me as if I were an amoeba waving at a microscope. "With the date on the file, it's unlikely. You weren't even in Avebury at the time, right? Yes, files can be manipulated, but our experts will work things out pretty quickly. Let me take this to HQ. The Sarge is the only one who can make the old water buffalo—DI Diloff see the light. But I need the stick."

How I wished Chris were still here. He could probably have exonerated me in two seconds flat.

"Get a Ziploc bag, would you?"

Alan snapped his fingers. "Good thinking." He dashed from the den.

I whisked around and pushed the print button in case I had missed something or there was a secret message hidden among auntie's words. I also saved the text on the computer.

Alan returned in a jiffy and held out a bag for me to drop the stick into. "I'll drive over to Swindon now. The Sarge is always in first thing in the morning. She can take over tomorrow." He regarded me with a frown. "You okay on your own?"

Those few words of compassion, spoken from a man who might be a grudging accomplice but not my friend, returned the tears to my eyes. "Yes. You get going. And thank you."

With a quick smile, he was gone.

The search was over. Now, the wait would begin, with the sword of Damocles hanging over my head.

Impossible. There had to be something, anything, I could do.

Like getting the mad buzz of thoughts in my head into some semblance of order.

I took a blank sheet from the printer and began to write.

Daisy.

She needed money. I stood in the way of her inheritance. She had to be involved. Who else would know about the carousel but her? But what about the petal incident? Whoever was behind it must have seen my aunt lying on the landing. Greg had alibied Daisy, claimed she had been at the pub when auntie died. With my erratic approach to sleuthing, I still hadn't followed up on that point. Not a good idea, since the person who nearly bashed my head in also left petals behind. I should have made the connection earlier. If Daisy's alibi held, it was unlikely she could be the individual who lashed out at me. No matter what else I did, I had to catch my cousin.

I called her number but got voicemail. "Daisy? Ring me, we must talk. It's about the money." In a way, it was. Once the pub opened, I would try there.

I perused my notes and wrote another name.

Chris.

Enigmatic helper, Neolithic-expert-gone-IT-specialist, and professional hacker. A nephew of one of the most despicable men in the country. A man descended from the witch hunters. He kept a reprint of the Malleus Maleficarum in his bedroom. Chris cast well as the villain. The trouble was, I found him fiendishly attractive. But who else would have witches on his mind? Yes, he was gone. But he knew his way around and the doors in this place were forever open. If need be, he could have keys replicated. And he could climb. Where had he been on the day I got attacked? What did he want to achieve with his odd hints and comments? I had no answer to either question.

Alan.

"You won't like his methods," Chris had said, and no, I didn't. Alan had struck me as a decent chap, not without insight, but he too had a darker side. He was ambitious and got abrasive when on the scent. He didn't care overly much for me. Or for Chris. Another, nastier thought wormed its way into my mind. I wondered how well the two knew each other. For all it was worth, they could both be members of the Ignatius tribe. They might be playing games, toying with me. Still, their motivations remained shady like the rain-besieged den. That last theory made no sense though. Alan seemed worried about his career. Why would he be if he didn't need to work?

There were others.

Greg, the kind-eyed giant of a temporary landlord on a mission for my cousin? I still didn't know enough about him. But the same way he alibied my cousin, she might have alibied him back. His involvement was improbable, but not impossible.

The Ragworts.

They turned up, and I got served with an ultimatum. Could I envisage Damian Ragwort dashing up and down staircases? Unlike his wife, he was fit. Cue the hiking gear. They knew something; I had overheard them talk about me this morning. Chris had mentioned them. No, not them—Damian. I circled the Ragworts' names with a red pen. I would find and quiz them, politeness be damned.

Jeff Burns.

Nasty bull of a man who threatened the "murder house" of mine. Might well be behind the hangups. They started after my visit to the farm and stopped when I threatened the caller with the police. Whoever was at large in the Witch's Retreat didn't fear the cops.

I added a question mark after his name.

I then added another, bigger question mark for "him," as my aunt referred to her enemy. He might well be the mastermind behind it all. He had been around at the time my parents died and came after my aunt in the present. That was assuming, of course, we were talking about the same person. It might be any of the people whose names I jotted down first or somebody else entirely.

The last lines were reserved for the family tree and the cookery book. Neither would have fitted into the small cavity. The hole was barely big enough for my hand. Nor had the Asher family tree shown any creases from folding.

No need to mention the gravestones. They were way too big for the cache upstairs.

I folded my brainstorm with care and, together with the copy of auntie's note, stuck it into an envelope. If only the disarray in my head could be compartmentalized so easily. No, I was still missing a link. I caught myself doodling on the envelope: headstones and witches with pointy hats, sitting on broomsticks. There would be no help from that corner, which was a shame since it would take real magic to get me out of this hole.

With a jerk, the pen raced off the envelope, leaving behind a blue streak.

Hang on—holes.

Headstones.

It was time for a visit to the country churchyard.

21

SKULLS AMONG THE BRAMBLES

"Damn!" I hit the disconnect button. The number I was trying to reach was unavailable and had been all afternoon. The pub and its car park were still closed, for which reason my rusty Ford now sat squeezed into the last free space between the Magic Mushroom Café and the gift shop. What had been heavy rain earlier had eased off to steady drizzle that floated in the air like sweet sea spray. I slammed the car door shut, winced at the rattle, and pulled the hood of my new orange anorak over my head to set out for High Street. Puddles dotted pavement and tarmac alike, and twice I had to jump aside to avoid the wash caused by passing vehicles. A warm air front had drifted in, but instead of spring weather, it carried along a drizzly mist swirling around the thatched cottages and cloaking the budding trees in their front gardens until only bleary forms in shades of gray and black remained, the color of old pyres.

When I approached the stony bulk of the church, it seemed to shy away from me and hid behind the gauzy layers that thickened the closer I came to the old churchyard. Apart from the sudden whoosh of the cars as they appeared out of the mist, the town was silent, as if bating its breath. The eerie quiet provided the backdrop to the scuffing of my Wellingtons on the pavement, pounding in rhythm like a funeral dirge.

Forty-eight hours. Forty-eight hours.

A dripping dark weight took shape to my right and morphed into the Victorian lychgate that guarded the entrance to the churchyard. In the moldy shelter provided by its wooden roof, I stopped and pulled the photo of the Coldron headstone from my wallet. With my surroundings gone bleary, as if seen through greasy lenses, it was difficult to get my bearings, but the markers I spotted appeared to be modern, the oldest of Victorian origins. I rechecked the photo. It showed greenery, and while bushes and trees were lacking at the front, tall beeches rose behind the church, their tips lost in the sodden haze.

Once I got closer, the church revealed itself to be of simple design: a straight Saxon nave with Norman trimmings, the vestry stuck on in later times, the square tower heaving upward on one end. Like the trees behind, the four spires of the tower pierced the mist, their tops invisible from where I stood.

A path snaked around the vestry, its latticed panes colorless like the belly of a reptile. The trail led me to a cluster of old yew trees that protected the fresh green nettles lurking among the weather-worn headstones. Drops of moisture were caught in the spider webs woven between them, a sad glitter. In one corner, bluebells flooded the ground between the abandoned headstones, reminiscent of the lost blue of the skies. Sparrows chittered in the bell tower, oblivious to my presence as if I were a visitor from another world.

Another glance at the photo made me head for the far end of the churchyard, which was covered in rotting bracken, brambles and creepers run wild. The ever-present mist made it hard to see things, but with some judicious squinting, I could detect three stones leaning at crazy angles toward the outer wall. I squelched across and after a brief tussle with prickly creepers, I faced two stones bearing crude engravings of winged skulls and a year—1601 on one and 1603 on the other—while the third one faced away from me. A clean, earthy smell drifted from the sodden ground where last year's leaves, new grass, and the rich soil composed their own perfume. I trampled on the creepers to stop them from nipping at my legs and lowered myself next to the first stone, the hem of my anorak tucked under, lest it trailed in the mud.

The torch function of my smartphone helped me decipher the name on the marker.

Rosalynd Asher.

Recognition nudged me in the ribs. That name had been on the last row of the Asher family tree.

I scrambled across to the second headstone and traced my finger along the crabbed and mossy writing, which had all but faded away.

Martyn Cowslip.

Another nudge. His name, together with a few others of his kin, had been on a printout.

Had they escaped the pyres and made it onto hallowed ground? They felt almost like intruders, hanging on for the sake of their eternal souls.

I rose, pushing my way through the vegetation to get at the third marker, and there it was.

Mary Anne Coldron. Departed 1604.

The stone that should not be here.

The marker from the photo. Last presumed to be traveling to Swindon with my aunt sixteen years ago.

The silence of the graveyard roared in my ears.

I held the photo close to the weathered sandstone, but I already knew I was looking at the same marker. In the same position. At the same angle. Impossible this stone would ever have moved.

The photo did not show that, due to its angle, the text on Mary Anne's marker was better preserved than the inscriptions on the other two. When I reached out to trace the writing on the stone, a thorn raked across my hand. I sucked at the cut, wondering which germs I might have caught. The thought faded away with the pain and the metallic taste on my tongue once I read the inscription on the headstone.

"Anno Domini," came first, followed by "left behind" and a catalog of what appeared to be names. It made me wonder whether this might be a mass grave.

Three stylized roses peeped over the discolorations that

covered the bottom of the marker. Roses. They must have been a lot more to my aunt than only her favorite plants.

I pushed aside the withered leaves, now heavy with moisture, but the soil in front of the headstone looked undisturbed to my amateur eye.

Nobody had dug here. Nobody had tried to hide "them," at least not recently. I wondered what auntie might have transported all those years ago, what she needed the protection of the Farnworth Security Detail for. Could it have been "them"? She had been about to leave the country, perhaps she thought "they" were no longer safe. But then, she had been all over the globe before. Did she do something that alerted the villain? In that case, it would most likely be one of her scathing features. All I had to do was go through the lineup of people she had slagged off over the years.

That would take me ages.

My thoughts raced each other, faster and faster, drummed on by my heart.

Had she dug up the bones of our ancestors? Did she bring them back when she settled in Avebury last November? Why would anybody want them?

Even stranger that Aunt Eve faked the transport of the headstone. Perhaps she had not. Perhaps I was wrong, and the stone had been moved. If that were the case, somebody, possibly my aunt, had gone to a lot of bother to replace it in precisely the same position.

The hood of my anorak slipped. Water plopped down from above and found my exposed neck. I shivered and wrapped my arms around myself, alone in the dribbling bramble hedge, the outside world shrouded in mist and my mind lost in the mystery.

From the other side of the church, the voices of children shrilled. I kicked myself out of my daze. There was nothing more for me to do here at the moment, so I struggled back into the open. I threw the crumbling gravestones one last glance, but they had already melted into the greenery that sheltered them from intruders.

Back on the slippery stone trail leading from the churchyard to the lychgate, I moved aside to let pass a clean-shaven man of middling size and age. Behind him followed a tall woman in spanking new outdoor gear, lecturing the two bored children she had in tow, presumably her daughter and son.

"*Entschuldigung*, oh I mean, excuse me. Would you be the churchwarden by any chance?" the man asked. His English was flawless but thickened by a German accent. I recognized it from the half-year I spent in Heidelberg to finish my studies.

"Sorry, no. There's a telephone number stuck on the church door. Maybe that might help you?"

The man winced. "Ah, I don't want to disturb anybody on a Sunday. Never mind. We couldn't resist a quick look before checking in. We believe an ancestor might be buried here."

It might well be a coincidence, but how many Germans would visit Avebury so early in the year?

"Are you Mr. Schlüsselblum?"

His face brightened. "Yes, yes. How did you know?"

"Oh, I work at the Witch's Retreat and saw your booking. Delighted to have you. Sorry if I don't shake your hand, but I've been dabbling in genealogy myself." I waggled my dirty fingers in front of my face.

"*Toll*. I mean, great. Are you Mrs. Eve Coldron? It's an honor to meet you. You have helped me so much with tracing my ancestors. And don't worry, I won't shake your hand."

"No, I'm her niece, Myrtle. I'm sorry to tell you my aunt has met with...she had an accident. But don't worry, your booking is secured."

"Nothing serious, I hope?"

"I'm afraid so. She passed away last Tuesday."

"Oh, how horrid. She was much too young. Angie, did you hear this?"

His wife nodded solemnly. "I'm sorry about your loss."

Their concern appeared genuine, despite the clichés, and I nodded gratefully. Once more I marveled at the bloke's command of the English language.

Language. With a flash of insight, I knew what they were looking for. "Follow the path and head for the blackberry thicket at the back of the church. Hidden within you'll find three headstones. One of them might be the one you are after."

"Are you sure?" Herr Schlüsselblum asked, hope brightening his face.

"I teach German conversation. A Schlüsselblume is a cowslip, and a Martin Cowslip is buried back there. Martin with a y to be precise."

Angie punched the air. "It's him. You two come here," she shouted at her children, who were playing hide and seek between the tombs. She then waved at me before shooing her offspring toward the brambles. Her husband lingered, though I sensed him straining at the leash of politeness, eager to check out his find.

"I'll see you later." I watched them go. With a bit of luck—a commodity I had to do without recently—they might even find something.

Any faint stirrings of hope my churchyard visit might have garnered died soon after. In their stead, a leaden weariness spread inside me. Roses, headstones, whacky Regency herbalists, hidden objects—and this morning's ultimatum in the form of an impertinent note. My life had become surreal ever since Sarah's phone call. I wanted back what I had before.

First, survive. Then worry about your way of life.

I turned my back on my guests and hurried out of the cemetery to my car.

I keyed in Daisy's number. She was still not answering her phone. A quick check-in with Greg told me she hadn't shown her face at the pub, where she was sorely missed. I returned to the B&B, blinking at the unexpected brightness spread by the setting sun, harboring the foolish notion my cousin might be there.

Fat chance.

With Daisy gone incommunicado, the Ragworts came next on my list. Alma and Cecily had gone, so who else could help me flush them out?

Jenna. She and her brother had appeared in the same set of shots featuring Rosie and Damian. They were local;

they should know where to find them. With renewed vigor, I snatched my keyring from the reception counter and dashed back outside into Long Street. I had reached the turning to Tadpole Lane, the farmhouse in my sight when the phone rang.

"Myrtle?" Daisy's voice hushed from the speaker. "It's me."

"Kind of you to ring back," I responded, relief curdling to anger. "You're a tick difficult to get hold of. We really need to have a word. Where are you, if I may ask?"

"London. I needed to get away." A shrill overtone in her voice hinted at the hysteria hidden underneath.

How typical of her to leg it. I wondered whether I should do the same. Somehow, I couldn't convince myself that would get me off the hook.

Static crackled in my ears. "Daisy, are you still there?"

"Yes. You sound odd. What's up?"

Her voice had regained some of her trademark sassiness, but she could not fool me. My cousin was running scared. A frontal attack was called for.

"I guess I'm entitled. First, I find rose petals all over the place and somebody using the attic as an emergency entrance. Next thing I know, presumably the same somebody tries to bash my head in and leaves more petals behind. The old carousel is going off at the oddest moments. To top it all, I get a threatening note with an ultimatum. Forty-eight hours to find 'them,' or else. These things ring a bell by any chance?"

"Huh? Carousel? Roses? What are you on about? But if whoever wrote the letter knows about them, we have a problem. That's so not good."

If somebody had whacked me with a headstone, I wouldn't have been more stunned. She knew. My cousin had heard of my auntie's hidden treasures.

"Daisy, you need to tell me what is going on here. Now."

"Can't," she said in her breathless voice. "Not over the phone anyway. See, that's why I had to get away. It's not safe there anymore."

Not safe for whom? Her or me?

"Myrtle?"

"Yes, yes, I'm still here. Look, you've got to come back. Please, I need your help. This is one big, scary mess."

"I know. I can't," Daisy said, the whine creeping back into her voice.

I leaned against a tree beside the road, digging my nails into the rugged bark. The alternative would have been a howl of frustration.

"Daisy," I said with all the calm I could muster. "I'm lost. I need your help."

Yet more static. When Daisy spoke again, her voice had gone pensive. "Mum said you'd take it from there."

"What do you mean?" I asked, changing the mobile to my other hand. The one holding it was slippery with sweat. From above me came the distant sound of an airplane crossing the skies.

"I'm not sure myself. Mum rang you, didn't she?"

"Yes, but she never managed to tell me anything. I was late for a blasted meeting and forgot to call back." I would never forgive myself. Never.

"Oh, I didn't realize." A sigh followed by a rustling and sniffing noise. "Can't you come here? That'll be much safer."

"Daisy, no. I need to sort this out once and for all. The answers are here. Or am I wrong?"

"No," she whispered. "All right. I'll come. Mum's death was no accident at all, is that what you're telling me?"

"I don't think so, no."

"Right. I'll be back tomorrow. You take care," Daisy said with an unexpected softness in her voice and disconnected.

I didn't know it at the time, but I had made a fatal mistake.

22

COPS AND ROBBERS

Daisy's voice was gone, and I stood by the side of the road with my thoughts bouncing from the attic to the churchyard and back again. I should be relieved. My cousin would return to explain it all. Well, not all, but hopefully enough for me to sort things out. There was no reason to feel like I did, all jittery and flushed with heat as if I had downed two pots of coffee in one go. I had done that before embarking on my first lessons; it was not an experience I cared to repeat. Back then, movement had helped, so I picked up the pace once more, with the anorak slung over my shoulder.

Daisy didn't sound like an evil schemer, more like a little girl lost. She was a decent actress, but not good enough to fake the undertones of naked panic I had heard in her voice. To my surprise, I didn't want her to be the villainess. She was all I had left.

Not entirely, perhaps. Team Myrtle now boasted two elderly caretakers, a stinky cat, and a shrewd sergeant. It was aided by a behaviorally challenged but otherwise useful bobby. I ached to share my latest discoveries with Sarah, but not only did she need her Sunday off, but I also mustn't expose her to the wrath of her moronic boss.

The sun was still shining, though the shadows were getting longer, greedily trailing after me. Suddenly, the clucking of what sounded like a million hens registered. The birds were out in the mud, enjoying the sunshine. So were the cows, kept in check by an electrified fence on my right. The beasts stood chewing the cud and staring at me with their dark, soft eyes, placid critters as malodorous as the rest of the livestock.

I turned into the yard in front of the farmhouse. Marty's white van was parked close to the steps and from behind the house arose the high-pitched squealing of the boys, full of cheer and free of care. Their presence likely meant Jenna would be around.

I banged on the front door before taking a few steps backward, ready to bolt if Jenna's obnoxious spouse was on door duty. It took a while until the door scraped open, and when it did, I beheld Farmer Marty's apple-cheeked face.

"Oh, hullo Ms. Coldron, is it about your bacon?"

Yes, could somebody please save it?

"Eh no, I wanted to talk to Jenna," I said.

"Sure, come on in. We're building a treehouse for my nephews," he announced.

Marty led me along a narrow, flag-stoned corridor past uneven walls in pastel-colors covered in family pictures and faded seascapes. The back door opened onto a walled terrace that might once have been the mudroom. Cluttered with mismatched plastic garden furniture, it led to the orchard beyond. In a week or two, with the pink blossoms out, the place would look gorgeous. A group of tall trees whose names escaped me stood clustered on the right and planks, hammers, and other utensils lay strewn on the grass beneath them.

"Myrtle." Jenna's gentle voice rang with genuine delight.

Out of the corner of my eye, I noticed movement. One twin was halfway up the mottled bark. The marrow in my bones glaciered.

"Uncle Marty, Uncle Marty, see, I can climb higher than Rob. He's such a chicken."

"Chicken yourself," shouted his brother, free-clambering after his brother. Visions of flailing limbs and small bodies crashing to the ground flared up in my mind. Jenna, however, not only stayed calm, her face glowed with pride. "Aren't they the cutest? Five years old and look what they can do."

Sure, they were brilliant. Even as a kid, I would have slipped down the tree like a sack of potatoes. Still, if I were a mother, I would prefer my offspring to stay on *terra firma*. The teacher in me wanted to bark orders and, for the umpteenth time, I congratulated myself for not dealing with preschoolers.

"Amazing kids," I said, trying to not to sound anxious. "Sorry for barging in on you like this, but I have a wee problem. Is there anywhere we can talk?"

"Sure." Jenna pointed back to the walled terrace. We sat down, accompanied by vigorous hammering. Jenna turned her fey face toward me, her maroon curls caressed by the evening breeze. "Jeff is gone," she said apropos of nothing.

"Oh dear. I guess that was my fault."

Jenna showed pearly teeth. "Definitely not. Please don't worry. Our separation was just a question of time. I threw him out after he acted up with you. It was simply the last straw." Her eyes, soft and warm, seemed to reach for my soul. "You did me a great favor there. What can I do for you?"

"I'm trying to get hold of Mr. and Mrs. Ragwort. See, I'm not convinced my aunt...I mean, there's something fishy about her death. Well, it's worse. Heavens, I'm totally lost." I hadn't meant my words to sound so desperate and pulled up my mental socks. "When I met the Ragworts this morning, they gave me the impression they might be able to throw some light on a few things."

I sank back into the hard confines of the plastic chair. The air was cooling down, and I shrugged on my anorak. Jenna, clad in a thin blouse, didn't seem to feel the cold. She jumped up and paced the terrace.

"Oh, sweet Earth, that confirms what we feared," Jenna said. "Such a shame your aunt didn't have time to tell you about—things. She wanted you to join us. But she said you were holding yourself back."

Questions erupted in my mind. Politeness forgotten, I let them rip. "Holding back? What things? Who do you mean by us? Are you talking about these funny families she was researching?"

Jenna let out a tinkling laugh. "I am. We all hail from Avebury originally, you know."

"Yes, as far as the Coldrons are concerned, I found the headstone to prove it." I didn't discuss with her my fears it might have gone walkies for a while. I didn't know her that well.

Her face fell. "They left our people behind, at the mercy of these—bastards. Too many didn't even get burials."

"They?"

She waved me off. "Sorry, shouldn't have said that. You'll think I've gone bonkers. Shall I call Damian for you? I'll make us a cup of tea. It's getting a tick nippy." Jenna whirled around and, without waiting for my response, strode inside.

By now I was freezing in my anorak and too antsy to stay in my chair. I got up and paced the patio, trying to ignore the banging and sawing coming from the nascent treehouse. An eternity later, Jenna emerged in an oversized poo-brown mohair pullover. Not even the scruffy garment could make her look ugly. She carried a tea tray laden with biscuits, eclairs, jams, clotted cream, and other calorific goodies and my mouth watered.

Jenna lovingly arrayed our snacks on an embroidered cloth. She then fiddled with a chrome-plated patio heater that soon radiated welcome warmth. Why couldn't we move into the kitchen? I had never understood this fixation of my fellow Brits on braving the great outdoors at the most unsuitable of times.

"All is well, I got hold of Rosie," she said once she had finished laying out the spread. "They're still busy with the builder. Are you okay with a chat tomorrow morning? In their new house. Soon they'll be part of our community. Isn't it exciting?"

Not really. She meant well, even if I would have preferred an earlier appointment. For a fleeting moment, I wondered whether these people all formed part of a weird cult, with my aunt egging them on.

Jenna smiled her lovely smile and pushed a beignet in my general direction. Politeness required me to accept, and a bite into the powdery sweetness launched me straight into vanilla heaven.

"Mmm, this is delicious."

Jenna beamed. "Glad you like it. Try not to worry so much. All will be well. Damian knows what he's doing. Now your aunt is gone, he's organizing things. Gran used to, but she's not fit enough right now."

"Damian knows I'm looking for something? And where it is?" Anticipation flooded my cheeks with warmth, and I leaned in.

Jenna buttered a muffin and placed it on her plate. "Ask him. I'm sure, though, whatever's been mislaid will turn up in good time."

The creamy taste in my mouth turned bitter. "I've got twenty-four hours left to find it. There's an ultimatum, see?" Even to my ears, I sounded like a drama queen. Perhaps I should try another beignet to boost my morale.

Laughter tinkled again. Then Jenna got serious. "Unlikely. I see you walking the Earth a long time from hence." Her face had taken on a faraway look. She bent forward, cradled my free palm in her warm, sticky fingers. She smiled. "Yes, it's like I thought. You'll be fine." She pressed my hand once before releasing it and reaching for a piece of shortbread she then munched pensively.

Mumbo jumbo, all of it, yet her words wrapped an invisible cloak of protection around my shoulders, a cover made of almond and butter, sugar and spice.

Even if it were only for palm-reading purposes, I couldn't afford to reject Jenna's helping hand.

Shortly afterward, I took my leave. Being reassured of survival was one thing, but I still had to make sure it happened. Plus, I could not have eaten more cake if I tried. Back at the B&B, I noted Alan's battered Panda was nowhere in sight.

The way my luck was running, DI Diloff had popped up at the cop shop and caused more trouble for Alan over the USB stick. On the other hand, his absence meant nothing. The constable might be cramming or got roped in to on a job. I pushed the niggles aside and squeezed past the old Volkswagen van parked next to my car. Initially reddish in color, the van was covered in cosmic eddies and swirls that almost took on a life of their own. The vehicle was owned by the druids, who now resided in Chris's Number Four. The dirty pickup truck next to the paper wheelie bin belonged to the archaeologist. He had checked out of Number One, but Alma let him leave his vehicle in our car park. The Schlüsselblums hadn't yet arrived.

Once inside, I hesitated to enter the kitchen, almost afraid of what the primula might have done. Nothing was the answer. Hopefully, the plant had reached its full size. Otherwise, it would no longer fit on the sill. I stroked the primula's velvety blossoms until an unearthly howl at my feet urged me to ignore the local flora and cater to the resident fauna.

"Here you are, Tiddles," I said and placed her bowl on the floor. The cat farted with glee and dug in. I wondered whether a different diet, fresh meat instead of this gruesome goo, might reduce her digestive problems.

My phone jangled the Harry Potter tune. I ought to change it. In the last few days, I had overdosed on the supernatural.

"Myrtle? What the blazes is going on?"

Sarah.

"Leave it be. Your boss made it quite clear he doesn't want you involved."

"Does he really? Now, there's a surprise. Here's one for you. I've got rid of the old water—DI Diloff. About twenty minutes ago, Hunter brought me the USB stick and told me about the note, and I went straight to the DCI. Shame you handed the ultimatum over to Diloff."

"What was I supposed to do?"

"Good point. One day I'm going to kill that guy."

"It's against the law. Plus, you happen to be a cop."

"Har har," Sarah said. "The constable was shrewd enough to take a photo of the message, so I had something to show the DCI apart from the stick. He hit the roof, I can tell you. Ta-dah. Case reopened."

Finally, things were moving. A warm sensation of

gratefulness spread inside. I owed Sarah a lot more than cake, coffee, and bubbly. "You are fabulous, you know? Don't you ever take time off?"

"We've caught our burglar," Sarah said. "And no, it wasn't Lentulus. She's now fingering the rest of her gang. It's why we're all doing hours. Believe me, I consider it worth my while. You provided some additional entertainment. Sorry. Didn't mean it that way. I'm tired. So is Hunter, and he still has to sit his exam this week. What have you done with him?"

"Huh? He helped me find the USB stick."

"I've never seen him so completely stressed out. Let's hope he doesn't flunk his exam. He's done that once already."

Her remarks made me wonder if chaos had infiltrated the cop shop by way of the Witch's Retreat. "Well, I didn't force him to help me, he offered. He did act a bit odd, now you mention it."

In a cartoon, a question mark would have bubbled from the speaker.

"Yeah, odd is one word for it. If I didn't know better, I'd say the man's scared. I'll try and have another word with him later. Calm him down a bit. Now, about you. I don't like you up there in Number Seven on your ownsome lonesome. Just on the off chance: Is there a bed free in your hotel?"

"Bed and breakfast."

"Whatever. Is there?"

"No salesperson tonight," I said, more to myself than to her. "We've got the Germans instead. But they're in four and five."

"Germans in forty-five?"

"Hang on, wrong—they're in five and six. What I mean is, Number One is free."

"Okay, good. Sleep in there tonight. I'll see if I can wangle some surveillance from the DCI. It wouldn't be fair to ask Hunter, even if he were fit. I hate to sound repetitive, but how about changing lodgings?"

"Where? The pub is always booked. The Crystal Dawn B&B is too—they're running a karma seminar. That's why we got Pierre and Arav staying. The druids I mean. Plus, I'm pretty sure whoever is after me will find me no matter where

I go."

"Okay, okay, don't stress. Wouldn't want you to unbalance your karma. Let me see what I can do. Make sure to lock every door you can find and shove a chair under the handle of your room. Do make sure your phone is charged. When does this so-called ultimatum run out?"

"Sometime Tuesday morning. I forgot to check my watch when I found the letter." A thought nudged me in the ribs, and I groaned. "Ah, crap, I still have to tell the headmistress I need a few more days off."

"I'd love you to hoof it back to Southampton. But here we can at least keep tabs on you." A sigh so heavy it almost stirred my hair came through the phone. "Myrtle, you need to keep your phone with you at all times and don't leave the hotel at night. The B&B, I mean. In case you need to, check with me beforehand."

"Thank you. I appreciate your help."

"All in a day's work." With a click, Sarah was gone.

That night, with a squad car sitting in the front yard, I slept like the dead and got woken up at the crack of dawn only by Tiddles, who wanted out and was howling at the door of Number One. She also wanted breakfast, but I went back to bed and zonked out again.

I woke refreshed, ready to do battle with the assorted villains. When prodded, the smartphone announced breakfast time. It was charged, having loaded all night, and it showed three calls in the middle of the night. No caller ID. I had snoozed right through them. Before fear could take hold of my throat, I went to shower it away and rinsed my hair with my favorite strawberry shampoo, wondering when I last had bothered. Once dressed in my new chinos and the olive tee, I packed my belongings in the plastic carrier bag from the outlet center, moved the chair away from the handle, and opened the door.

I will freely admit it—I halfway expected another letter to be waiting for me. Instead, the aromas of bacon frying, accompanied by the sound of Sarah's voice, wafted up from downstairs, making me realize how hungry I was.

Once I arrived on the second floor, I found Number Seven still locked. I inched open the door, but both floorboards and beds were pristine, and no assassins were lurking in the bathroom. In their stead, I found the laundry hamper filled to the brim, so I dropped my clothes on the floor. Survival came with strings attached; I would need to run a machine load later.

Back in the kitchen, I met Sarah, who appeared to be wolfing down a super-sized bacon sandwich, and the Simpkins sisters, busy with preparing the breakfast.

"Morning," Sarah said between bites. "I wanted to see in person how you were faring."

"So, so," I said. "Thanks to your bodyguard I slept well enough."

She raised her chin at the stout backs of Alma and Cecily. "Let's go across to the conservatory, shall we? It's still empty."

We sat down at the table for Number One, decorated with an orange numeral and a grinning black cat.

"You needn't worry about Alma and Cecily. They were around when I showed Alan the note," I said.

"That's what I fear. They'll be tapped into the local gossip mill."

Of course, Sarah was right. But without Alma and Cecily's staunch support, I would have flipped a long time ago. "I know. To be quite honest with you, I don't care. I don't have the intention of staying here. They've gone out of their way to help me. I've no idea how to find employment for them. But I will."

Sarah regarded me calmly. "If I interpret the will correctly, you'll be saying goodbye to an awful lot of money."

She was correct, but I couldn't care less. "Yes. I absolutely refuse to be sucked into Aunt Eve's crazy schemes. I'll sort this out, and then it's sayonara. I still need to find a way to help my cousin. She's in real trouble. No idea how to do that either, but again, I'll find a way. Assuming she doesn't turn out to be the baddie."

Alma chose that moment to appear with the teapot and a

cooked breakfast. "You'll be needing something to keep you going," she said with determination and marched back to the kitchen.

Sarah waited until the clattering and clanking had started afresh. "I understand," she said soothingly. "Perhaps, you would care to update me on yesterday's developments?"

I did. And this time I didn't forget to mention the crank calls.

Sarah was an excellent listener. She asked a few questions and took a few notes, but otherwise gave me her undivided attention. It made a pleasant change from the approach the DI had taken.

"Oh my, the whole story sounds like the script for the latest blockbuster with your aunt in a leading role," she said when I was done. "Mrs. Coldron must have been desperate. What I don't get is why she didn't come to us."

That would have been way too easy. "Let's not forget, somebody called me a witch. Auntie was by far not the only drama queen on the set." Renewed anger rose on a bubble of acid that soured my throat.

"Water under the bridge." Sarah sounded so calm she could have stilled Niagara Falls. "Now to your suspects. Forget about Hunter. Haven't worked with him before so I thought it might be the exam. But when I probed a bit deeper people told me he's indolent, as bright as he might be. Thinks he's sharp and goes for the easy pickings. Or what he believes are easy pickings. Sucked up to Diloff and got burned. But he's no criminal mastermind. Your cousin, hmm, I don't know her at all. Never got to question her—the doctor wouldn't allow it. Then, the case was closed. Let me know what she has to say for herself."

"What about good old Jeff?"

"Oh, Mr. Burns tops my inbox. The guy has a record of stalking his ex, his mistress, and a couple of neighbors while he was at it. Guess what he did?"

"Anonymous calls?"

"Bingo," Sarah said. "But not only that, otherwise my colleagues wouldn't have caught him. He trumped up complaints, crowded his victims in supermarkets, that sort of thing. A nasty piece of work, our Mr. Burns. Not convinced he's the mysterious "him" your aunt mentions, though."

"You mean because of there being a "him" at work sixteen years ago?"

Sarah laughed. "Bingo again. It almost sounds like there's an old archenemy who's now shifted his attention to you."

"Hilarious, isn't it? Could the police find out whether the headstone ever moved? Or if the grave was dug up?"

Sarah pursed her greasy lips. "I would imagine so. Our techies never cease to amaze me. I would prefer to wait until you have talked to your cousin, though. Let her tell you her story, and we'll take it from there."

I hated to say it, but it had to be said. "Otherwise, there's only the Ignatius angle. Or Chris, rather. He knows something."

Sarah stared at her empty cup. "That has occurred to me as well. I've got no idea, though, what Ignatius could have wanted from your aunt. Somewhere, I read he might have dropped a few billion when the stock markets crashed. Not sure he's even going to notice. No, that can't be it. In any case, we need to tread carefully here. One wrong move and he'll sue our pants off. I wished you hadn't thrown Lentulus out on his ear. I could give him a good grilling."

"I didn't throw him out," I protested. "He left under his own steam."

The door to the corridor opened the same moment, and the Germans trundled in, freshly washed and combed, cheerfully wishing me a good morning. The two kids carried large paper rolls, which they placed next to their chairs.

Sarah rose. "Try not to get in harm's way for a while. I'll be in touch." She gripped my shoulder briefly, and then returned to the kitchen. A second later, Cecily barged into the conservatory bearing a notepad to take breakfast orders.

Once she had gone, a hushed conversation ensued at the German table. Once in a while, the boy or the girl would shoot me a glance when they thought I was not looking.

I speared a tomato, blew on it and swallowed.

The Germans were whispering among themselves, making me wonder what they were on about.

I stared out of the window. Sunshine flooded the lawn in the garden, painting golden halos around the new leaves. Kitschy, but pretty. If the pleasant weather kept up, we would serve breakfast on the terrace soon.

The Germans had reached a decision. Mr. Schlüsselblum stood up and approached my table, carrying one of the paper rolls. He beamed at me. "We found something yesterday. On a headstone. Are you interested?"

23

THE TEMPEST

"May I?" Mr. Schlüsselblum pointed at the empty chair in front of him. I nodded and used the napkin to wipe the buttery smear from my face. Mr. Schlüsselblum sat and unrolled his paper. Its edges got too close to my greasy plate, so I slapped it on the free seat next to me.

"Angie and the kids tried stone rubbing," my guest said. "Not enough time to try all three markers in one session. We started with Martyn's but did the Asher one next. The Coldron stone is at a funny angle. Which makes it difficult. But we'll have a go."

"Stone rubbing?"

"Like brass rubbing. You take a large piece of paper, place it on the surface of whatever it is you want to copy and run a pencil or crayon across. We used crayons. It brings out the text, and you get to figure out a lot more than with the undressed eye."

My inner grammar and style nerd growled. "Naked," I said.

Schlüsselblum grinned. "Yes, better to cover the stone."

Had the guy cracked a joke?

His face got serious again. "Anyway, we rubbed both the Cowslip and Asher headstones, and found some interesting stuff."

He pointed to a passage in the middle of his headstone-sized sheet of paper. The "left behind" I remembered from my ancestor's memorial, but the Schlüsselblums had dug up, or rather rubbed off, even more. Or would that be rubbed out? I read. "Left behind when the others passed through the circle" was followed by a long record of names including many illegible scribbles but also familiars like "Cowslip" and "Ragwort" on top of some strange, foreign-sounding ones like "El Cáñamo" and "Marguerite."

"When we rubbed the Asher stone, we discovered the same text. I suspect it might have been used on all the headstones. And look at this passage." Mr. Schlüsselblum poked the paper. "This reads 'found wanting.' Sounds almost as if these people weren't good enough with something and that's why they got left behind. I have no idea what they're on about, but isn't it fascinating?" He looked at me expectantly.

I caught myself curling a lock of freshly washed hair around my sticky fingers and dropped my hands. "Those graves date back to the times of witch hunts. I fear those people, our ancestors, were left to die."

Mr. Schlüsselblum nodded slowly. From the table where his family sat came the all-too-familiar sounds of bickering siblings. "Sounds horrid, but plausible. I was hoping Mrs. Coldron could shed some light on things. What do they mean by 'the circle'? The one in Avebury?"

I stared at the paper. Mr. Schlüsselblum was right. The word read suspiciously like a circle.

"How odd." A pagan death ritual featuring the Avebury ring of stones? Supposedly this was a Christian burial. What exactly had all those people been lacking? It baffled the mind, so I changed the subject. "Do you have any idea why they might have been buried together in that corner?"

My guest rolled up his paper. "The graves are located on the northern side of the church, marginally within the limits of the old cemetery, but we'll have to verify things. Maybe they were even outside at one point. I need to talk to the churchwarden. Or get maps."

The ghost of lectures past made its appearance. "You

mean they committed suicide?"

"Either that or they broke another rule. Society was very strict in those days. Sinners or other miscreants would be buried outside of consecrated graveyards."

Alma trooped in, bearing the Schlüsselblums' breakfast, which put an end to our conversation.

I emptied my second cup of tea and only afterward noticed it had gone cold. Over 400 years ago, something extraordinary must have happened in this place, the aftereffects of which rippled into our time. I reached for my phone to call back Sarah but dropped my hand. No, better to let her pursue rational things like motives and alibis while I burrowed into the whacky stuff.

I wished the Germans a good day, hoping they would unearth a few more secrets on my behalf.

Back in my room, I cleaned my teeth before trying to get hold of my cousin. I drew the usual blank. Stupid of me—even assuming she had delivered on her promise and returned to the village, she would still be in bed. Then I called the headmistress. I hadn't been looking forward to that conversation, and she wasn't making it easy for me. Hating myself for my underhand methods, I groveled and wheedled and got unpaid leave until Friday.

Duty done, I could go after the Ragworts, but to find their new home I needed directions from the ladies.

All was not well in the kitchen. "The Ragworts are already in their new house and have rung in for food. We're no takeaway," said Alma.

"It's okay, they're entitled to breakfast, and I'm going there anyway."

"Oh, are you?" Alma said.

"How about more bacon butties?" Cecily asked.

"Will the sandwiches stay warm enough until I get there?"

Alma huffed but grabbed the nearest skillet and turned on the hob. "It's not so far. Turn right into Nightingale Lane when you get out of here, then follow the road where it becomes

Field's View and keep going."

"It's in the scullery sack, Number Forty," Cecily said.

Alma banged her consent with the pan. "The shabbiest of the lot, that's what it is. My friend Lizzie took a peep when it was up for sale. Still, cost a pretty penny, I would say. But those two insisted on settling here."

The bacon sizzled its protest at the rough treatment. It browned nicely though. I nearly asked what a scullery sack was, but the answer dawned on me: cul-de-sac.

"You could take your aunt's bike. You might get there faster. It's in the shed." Cecily had the toaster going overtime and was buttering crumpets with abandon. "Shall I prepare a thermos flask with tea?"

"Please." I watched tea sloshing into the silver flask followed by the two butties getting placed in two greenish Styrofoam blocks that would keep them warm. I could use that back at school.

Cecily placed the food in a large wicker basket. "Mrs. Shuttlecock left us these. She's from PlastiElasti Limited. Very practical. Could do with more. She should be back soon."

Alma nodded. "Tonight. At six."

With another salesperson coming I could only hope I wouldn't need more emergency accommodation in Number One.

The basket under my arm, I left through the kitchen's back exit and crossed the gravel to the annex. The bike was in the shed, next to the construction debris, like Cecily had said. She had forgotten to mention that the whole contraption had been painted bright orange, probably the result of one of my cousin's bursts of creativity.

It was a gorgeous Monday morning. I pedaled my way along the quiet street, framed by the shy greenery of the hedges and long rows of detached houses in brownish brick, hunkering in the gardens like fattened toads.

A few more days and once the cops, I or both of us together had put an end to this nightmare, I could escape.

"There's something like free will, you know," I said to the now-defunct telephone box while cycling past.

It was great to be out in the open and not fretting all the

time. The air was fresh but not chilly and carried the promise of summer. The skies rumbled and I stopped the bike, placing one foot on the ground, and looked up.

A towering mass of black billowed into the heavens, spreading cauliflower outbursts that bubbled toward the sun. Lightning flashed. A flock of ravens was speeding across the clouds, cawing loudly. In the short time I stood there, the world changed colors to a leaden gray, the memory of brighter times nothing but a glowing fringe under the dense mass of clouds.

Just when I had thought things were getting better, this place delivered another slap in the face.

Field's View was not a long street, but it turned into a racing track—a challenge between me, the oncoming storm and the shiny windows of the houses, every one of them gloating at my sweaty plight.

Drops so cold they burned like ice splashed onto my exposed neck as I careened across the road. The wind blasted straight in my face with banshee howls, turning every push on the pedals into a fiery pain.

The bushes quivered and rustled. Hail, not rain, was pelting my neck.

I zig-zagged over the street. My destination, the driveway of Number Forty, wobbled and waved. Another flash from above, followed by a loud bang. That had been way too close. Not a good idea to be out on a bike in a thunderstorm.

Only a few more meters.

Crrump.

Yikes.

I abandoned the bike and raced toward the flimsy safety offered by a sagging porch with its roof covered in sulfuric streaks of fungus.

Another flash, another thunderclap.

I banged the knocker, and frigid blasts of the north shrieked along the sleepy street. Some unlucky fellow in a dressing gown a few houses down dashed out to grab the paper and then raced back inside. The raging wind made it hard to hear what was going on inside the cottage, so I almost jumped into the air when the door opened, releasing the musty odors of long-forgotten lives together with Mrs. Ragwort.

"Oh heavens, luv, what rotten timing. Come in, come in, isn't this weather simply atrocious?"

No further invitation was needed. I dripped after Mrs. Ragwort into her new home, where vector graphics in green, red, and orange ruled supreme on the walls.

"It looks a fright, doesn't it?" Mrs. Ragwort led me into a living room decked out in scuffed harvest gold linoleum and drab olive walls. The whole place was a gruesome study in autumn. Other than a camping table and two chairs, I saw no furniture. Alma's friend had been spot-on. Whatever the Ragworts had paid for this museum, it was too much.

I shook myself like a dog, sending drops flying. "Here's your breakfast." I handed over the basket, which Alma had filled with plastic cups and plates, grumbling all the time.

"Oh, how kind of you. You must have the first cup. And take my blanket. You're soaked. I'm afraid the electricity is not on yet, and this place is not so warm."

That was the understatement of the year. The house must have stood empty for a long time and had become a hideout for winter. Each of Mrs. Ragwort's words floated on a puff of white, and she kept rubbing a pair of hands veined in blue.

"Damian?" Mrs. Ragwort shouted down an open door on the other side of the living room from where issued icy drafts and, soon afterward, a male voice.

"Coming, Rosie."

I heard rapid steps. Outside, a white plastic bucket flew past the latticed windows, which were being pelted with hail that covered the garden in instant white. Grateful for being under the Ragwort's ramshackle but seemingly solid roof, I wrapped the musty blanket around me and sipped my tea, the only warm thing in this igloo of a house.

Apart from the Ragworts and me.

"Crikey. Methinks the end of the world is nigh." Damian remarked when he joined us. He pushed the glasses farther up his nose and peered at the window, but the rain now obscured the panes and visibility was almost nil.

Once Damian noticed me the muscles in his face tensed. He sucked in a deep breath, which he released ever so slowly.

"Don't tell me you braved the elements to get our breakfast?"

"Well, I didn't know what I was letting myself in for," I said, with a polite smile.

Rosie had uncovered the sandwiches. "Oh gosh, they're even hot, but there's only two. We can't have you starving."

She was looking for a knife, but I covered her hand with mine. Like the inside of their new home, it was clammy and cold, her papery skin covering bones as fragile as her hold on life. "It's okay. I've already eaten. Thanks for sharing your tea. I needed that."

Damian leaned against the windowsill and motioned at one of the camping chairs. "Please do sit down."

"I'm all right," I said. "Enjoy your breakfast first. If you don't mind, I would have a few questions later." My voice sounded croaky. Silly of me, there was no reason to stress. I was here so Damian could throw light on a few of auntie's secrets. Nothing to worry about.

"I know," Damian said. "That's why I would like you to sit down."

The drafts from the cellar, or wherever Damian had emerged from, found my spine, but my parents and my aunt between them had raised me well. "Please, do me a favor and eat first. I can wait."

Damian sighed and joined his wife at the table. He lifted the sandwich to his lips and then placed it on the plastic plate once more. "If you would like to have a peep, be my guest," he said with a sweeping motion of his hand. A crooked smile tugged at his thin lips. "It doesn't look like much right now, but it will once we are done with the renovations."

I assumed he wanted to talk to his wife about how to best break whatever news they wanted to share. I did the honors and left the room. Under normal circumstances, I would have enjoyed exploring this place. Right now, I suffered from the same stomach cramps that assaulted me whenever my advanced German conversation class was due. The group was a real handful and keeping order impossible, so I dreaded the biweekly sessions the same way I dreaded what Damian might have to tell me.

As I ambled through the corridor, I concluded from the

thick walls and solid oak beams overhead that the cottage had to be older than its exterior let on—maybe Georgian, like my B&B. I checked out the first-floor corridor and peered at empty rooms filled with peeling wallpaper and damp desolation. The bathroom, despite the appalling tiles in liver-sausage brown, appeared to be functioning. I allowed myself relief. By now, the Ragworts should have consumed their butties, so I descended the stairs and once more entered a living room still shrouded in the dimness of the downpour outside.

If possible, the place felt even colder than before.

The Ragworts sat at their collapsible table, silent, facing their half-eaten sandwiches. "Shall I come back later?" I asked, fearing a no as much as a yes.

"No, please stay." Damian got up. "Or, rather, please sit down. My news might come as a bit of a shock."

I sank onto a seat marginally warmer than the freezing walls.

Damian stopped at the window, his hands clasped behind his back. "Do the police have any clue why Eve died?"

"Aunt Eve believed somebody was after her. Or after something she owned. The sergeant in charge has now reopened the case."

Damian seemed absorbed by the vista of hail smothering his ragged lawn and spoke facing the window. "Your aunt was indeed concerned, especially at the end. Unfortunately, she never told us what bothered her. It doesn't surprise me. Keeping secrets must have become second nature."

He heaved a sigh and faced me. "Right, let's forget that for a moment. You'll think we're nuts. Please, promise you'll listen, even if I sound batty. When your aunt broke the news for the first time, we both got rather concerned for her sanity. She did convince us, eventually. Right, here goes." He paused, giving me an intense look. "Do you believe in witchcraft?"

The fairy tale theme again. But somehow, I had known.

Without electrical light, Damian's face formed part of the shadows. What I saw looked grim, determined.

"Eh, no? Sorry, I'm a practical sort of person."

"You might well be." Damian hesitated. "But I strongly suspect like your aunt, like Rosie and myself, and like quite a few of the people gathered these days in Avebury, you're also one of the last witches on Earth."

24

HEXED

What do you do when confronted with a bunch of lunatics? Politeness makes for a good start. Nodding and smiling will help. The exit comes next. Outside, torrents of rainwater were hammering against the windows so hard, the old panes rattled and shook. Any more of this, and they would break. The wind must have changed direction; the white plastic bucket flew past again, this time from the other side.

I clutched the armrests of the camping chair like a passenger in an airplane bucking through the skies. It made no difference, but it reassured me. A decent chair on solid ground.

In a witch's house.

"You don't believe it," Rosie said. "I can't blame you. We didn't either. Not at first, especially since Eve told us we both were descended from witches."

Her husband nodded. "Too much of a coincidence, but it must be correct. The Coldrons always knew about their heritage. Even if they didn't settle at Avebury like, for example, the Wytchetts. See, the last witches split up to have a better chance of survival. Throughout the centuries most of us forgot who we were. Nowadays, society is much more tolerant. Dottie Wytchett is adamant we can safely be together again. She contacted your aunt, who agreed to trace the missing families."

"Forgive me, this sounds rather outlandish. This world is all messed up and Aunt Eve would have been the first person to agree with me. All she ever did was harbor this Wiccan spleen. It was a bit of an obsession with her."

Careful, girl, careful.

Damian wandered through the room. "Our tradition is older than Wicca, and it's no spleen, I'm afraid. Even if most of us these days have only weak powers if any. Jenna is a spiritual healer, and so is her grandmother. I don't know what your aunt did exactly. Apart from keeping track of our history and the spells. She wanted to build a database for our lore."

Petunia's floral script swam into my mind. *I will note our lore, lest it be lost.* I blanked out the thought, only to have another one blip up.

"Is that why she chose Avebury? Because of the circle and the ley lines and stuff?"

"We have little clue how things work," Rosie said. "The lore was passed on orally and has been forgotten. Mostly. Apart from the Coldron recipe book and the Wytchett laundry list. But yes, Dottie guesses the powers might be somehow connected to the stone circle."

The rain and wind eased off as suddenly as they had arrived, and a ray of light pierced the gray above, illuminating the bucket that had come to rest under the hedge. From the gap in the clouds, a rainbow spanned an ethereal bridge across the skies.

Witches powered by a Neolithic relic—it had to have been something outlandish like that.

The Ragworts were not young, neither of them. If I ran fast enough, I would make it. It was worth a try.

"Care to show your skills?"

Rosie shook her head with a sad smile. "It doesn't work that way, dear."

Of course not.

"We can't," she explained. "We lack the magical energy, as Damian told you. In groups, it's supposed to be easier. That's also why Dottie and your aunt were keen to bring together the old families."

"The idea was to explore what exactly we were capable of," Damian said. "Then we can try to pool our remaining skills to do good. This world needs us. But one step at a time."

The world was safe enough for the witches to come out of the woodwork, but at the same time, it needed a magical fix. Super. My aunt had gone off her rocker together with the rest of them. Witch's Retreat, my backside.

"Explore?"

"Well, we have tried nothing yet," Damian said. "We still need to get to grips with who we are."

Witches didn't exist. Still, those two nutters unsettled me. Auntie—and my parents—had died for a bundle of airy-fairy beliefs.

"I understand," Damian faced me. "This is too much to take in all at once. You're right. We don't have proof. We don't even know how magic works. I wish we did." He faced his wife, a deep longing on his face.

Horror flitted across Rosie's pallid features, and she made shooing motions with her hands. "Don't you dare, Damian. Dottie and Eve both warned us not to try things—it's too dangerous. Our ancestors must have messed things up pretty badly, or why else were they left behind?"

Left behind. Found wanting. I thought about the writing on Mr. Schlüsselblum's sheets.

Damian nodded sadly, echoing thoughts he couldn't hear. At least, I hoped he couldn't. "Magical weaklings. All of us. The true witches escaped in the sixteen-hundreds. Don't ask me where to. Or how. Our ancestors were not skilled enough to join the exodus and fell prey to the witch hunters. Far too many of them burned."

No. This was sheer lunacy.

I had to get out of here. Now.

I rose and beamed at the Ragworts while fighting the queasiness bubbling in my throat. "Well, thanks for being so honest with me. I'll have to digest this. We'll talk later, okay?"

Damian dug a business card from the pocket of his woolen trousers. "I knew you'd think we'd lost our minds. Promise you'll ring us if you need to talk. We'll be around."

Witches with business cards. Well, this was the 21st century. I accepted the little rectangle. Then I shook his hand, breathed a sigh of relief when I didn't get zapped, felt foolish for it, and fled through the front door. Nobody came after me.

Outside, I doubled over, gasping. When the world stopped wobbling, I retrieved my bike. Its saddle was soaked, so I would have to push it. Before I set out, my smartphone buzzed somewhere in the pocket of my anorak. I leaned the orange auntiemobile against the Ragworts' porch and checked. A message had come in. Quite a few of them.

There were no hang-ups though.

Miller's Funeral Home had rung first, at nine this morning on the dot. My aunt's urn was waiting to be picked up.

The next voice I didn't recognize. The chap introduced himself as being auntie's financial advisor. He apologized for not contacting me earlier, but he had been on a business trip. Would I be available for an appointment this week?

The last message was from Daisy, forty minutes ago. "Hullo, I'm at the Whacky Bramble. We can talk." She sounded perfectly calm and coherent. The pub it was, then.

I started off by pushing the bike along Nightingale Lane. A few minutes later, I gave up and heaved myself into the soggy saddle. My trainers slipped on the pedals, and I had to swerve around puddles and potholes the whole time I struggled up Long Street. On my right, a tractor was meandering over the open field, water pooling in the ruts left in its wake. On my left, drippy hedges were only too ready to dump their load on me whenever I avoided the oncoming traffic. After the Ragworts' house, the air was near balmy, even if steaming with moisture. Everything airborne was out in force, all at once. Birds, butterflies, and bumblebees chirped, fluttered and hummed across my path, enjoying themselves.

I did not.

However, cycling helped in a way since it kept the dark thoughts at bay.

At the T-junction, I turned right onto Broad Street, which was anything but. Cars parked along the lane forced me to weave my way around them and straight into the next puddle.

The bright light of a freshly washed sun flooded the

gardens and super-posh houses with a sea of fire. Half-blind, I squinted at the glare.

With a roar, a car shot from a side street across my path. I jerked at the handlebars to avoid a collision. The bike slipped, and I offboarded. When I pulled myself up from the ground, fortunately with my limbs still intact, I could swear I heard giggles from the windowpanes of the nearest house, glittering from under a gray fringe of thatch.

Avebury had scored again.

I cycled on. The name changed, but the street got no wider. It was lined by long rows of cutesy "Olde Worlde" homes, their front gardens too bonsai to keep the wisteria in check and allowing it to creep all over the stonework.

Once I emerged into the main road, I jumped off the orange contraption and gingerly pulled the wet bottom of my pants from my crotch, hoping nobody would notice.

The Whacky Bramble was besieged by wanderers, waving their pints at the once more innocent blue skies. Having chained my bike to a pole sprouting the local bus timetable, I went in search of Greg. He chose that moment to pop from the entrance to his pub, bearing a tray laden with pitchers and glasses.

"Hi there, have you seen my cousin?"

His eyes white in his dark face, Greg gave me a funny look. "She arrived yesterday evening but left again half an hour ago or so. Said she wanted to talk to you. Is she not at your place?"

This was turning into a farce. I checked my messages and hey presto, Daisy had indeed tried to reach me while I had been pedaling my way through the village.

"Myrtle, I'm tired of waiting. I'm now at the Witch's Retreat. Where are you? I thought you wanted to know what mum told me?"

"Oh blast."

Greg returned with a tray crammed with empty glasses. "Everything all right?"

"Nope. You were spot-on. I've got to cycle all the way back." With a wet and numb bum.

"Uh, sorry to hear that. If you do find Daisy, could you ask her if she can join me here? We're kinda rushed off our feet."

As if in response to his comment, a table of tourists banged their glasses onto the wooden table. "More beer, more beer…"

"Coming right up. Sorry, ma'am." With that, Greg threw himself at the entrance, where he collided with Marty. The farmer was balancing a pile of empty plastic crates. The onslaught knocked him over and sent his load flying, much to the merriment of the thirsty visitors.

Applause crested over Marty and me while we were picking up his containers.

"Thanks, Myrtle," he said. "I hope you didn't come here for lunch. Pub's a wee bit busy."

"What I'm looking for is my blasted cousin. She's got ants in her pants. I cycled all the way across from the Ragworts, and now she's back at my place."

"Really? How about if I take you then? Got a delivery to make anyway. There's plenty of space in the van for your bike."

"You're a lifesaver."

Once Marty had loaded the auntiemobile into his transporter, I hopped on board, and with a wave at a sweating Greg, we were on our way.

Marty's callused hands gripped the wheel, the skin chafed and red in places. He smelled of Jenna's baking with a whiff of manure mixed in, a hard-working farmer struggling to survive the economic downturn. A decent man, a good uncle. And a male witch, if Damian was to be believed.

I was considering whether to broach the subject when Marty spoke. "Has Damian told you?"

"Ye—es," I said, still unsure whether I wanted the chat to continue.

He threw me a glimpse, mirth tugging at the corners of his mouth before he once more concentrated on weaving his van past the rows of parked cars.

"Let me guess, you don't believe him," Marty said. "It does sound wild, doesn't it?"

There was no answer to that, so I remained silent, wondering instead what his "skylle" might be.

Mind reading shot right up the ranking when he responded. "I haven't got it. Jenna does. Had it all her life. Drove our mum crazy. Gran was proud, though." The exhaust popped in protest as he braked to turn into Long Street. "The boys also have it."

"Oh, God," I said. The thought of two small kids endowed with magical skills boggled the mind. I couldn't help myself. I had to ask, even if this was the second conversation of the day that couldn't be happening. Damian had called her a spiritual healer. "What is it your sister does?"

Marty pursed his lips and slowed the van. "Hard to explain. A bit like fortune-telling. She has an inkling of what's most likely to happen. And she can, well, not heal, but calm things down? Puts her hand on your head or wherever and everything looks a lot better than before. Well, on a good day."

For a young mother of two rambunctious boys, it was a useful talent to have.

"What about her husband?"

"He's not born to the families," Marty said. "Doesn't matter really. It gets passed on mostly via the maternal line."

He set the indicator and turned into Nightingale Lane, but stopped at the side of the road, the motor idling. He regarded me once more, a quizzical expression on his face. "Jen said she could sense it in you. Even before she touched you. Really strong it was, she said."

"What was? I've noticed nothing." I crossed my arms, trying hard not to think of the darned plant. And the carousel. Perhaps even the petals were part of it?

I shooed away my thoughts. I had never done anything magical in my life.

Not before I got here, anyway.

"Some sort of buzz. You come across as green. Can't tell you more. Anyway, it reassured her. Something about you having to discover your talents without being told. Looks like you have."

The lid on my memories flew off and within my mind rose an image of the over-affectionate recipe book. I crammed the lid back on and sat on it.

"You girls need to have another chat," Marty said. "Or you talk to Gran once she comes out of hospital." The van moved again.

"Is she ill?"

"Arrhythmia. Normal at her age."

Nothing witchy, then. The thought ushered in another one. "Do you also have, eh, warlocks?"

Marty's expression became pained. He stopped the car once more. "I believe you're talking about male witches. The answer is yes. Though the majority are female. About two-thirds, I would say. About the word you used—I suggest you don't use it again."

"Why?"

"Warlock means 'oath breaker.' Somebody who betrayed his coven. Appears it was the male of the species who sold out their womenfolk when the witch hunters came a-knocking. Doesn't make me feel good about being a man." The car started again and crunched across the gravel into the Witch's Retreat.

I shivered, and not because of my still-damp trousers since the van was warm enough. Farmer Marty's no-nonsense demeanor made the whole surreal business far more real than when I had been with the Ragworts in their so-not-gingerbread cottage.

"Do you want to get out here?" Jenna's brother seemed glad to change the subject.

He wasn't the only one. "No, please take me around the back. I'll drop the bike in the shed. Ah, there's my cousin's car."

It stood crosswise between the wheelie bin and my Ford. The two vehicles looked like refugees from the local junkyard compared to the technological miracle parked lengthwise on the other side: a shiny monster of an SUV. A quick check showed German number plates. I expected no less.

Marty steered his van through the narrow access to the back and stopped it on a determined final bang from the exhaust.

"Doesn't sound healthy."

"Nope," he said. "No time to have it seen to, though."

The back entrance to the kitchen opened, and Cecily appeared, waving cheerfully. Marty retrieved my bike, and I rolled it into the shed. The task was mundane, but it helped quieting the whispers in my brain that wanted me to believe what I had heard was true.

With a strange detachment, I noted that one bag of cement had fallen over in the storm. The deluge had also dumped large amounts of water on the packed earth floor, which had become sludgy and slippery. I leaned the bike against the wall closest to the entrance and returned to the kitchen. My trainers looked a fright, so I took them off on the stoop, placed them on the mat and padded inside.

The whispers never left me.

25

STRINGS OF WOOL

The moment I entered the kitchen my gaze got sucked in by the balloon-sized yellow and pink monstrosity on the windowsill. I had closed the back door behind me, which should have blocked the drafts, but I could swear the thing had quivered. And now something glittered at the tip of a leaf, then vanished again. The sparkle reappeared on a blossom and raced across the top of the plant. A split-second later, it was gone.

I closed my eyes, balled my hands into fists and counted.

One, two, three, four.

Before I got to five, my eyes popped open against my will. Facing me sat one peaceful, cheery primula. My vision wobbling not for the first time today, I grasped the backrest of the nearest chair.

"You all right?" Alma asked.

I ignored the queasiness in my stomach and faced the others. "A bit weary. Must be too much of the fresh country air. Have you seen Daisy by any chance?"

Cecily nodded and grabbed the packets of bacon and a lump of something Marty was handing across.

"Homemade tofu," he said proudly.

"For the druids," Cecily said. "Your cousin was looking

for you earlier. Threw a hissy fit, then climbed upstairs to her room. I think she's left again, though. It's been quiet for a while."

"Her car is still outside," I pointed out.

Alma was busy storing the packets in the fridge. "Maybe she's gone for a walk."

Walk? Not Daisy. Perhaps she was enjoying a power nap. I said goodbye to Marty and thanked him once more, though whether it was for the lift, his openness, or the delivery, I didn't know.

"Let me see if I can find her upstairs." I left the kitchen by way of the swing doors.

On the first-floor landing, the little ceramic tiles on the doors to Numbers Five and Six, a wand and a raven, caught my eye, forcing my thoughts back to the witch theme with a vengeance. From there, they darted to my aunt. Preoccupied with protecting "them" from "him," auntie had ignored the symptoms of a nasty illness. But her injuries didn't fit the picture. Nor had anybody found a solution for the trap door mystery.

A Kind of Magic started playing in my head.

I tried to tune it out, but no go.

I dragged my thoughts in another direction. To find out what "they" actually were, I needed my cousin to tell me.

And here to receive the wooden spoon for last place in the annual Miss Marple award, Myrtle Coldron.

Imaginary catcalls sounded in my ears while I continued up the stairs.

There was no point. The witch theme elbowed its way back into my mind, and this time I let it. The cauldron of delusions I had stirred up made me suffer from hallucinations myself. The last witches were gathering in Avebury.

Yeah, yeah. Step.

The image of the flickering, rustling plant rose with a vengeance. I swatted at my thoughts. After all this stress, I needed a medical check-up. Step.

The burned rock where my parents breathed their last. On a mission for auntie, killed because somebody flipped when he didn't get what he wanted. Step.

While she was traveling with a headstone—hang on, no. I might be wrong, but I could swear the headstone never moved. Step.

Were mum and dad killed by "him"? Or by somebody in his employ? Most likely the latter, for "he" still hung around. Step.

This was sheer lunacy. Stars swam across my vision, and I grabbed the banisters. I was dealing with reality, not a cheap thriller where mysterious villains masterminded evil plots. Undeniably, however, somebody seemed to be doing just that.

Another image took shape in my mind. The proverbial dark-clad baddie, sporting a stereotype mustache and a black hat with a buckle. I had seen the picture of the woodcut on the Internet. It showed Robert Enrique Ignatius, witch hunter by profession, dead since 1642. It couldn't be him. Not unless some tosser had thrown ghosts into the mix.

How about Chris?

No, he couldn't have been involved then. Not only because I didn't want him to be. Sixteen years ago, he would have been much too young to confront a woman as formidable as my aunt. But what about now?

What about his blasted uncle? Could he be hunting witches? Or hunting for something belonging to the witches?

The pressure on my chest mounting, breathing became a beast. I needed a rest.

My next step hit the empty air, and I stumbled. I had arrived on the top floor. Out of the corner of my eye, I spotted Tiddles darting along the corridor and slipping through a gap in the curtain. My legs refused their service, and I sagged onto the corridor floor, fighting the tears. It was all too much. Murder, mystery, and witchcraft. Never mind the routine chores, such as doing the laundry. Or burying my aunt. From behind the curtain came an impatient yowl the same moment my telephone rang. I thumbed the call away. The phone rang again. Caller identity unknown.

"What do you want?" I screamed at the phone, expecting more heavy breathing.

"Myrtle?"

"Chris?" I flushed hot, then cold. I couldn't talk to him,

not now. Perhaps not ever. Not while I could trust neither my own feelings nor him.

"I've got nothing to say to you. Please leave me alone." I cut the connection. The next second, I wished I hadn't. Perhaps he would call back.

I waited. He didn't call.

A sob escaped my throat.

"Merow." The blasted cat again.

"Oh, go away."

With another yowl, a furry body appeared from between the gap in the curtain. The cat's flattened ears and the bristly tail lashing the fabric told me something must have disturbed the old animal.

"Aw, all right."

If I wanted this horror to end, I would have to find my cousin, sooner rather than later. I dragged myself after the cat, who disappeared through the half-open door of Daisy's room.

I hesitated and then rapped on the panel. "Daisy?"

No response. I rapped once more, with the same result.

Was Daisy lying in wait behind the door, ready to pounce? *That's downright ridiculous.*

Maybe, but then many things were these days.

I held my breath when I pushed open the door and waited. The second hand on my watch did a full circle. And another. I heard no sound and saw no movement.

"Meow."

Other than tripping auntie up, Tiddles was unlikely to be involved in her death, so I pushed the door ajar.

The interior design would have had the Barbie doll in raptures owing to the fifty shades of pink. However, a small tornado had hit the bedroom, leaving disaster in its wake. The wardrobe gaped open, cheap clothes spilling out in a colorful rush spreading from the floor to the bed. Silken sheets and pillows had been ripped apart and tossed aside like junk. My arrival had stirred the air, saturated with the cloying scent of my cousin's perfume. Tiny feathers swirled through the room; they teased my nose with a sneeze that never came.

Drawers hung open, sideboards yawed, and the curtain

had been pulled down. I beheld a chaos similar to the one in auntie's bedroom. However, Daisy's place had been locked, so the police never got in here. Instinct and the floating downs told me the mess might be recent.

Something cold and spiky stirred in my stomach.

"Daisy?"

No answer.

I scrambled over the clutter and threw open the door to the bathroom. Somebody had swiped my cousin's toiletries off the shelf under the mirror. Creams and lotions mixed with glass shards caked the sink and soiled the rose-tinted tiles of the floor. If I needed proof the intrusion happened not long ago, I stumbled upon it. The fluids were still runny. But of Daisy, I found no trace.

She must have been here. How else would the room be unlocked?

Back out of the bathroom, a splash of color in the corner next to the window caught my eye, and I stepped closer. Balls of wool sat on a low coffee table—fluffy angora, knobbly tweed, and baby-soft mohair in the bright yellows, oranges, and reds that matched the handiwork left in auntie's knitting basket. Carefully piled on top of each other, they formed a hairy pyramid. Next to them stood a photo of my aunt, a black bow tie affixed to one corner.

Drawings displaying an equally cheerful color scheme had been tacked to the wall behind. Created by a childish hand, "For Mum from Daisy," they still were remarkably good. Right at the front stood another box.

Like mother, like daughter.

Decorated with glittery stars and buttons, it brimmed with photo snippets showing my aunt and my cousin. Or only my aunt. There was not one photo of me. Some pictures were familiar but smaller than usual. I had been in them. Daisy had created a shrine and cut me out of the picture. Perhaps it was childish of me, but the cold, spiky thing in my stomach took offense at the slight and shifted around in my body, rubbing my insides raw.

The melted stubs of candles on the wooden floor became a blur. Tears rushed from my eyes as I grabbed the top ball—

angora the color of mimosas—and pressed it to my cheek. I hoped for a memory of auntie's perfume, but the air was too heavy with Daisy's invasive scent. Instead, I smelled cat drool. Tiddles loved messing with wool.

The minutes faded away, and most likely became hours while I squatted close to Daisy's shrine, sometimes fondling the yarn, sometimes crying, while outside the day slipped away.

The roar of a motorcycle on Long Street shook me from my crying spell. I sniffed, wiped my eyes on my sleeve, and then got up and used the tap over the tub to splash water on my face. I stood, and from the cracked mirror my bloated, blotchy and distorted face stared back at me. Some women cry prettily. I wasn't among them. I sat on the fluffy cover of the toilet seat and checked my phone once more. No new messages, no calls from either Chris or Daisy.

No calls from Sarah either.

Hoping my voice wouldn't betray how I had spent the last hours, I opened the window for some fresh air before ringing my cousin's number. I got voicemail.

Next, I called the pub. Accompanied by the clattering of crockery, soft jazz, and loud conversation, Greg's Southern accent flowed into my ear.

"Is she back with you?"

"Who? Daisy? No, ain't seen her the whole day. She not at the inn?"

She was not. Where was she?

With a soft "mrrp," the cat appeared from under the bed. My crying fit must have driven her into hiding. Tiddles stretched, and then reached for the woolly pyramid.

"Don't you dare!"

Too late, the balls toppled and tumbled to the floor, much to the delight of the blasted animal who batted them all over the place. I laughed, and it felt good.

Tiddles might well have been geriatric, but she still gave me a good chase, spreading gaudy strands of wool across the floorboards. One had slipped off the folded paper rectangle it had been wrapped around, forcing me to rewind the whole ball.

Around and around went the strings of wool, almost covering the elegant handwriting on the paper. I must have been exhausted from my breakdown. Otherwise, I would have reacted much earlier. But now my cerebral synapses sparked, and I recognized the handwriting to be Aunt Eve's.

"Cripes."

The strand of wool ripped apart in my hands. With a dry mouth, I unraveled my handiwork and unfolded the paper. It showed dates, followed by activities.

It looked like...

"A diary," I shouted.

Tiddles shot under the bed.

"Sorry, cat."

Pressing on the wool to keep the balls intact, I pulled out every folded core in such a hurry that more strings ripped and unraveled until the lot had disintegrated into a gaudy mess. I would deal with the wool later. Right now, I cared only for the notes.

Most of them were humdrum. Daily events at the B&B. Observations about Aunt Eve's guests, the villagers, and the village, ripped from a notebook, crossed out, and then rewritten. My mood plummeted. She had restrung her wool on discarded diary entries. With a sinking feeling in the stomach, I scanned the remaining bits of paper. When I picked up the second to last, an electric current ran through my body.

I had found the message from my aunt I had been searching for.

April 6: Myrtle, if you find this message, something has gone wrong. Please read to the end. No, I'm not mad. Bob Ignatius is after two items we Coldrons have been entrusted to keep. I should have left them where they were, but I wanted them close. He has threatened me and has planted a mole in my house.

Even if I can't prove it yet, I'm pretty sure that person has tricked poor Daisy. It's all my fault. I poked the bastard years ago. Back then, I threw him off track. But at what price. I'll never forgive myself for the death of your parents. Search the boxes, and you'll understand. And read the recipe book. I can't explain more. You need to find out for yourself who you are. And I'll catch that bastard.

She had added a postscript on the side that tore at my heart. It was written on the seventh of April, the day of her death.

He's in the attic. This is it. I'm going after him. Daisy has the key. She'll be the new guardian if I don't make it, and you can't. Or won't. Please help her. I never wanted it.

I love you,

Eve.

Hot tears coursed over my cheeks. Auntie must have hidden the note among the other balls of wool in the knitting basket, knowing I would look for a message. To her fevered brain, it must have appeared like a logical hiding place. Daisy then dragged the wool into her den.

I wiped my eyes with the heels of my hands and checked the remaining note. It featured a recipe for *Tarte aux Pommes*.

Tiddles had left the shelter of the bed and sat in front of me, her head tilted with a curious expression in her rheumy eyes. The beige tip of her tail curled and uncurled over a pair of matching beige front paws placed next to each other.

I drew a deep breath and ended on a hiccup.

Tiddles' ears flattened.

"Don't worry, dear, I won't cry again," I reassured the cat. "All I need to do is get hold of my cousin, and all will be well." Not quite. Better, perhaps.

Tiddles farted. I assumed she agreed with my reasoning.

I tried my cousin's number once more. It rang and rang

until it landed on voicemail. Strangely enough, I heard another mobile shrilling somewhere outside.

I tried again. Ringing—in my ear and outside. Then voicemail. The ringtone in the car parking, or wherever it was, stopped at the same time.

I rose and tried Daisy's number yet another time. Loud and clear, an old-fashioned American telephone ring shrilled into my ear. But not in the car parking. Somewhere in the landing outside the room.

Uneasiness spread inside me like a dark cloud.

"Daisy?" I whispered.

No response. My stomach responded to the pull of gravity. I opened the door to Daisy's room I must somehow have closed earlier and entered the landing. Dim and silent, it lay in front of me, the pine panel of my aunt's door closed, the aluminum ladder pointed at the dark maw of the trap door. Once more, I pushed the repeat button on the phone—and from behind the old settee trilled my cousin's unmistakable ringtone.

Three rapid steps brought me close. I hoped for a lost phone. Instead, my gaze hit on the dirty soles of a pair of trainers, followed by flowery leggings on long, shapely legs.

The rest of my cousin's body lay hidden in the shadows, twisted and bent. Thrown away like so much rubbish. I saw a tiny hand, palm up, pale like bleached coral. A familiar whiff of perfume hit my nostrils.

"Oh no, Daisy!"

She couldn't be dead. No way.

I dragged aside the sofa, and it screeched over the wooden floor.

Crime scene. Do not touch, my inner voice screeched in response. I didn't care.

I kneeled down next to my cousin, grabbed her arm and fumbled for her wrist. Her skin was clammy under my fingers. Clammy, not cold. Her limbs were still pliable, not stiff. Her nail varnish sparkled in the half-light.

I called her here.

I got her killed.

She mustn't be dead.

My fingers touched the slim wrist, seeking a pulse and tracing a faint flutter.

Don't leave me.

I gulped down my panic and called 999.

The calm voice at the other end promised ambulances and medical care. It asked for my address. I gave it, begging the voice to hurry. Then I tried Sarah's number once more.

I got her voicemail.

Desperate, I pulled out Damian's business card. The phone rang, but nobody answered. Were there no people left anywhere?

I was alone with a dying Daisy.

The Simpkins sisters. I called their number and finally got a human voice. Alma responded. She promised help.

"Do you have Jenna's number? Can you chase up the Ragworts?" I shrieked at the phone.

Alma did. She would ring a friend who lived around the corner from the Ragworts. I was to stay with my cousin.

I cowered on the hard planks of the landing, holding on to the little hand, her pulse faint, willing my cousin to live. Daisy was no killer but instead another victim. My cousin, my quasi-sister, and the only surviving family member I had left on Earth.

I thought back to the gravestones and heard Rosie's words: left behind.

From the window in Daisy's room, the siren of an ambulance wailed its urgency into the coming night.

26

TOIL AND TROUBLE

"Your sister is suffering from cervical acceleration-deceleration syndrome. Better known as whiplash," the surgeon in his rumpled royal blue scrubs explained. The hawk-like features hinted at Middle Eastern origins. Fatigue lined his sallow face, the raisin eyes almost disappearing into purplish sockets. "Happens often during a car crash. Was she in an accident?"

"No," I responded, feeling strangely lightheaded, though the wooziness might have been caused by the acrid sting of disinfectants permeating the whole place. Alma patted my arm. Her touch gave me the courage to continue. "If not an accident, what would lead to such injuries?"

The doctor fingered the face mask dangling on his chest. His body half-hid the clock on the stark wall behind him, which hinted at this being the small hours of the morning. "Not sure. There was a minor cut on her neck, and we found hematoma in her upper arms. Somebody must have grabbed and shaken her. The brain is bruised, and there's considerable swelling. We must keep your sister—cousin—in an artificial coma for the moment."

I licked my cracked lips. "Sister is fine. Will Daisy live?"

"I can't tell you right now. It depends on how things

develop. If there's no swelling and no further damage, Ms. Coldron should recover. If not, I don't know."

I'll stay in Avebury. If that's what it takes. I pleaded with nobody in particular. *Just let Daisy live.*

"Can I stay with her?"

He ran his hand over a chin that had not seen a razor in days. "Sorry, no, not right now. You can wait out here if you wish, but it's unlikely we'll see any change in the next hours. Try to grab some sleep yourself. Ring the ward around nine. If anything happens, we'll let you know. You found her in time. Just." His expression was not unsympathetic. He was a professional. Daisy was in good hands.

A beeper went nuts in the pockets of his scrubs. "Sorry. Got to go. Ask the head nurse for the number." Another nod and he left.

I sank onto one of the grayish plastic chairs. After the mad ambulance chase to the hospital, I couldn't walk away now. Alma said something, but I blended her out and let the memories of the evening wash over me.

Waiting in the landing, I had listened to the siren come closer, but the people of Avebury appeared first.

The Ragworts arrived ahead of the others, hastening upstairs as fast as Rosie could make it. Alma and Cecily followed on their heels. They were joined by others I might have come across during my ramblings or encountered at the pub. People like Mrs. Mornings, like the Colonel, like Mrs. Bingham. Now, their quiet whispering filled the corridor and the landing, like a lifeline of humanity. Somebody switched on the light, but it changed little, other than to throw moving shadows across the ceiling.

Marty and Jenna joined me behind the sofa. She had brought the twins, and the three of them kneeled next to my cousin, tiny fingers intertwining with Daisy's limp ones. Jenna's palm was resting on my cousin's forehead, whispering urgently. How I wished I could believe in magic.

"Mum, why is the lady lying off and not on the sofa?" Robbie or Johnnie asked. Even their voices sounded alike.

"Shhh, love. Think of her, how she gets better," Jenna said.

"I don't like this place, it smells of spiders," the boy persisted.

"Mum, I need to do number two," wailed the other twin and broke contact.

The echo of the siren bounced between the houses. It was followed by strobes of blue light that shredded the evening. The yowling died on a wail, and the murmurs in the corridor became more urgent. Feet shuffled, and the sound of boots thumping up the staircase reached my ears.

The Simpkins sisters will need to hoover again.

I would do it for them if Daisy lived.

Two paramedics in forest green bearing a stretcher barged onto the landing. Jenna and her boys faded into the background once the pros took over.

Marty wanted to drive me to the hospital, but I knew he would need to get up early to milk his cows. Alma offered to take me instead, and I let her. The middle-aged lady in her clapped-out vehicle was a closet racing driver. I clawed at the dashboard every time we shot through the crossings, but Alma kept the car stable and never lost sight of the blue beacon flashing ahead of us.

"Do you want to stay?" Alma's voice interrupted my flashback. "I'll wait with you."

Before I could answer, the doors to the hospital corridor swung inward. I turned, expecting the same old man I'd seen before to be lurching past in his striped dressing gown and dragging an IV drip behind him, the reek of smoke in his wake, stronger even than the chemicals. Instead, a uniformed police officer entered, followed by Sarah, her taupe blazer as creased as the surgeon's scrubs. The bobby was not Alan. The face under the helmet was black, not pale.

Sarah sank into the chair on my left while the constable guarded the door, his brawny arms crossed over his uniform jacket. "I'm sorry, but I'll have to ask you a few questions," she said.

"Is Myrtle a suspect? In that case, we must get a lawyer."

Alma glared at my cop friend, suspicion written all over her homely face. If I hadn't been so scared, I would have laughed. An aging housekeeper was acting as a bodyguard.

Sarah ran her hands through the spiky mess on her head. "Look, Ms. Simpkins. I'm trying to do my job. I need Myrtle's testimony. What Dr. Rasheed has explained about Ms. Coldron's injuries tells me there's a rather vicious person out there. I want to catch the bugger."

"Who also did in Mrs. Coldron—I knew it." Alma glared at Sarah and rose from her seat.

"Well, it's possible. The vic—Myrtle's cousin was attacked by a perpetrator displaying significant physical strength and unnecessary violence. If you asked me, I'd say this isn't premeditated. Somebody flipped."

"Like Alma said, something similar must have happened to my aunt."

Sarah massaged her temples. "One step at a time. In any case, we have a search warrant out for both Burns and Lentulus."

Staccato glugs boomed from the water dispenser placed on the opposite wall, and Sarah caught my gaze. "Bear with me. I need to run a lot of detailed questions past you. Timing is critical."

A plastic cup with water appeared before my nose. Alma to the rescue, yet again. The cold water flowed down my aching throat, quenching a thirst that had gone unregistered. I emptied the cup in one go, and my stalwart housekeeper snatched it from my hands and returned to the dispenser.

"When did you last speak to your cousin?" Sarah asked.

"Yesterday?" Disjointed images came back. The tree, the farm, Daisy softening on me. Had it been only yesterday?

"No, hang on, the day before yesterday. Sunday afternoon. We spoke on the phone. She was in London. I asked her to return here. She knows something, but she's in a real muddle and not only because of her money issues."

"I see. She returned when?"

Alma reappeared, passed me another cup of water and pulled a chair closer to sit down.

"No idea. Greg, the landlord, told me she had gone again.

She left messages on my phone. We kept missing each other."

The events of the past two days were nothing but a confused flurry of images. I dove for facts in the mush my brain had become and resurfaced with a thought. "My cousin said she was waiting for me at the pub. Only, when I got there, she wasn't. Instead, she left another message that she'd gone to the Witch's Retreat, so I went there."

"And?" Sarah asked.

"I spotted her car parked in front. And Alma confirmed Daisy had been looking for me."

"Indeed," Alma said. "Wouldn't wait until we had the lunchtime tea ready, drank two glasses of orange juice instead and kept checking her watch. Then she raced upstairs. Ever so jittery she is, that young woman. At the time I thought it must have been the juice. Was she attacked in her room?"

"Do you mind if I ask the questions?" Sarah snapped.

"Hah," Alma said, unperturbed. "My money is on the young copper."

Sarah rolled her eyes "Ms. Simpkins—"

"Don't Ms. Simpkins me, young lady. He arrived twelvish and left again twenty minutes later. She never did. We would have heard. There's only the saloon door between the kitchen and the corridor, see? She always makes a lot of noise, Ms. Coldron does. And we were there until gone one."

Sarah's cheeks had flushed, and there was a dangerous glitter in her eyes. "It's Sergeant Widdlethorpe to you. Hunter was called in for a search. A child has gone missing in Marlborough forest. We still haven't found her."

"Aye," said the constable guarding the door. He had a strong Scottish accent. "Laddie volunteered when he should have been poking his nose into books."

Alma narrowed her eyes. "Huh. Come to think of it, the other one also popped up shortly before the copper left."

"What other one?" Sarah asked, exasperation in her voice.

"Mr. Lentulus. I was dusting in the living room. Well, I didn't see him. Only his car. 'Twas gone pretty quickly, though."

Something sharp and hot stabbed my chest.

"When would that have been?" Sarah asked.

"After lunchtime. We finished our tea. Then, I did the dusting. The other bloke came before, though."

"What other bloke?" Sarah and I chorused.

"Jeff Burns. Barged in through the back door, looking plenty pissed off. My sister came after him with the pan and he ran. Myrtle and Marty showed up last. Twenty-five past, I reckon."

Sarah pinched the bridge of her nose. "I wished you'd mentioned that earlier, Ms. Simpkins."

"You didn't ask me," Alma said, her voice dripping with glee.

Sarah waved at the constable. He uncrossed his arms and joined us.

"Take a record of Ms. Simpkins's statement, Cameron, will you? I need to know who came and left when. I'm aware you're technically only a part of CID as of tomorrow, but who cares."

"Aye, Sarge. It's tomorrow already." He ushered Alma to a chair close to the water dispenser.

"I've got another suspect for you," I said.

Sarah slumped in her chair. "Let's have it."

"It's complex. While I was waiting for Daisy to reappear, I found something in her room. A note from my aunt. Hidden in a ball of wool. Well, the cat found it. Sort of."

"Your cat found a note in a ball of knitting yarn? How convenient."

"No, she hid it in the wool. Deliberately."

"The cat?" Sarah seemed to take an interest in a brownish water stain on the ceiling, shaped like Australia. "Myrtle, do me a favor and focus. Who hid what where?"

"My aunt. The cat played with the wool, and I noticed it had been rolled up on pieces of paper. Most of them were meaningless, but one wasn't. Auntie hid a note in the wool. It was a message for me. It said something about a key that she has given to Daisy. It also mentioned Ignatius."

At this moment, the solid blue metal doors to the ward opened, releasing the old man in his dressing-gown, the IV unit still creaking behind him. He saw the police officer, gulped, and exited posthaste. The doors squealed shut behind him but the stink of stale smoke lingered.

Sarah stared at me. "I must see the note."

My guts cramped with shock. Where were auntie's papers?

I had them in my hands while I was dialing, that much I remembered. When Daisy's phone rang in the landing, I forgot about everything else. I rummaged through the pockets of my cardigan in increasing desperation. No notes.

"Oh, no," I said. "I kept ringing Daisy's number until I worked out what was going on." Tears shot into my eyes. "I can't remember…"

Sarah jumped up and paced the floor, her rubber soles squeaking on the scuffed linoleum. Then she stopped. "Cameron? Write up the statement later. We need to drive to Myrtle's hotel. Let's hope the papers are still—where did you say you left them?"

The stern voice and the direct address did the trick, and my memory returned. "Either Daisy's bedroom or the landing. Can I come with you?" Somehow, I felt safer in her company.

Sarah gave me a sharp look. "We don't run a taxi service. But, fair enough, you can fill me in on the rest on the way there."

She stretched and suppressed a yawn.

Alma joined us, her face leaden with fatigue. I was keeping a hard-working woman from her bed. "Alma, I'll do the breakfast with Cecily tomorrow—I mean later."

She waggled a finger at me. "Oh, no you don't. That's my job. I've never missed a day in my life. Won't start now."

I was too tired for a comeback.

We filed out of the hospital. All the time the police car, calmly steered by Officer Cameron, rolled through a sleeping Swindon and into the countryside, Alma's headlights kept a safe distance behind us. The two-way radio chattered away at the front, sputtering cop lingo full of codes.

Sarah yawned once more and rubbed her eyes. "Gosh, that was a Monday from hell. Glad it's over. Would you have the exact timings of your cousin's calls?"

"Let me check." I pushed buttons, and the *Flight of the Bumble Bee* exploded from the smartphone. Officer Cameron drove on as if nothing had happened.

"Give me the phone, will you?" Sarah snatched the device from my hand. Her fingers danced over the screen and soon she scrolled through my messages. "Ah, here we are. First call came in at eleven oh one on Monday morning, the second one fifty minutes later, while I understand you were still cycling." She stared out of the car window at hedges and signposts that sprang up from nowhere, only to vanish again. "Hmm. Ten minutes to drive from the pub to the hotel, which places your cousin at the Witch's Retreat latest at ten to twelve."

"I must have just missed her. I got to the pub not long after noon and Marty took me to the Witch's Retreat soon afterward. We stopped a couple of times." To discuss the impossible. I shelved the thought and focused on facts. "Once Alan is back, check with him. Maybe he saw her."

Sarah's face was illuminated by the light of the radio. "The search for the kid started around one-thirty, so they might have met. Though from what you told me, your cousin doesn't strike me as being a patient person. I suspect she would've moved on a lot earlier unless she got stopped."

"I can't remember what time it was I found her."

"Well, I checked, your call came in at half-past four."

It had felt darker than that.

For a moment all I heard was Sarah's breathing and the cop babble from the dashboard.

The headlights of the police car slid over the stones of the henge and one by one they popped out of the dark like spooky wardens guarding...what?

Cameron steered the car through the s-curve that led through the village and Sarah rubbed the heels of her hands over her eyes. "This is one crazy case. I need sleep, or I'll never sort this out." She fell silent.

I was too groggy to talk, let alone think.

The car drove on until it eventually turned and passed the white B&B sign, where it stopped. Over the porch, a light came on, a motion-sensor triggered by the headlights of the squad car.

The sudden brightness woke me from my stupor. "Why don't you stay the night? Number Seven has got twin beds. If you don't mind sharing a room."

Cameron spoke through the headrest. "Sarge, that's nae a bad idea."

Sarah rubbed her neck. "You know what, I'll take you up on your offer. I'm bushed. Crikey, what a day. What am I doing here? Ah, right. Let's see whether we can find these notes of yours and then we leave it at that. My brain's shutting down."

Her tiredness showed. Sarah was rambling when in my experience she never did. Cameron left the moment Alma turned up. She would have dashed inside to prepare an early morning snack and air the sheets in Number Seven had I not put my foot down. Once she had reversed out of the front yard, I rushed upstairs, leaving Sarah to pant up behind me. A flurry of notes strewn all over the carpet in Daisy's room was my reward. Even the message was still there.

Sarah skimmed over the note and shook her head. "I must be half asleep already," she said. "This is beyond madness." She snapped open her briefcase and deposited the papers inside. Interestingly enough, she didn't ask for Ziploc bags.

We returned to Number Seven, and I handed over my spare nightie. "There are toiletries in the basket and a fresh towel on the rack. Otherwise, feel free to use my stuff. I'm going to lock the door and put a chair under the handle."

She nodded, heavy lids half closed over her reddened eyes. "Good girl."

She disappeared into the bathroom while I pulled up the drawbridge. When Sarah emerged again, wearing my old Garfield sleepshirt, I half-expected her to plonk a gun on the nightstand. All she did was remove a sleepy Tiddles from her duvet and park the cat on my bed. "You better stay with your mistress, my little friend. Nightie night, Myrtle." Then she slipped into bed. When I returned from the bathroom, Sarah was already lost in slumberland, her breathing light and even. I discovered having a police officer in the room was better than any sleeping aid. A few breaths after turning in myself, I sank into oblivion.

27

A NEW DAWN

I struggled my way back from a deep yet troubled sleep where nightmares weighed on my chest. For a moment I thought I was back at school and had forgotten to prepare for my lessons, but the light in the room was all wrong. The *room* was all wrong. Those weren't my teacher's quarters. And who did the dark head in the other bed belong to?

I noticed a weight on the duvet and turned to face it. The reason for my breathing problems squatted on the duvet a few inches from my face, purring and tickling me with its whiskers. Tiddles' fish breath pulled me back to the here and now. No, I wasn't safely back in Southampton, facing a load of hormone-crazed teenagers. Instead, I was marooned at auntie's B&B with a killer on the loose. At least I was sharing my room with a police officer, my new friend Sarah.

I ran the heel of my hand across my eyes and found them to be wet. Had I cried in my sleep? Thinking of tears brought back the memories of the previous day, and an electric jolt zapped through me.

Daisy.

Oh my gosh, I need to ring the hospital.

I shot upright in the bed, and the cat toppled from my chest with a hiss. My phone lay on top of the sheet of paper with the number the nurse had given me. Not wanting to disturb Sarah, I threw on my gray fleece bathrobe and shoved the phone and the sheet of paper into one pocket. Once I had removed the chair from under the handle and unlocked the door, I slipped into the corridor. The cat followed me but started off down the stairs in search of breakfast. It was early and the hesitant rays of light didn't reach far into the corridor. I placed myself next to the window to squint at the screen. For once, the window had remained closed, locking in a stale miasma of sweat and desperation. The soft carpet under my bare feet was gritty with the stones and sand dragged in by the shoes of the people who had been there for me yesterday evening.

Hands slippery with sweat, I hit the keys but misdialed, which forced me to start again. I got a ringtone followed by distorted piano strains running in an endless loop. If the plinking was supposed to be therapeutic, somebody needed to try a lot harder.

Finally, a click, followed by a nasal voice. "SwindonCentralHospital. HowcanIhelpyou?"

I had landed at the switchboard, not the ICU. The pressure in my chest mounted as I answered questions. Did I have the name of the patient? Yes, I did.

Did I have the number? No, I didn't. I should have but I didn't.

The name of the doctor? No—Yes! Rasheed. Dr. Rasheed, Sarah had said.

Leaning against the windowsill, my throat tight, I was hyperventilating. I waited, listening to the damned piano again.

There was a rapid clicking in my ear, followed by "Intensive Care Unit, Nurse Baker speaking."

"Yes, it's—Myrtle Coldron. Would you tell me how my cousin is doing? Daisy Coldron. She arrived last night, eh—this morning." I didn't know how to continue. I shouldn't have left. I should have stayed with her.

The brisk voice on the other end was softened by a lilt that had flown north all the way from the Caribbean. "Ah, Ms. Coldron. Dr. Rasheed said you would call. I'm to tell you he's cautiously optimistic. Your cousin's still in a coma, but her vital signs have improved. You may visit her later."

Had Nurse Baker stood next to me, I would have hugged her. "She'll be okay?"

The voice hesitated for a moment. "It's too early to say, but your cousin is young and healthy. That helped. Don't expect too much. Your cousin won't be very responsive. It might help if she hears your voice. If everything continues the way things are going now, we'll see if we can wake her up later today. The MRI looked promising."

I didn't understand what she was talking about, but if things looked promising, Daisy might live. "I'll come. Can I bring her anything?"

It appeared even a single grape was an anathema in Intensive Care, so I rang off with a vow to visit once I was more presentable.

All of a sudden, the world sparkled with light, the skies were blue, and the pressure on my chest had vanished, together with the cat. I remembered the call from the funeral directors and promised myself I would pick up the urn later today, once I was finished at the hospital. After leaving a message with the locksmith canceling our appointment, I tiptoed back to my room. The bathroom door was locked, and I heard splashing inside. Sarah was up. No doubt she would want to investigate Daisy's room. She might not let me tag along, but I could at least try to weasel my way in. That meant I had to get ready pronto. I rummaged in my drawers, found an old T-shirt I had not been wearing for ages since it was too tight for me, and left it on Sarah's bed. That would give her something to change into. Then I grabbed my last clean blouse, cream to match the blazer, together with underwear and jeans and dashed along the corridor, heading for the shower in auntie's bathroom.

I emerged in time to hear the door to Daisy's room creak open. "Sarah?"

She whirled around, one arm stretching out, the other pulling back in one fluid movement. While her fists tightened into wrecking balls, Sarah's feet sprang apart and her eyes narrowed to slits, completing the transformation. I was confronted with a lethal stranger.

My mouth an instant desert, I backed into the wall. "Uh, careful. I'm harmless."

The tension left Sarah's body and her arms dropped to her sides. "Watch out. It's never a good idea to ambush me like that."

"Black belt?"

"Among other things."

She entered Daisy's room and I followed, unbidden. Sarah had donned my shapeless old tee, which had once been ruby red. It looked out of place on her, but she wore it with grace.

She wrinkled her nose as her eyes scanned the room. "Phew, what a stink. And what a chaos. You rang the hospital, I presume?"

"Yes, Daisy's better."

"I know. I also checked. Thanks for the tee, by the way."

"All part of the service."

The corners of Sarah's mouth twitched. "We'll make a landlady out of you yet. Ah, there's something I wanted to ask you—did your cousin wear a necklace of some sort?"

"Why?"

"Well, the doctor found a wire-thin cut at the back of her neck, as if a small chain or necklace got ripped off with quite some force."

A necklace. A thought swam to the surface of my mind, only to sink again. "She always wears a lot of bling." The thought resurfaced. "Actually, yes, I remember a necklace. You know, one of those with the little charms on them?"

My friend jerked her head around with quick, birdlike movements. "Would be good if I could find that," she muttered, more to herself than to me.

"Do you want me to leave?" I asked, hoping she would say no.

Sarah sighed and faced me. "You've been all over the place yesterday, and I don't know how many people nosed around in here after you. The scene is already compromised, so you might as well stay."

"Much appreciated. I can make myself useful and find out if Alan is up. He could help you."

Sarah's gaze flitted aside. "No, he stayed with a friend in

Swindon. I'll check him out later."

She was the mistress of the poker face, but something about her remark struck me as off. I let it slip for the moment since I had other fish to fry. "What about the suspects? Ignatius or his nephew? Or Burns?"

"You never give up, do you?" Sarah clambered over the clothes, peeped into the bathroom and grimaced. "Good heavens."

She swung around and looked me in the eye. "I checked out Ignatius. He wasn't in the country for the last few days. Seems to be rallying more funding for his latest project. Asteroid mining or something. Looks like the crash has delayed things a bit. Anyway, I can't see the guy getting his hands dirty. But like your aunt wrote, he would have helpers, and they're the ones who interest me. For now, however, I would like to stay with the scene." Sarah knelt and checked under the bed. She got up, shook first her head and next the pillow. Something glittered and fell to the floor.

"Hah, gotcha." Sarah pulled a handkerchief from her pocket, wrapped it around her hand and grabbed the shiny object. She faced me, a broken silver chain with a pendant—a silver bunny—still caught on the links dangling from the folds of the hankie.

"I was hoping for this. It proves the perp attacked your cousin right here without ever realizing he ripped the chain."

The glittery trinket swung back and forth like a pendulum.

"There should be more pendants," I said.

"Then let's find them."

My breath caught. "One of them was an odd-looking key. Auntie mentions a key in her note."

Sarah grabbed a tissue from the box on the nightstand and used it to wrap up the chain. "You reckon your aunt gave it to your cousin, and she wore it as a pendant? How bizarre."

"Why not? A bit like hiding things in plain sight?"

Sarah's expression grew skeptical. "Why didn't Daisy ever tell you what she knew?"

Good question. "I have no idea. Spite? Confusion? It might have been a mixture of everything. I told you, she was stressed. Plus, from the way she acted, I reckon she must have been convinced I was on top of things when I wasn't. Daisy was aware auntie rang me, but what she didn't know is we never talked."

Sarah snorted. "Questions can be useful once in a while."

"She might have asked them had she not been distracted by her financial worries. Her brain can only deal with one problem at a time, and whatever bothered her took priority over auntie's troubles. She's that sort of person. Not bad. Just flighty."

Sarah pulled a face. "Hmm. Both your aunt and your cousin are well-suited for MI6. They could muddle for England. Well, let's run with that for the moment." She stepped around the bed and shook out the duvet. Another glittery flash. This time, it was a sparkly cross. It too got wrapped up in tissue.

I ran my hands along the sides where the sheets had been tucked into the mattress and found nothing. Sarah mirrored my movements on the other side and waggled a mariner's knot in my face.

I stretched and then scanned the room. Where was the darn key? My police escort was rifling through the photos in the box. I left her to it and fingered the curtain heaped on the floor. Nothing.

I spoke over my shoulder. "Why did the attacker drop Daisy outside instead of leaving her here?"

Sarah rose from the floor and tapped her chin, her eyes darting from left to right. "Two possibilities. Either that guy—think it was a guy, really hated her guts. He attacked her, but she was still breathing so he hid her, hoping she would die before she was found. Alternatively, he believed she was dead and wanted to give himself time to escape."

While she was speaking, I sifted through the wool and fumbled through the clothes on the bed. Nothing. "There's Daisy's purse."

"Where?" Sarah turned around.

"Under the radiator."

She nodded and shook it out. A pinging noise made us look down and Sarah knelt down next to the heating. She picked up something with her hankie-wrapped hand and presented it. "Could this be the infamous key?"

It was the one I had seen on Daisy's chain. Tiny, with a round bow and zig-zaggy cuts with holes in them. Upon closer inspection, it showed a number stamped into it and didn't appear decorative at all. Perhaps that was why I had remembered the thing.

Sarah used the last tissue to pack the latest find.

"Now, we need a lock that fits it," I said.

A smile blipped on Sarah's face. "I would say bank vault or safe deposit box, but one thing at a time. First, I need to work out why your cousin got attacked. And by whom." She let her gaze roam over the room which, after our search, was even messier than before. "No idea about the culprit, but I would say somebody came across your cousin when she was waiting for you. Either she provoked him, or he wanted something she couldn't or wouldn't give him. And don't get me wrong, I'm not saying it was her fault."

Sarah's words triggered a brainwave. "Yes. Your perp might have overheard the message she left on my phone. He wanted to make her talk, shook my cousin, and the chain broke. That also means he must have been following her in the first place."

"Remind me to hand over the application sheets for the CID. You'll make a good detective." Sarah straightened and rubbed the small of her back. "Okay, I need to get this stuff to HQ. You visit your cousin."

Once Sarah had been picked up by Officer Cameron and had been supplied with cheese sandwiches and a thermos flask filled with coffee courtesy of the Simpkins sisters, I shoveled a load of cornflakes down my throat before I hit the road myself.

Daisy was expected to live. After a long, dark night, the sun shone again, the birds sang while puffy clouds drifted across deep blue skies. Somewhere inside me, however, lurked yesterday's horrors, yesterday's desperation.

What if Daisy lived because of something that didn't exist?

Something belonging to the world of fairy tales and make-believe.

Magic.

28

ANTISEPTIC

The noise in the Intensive Care Unit was deafening. In my mind, this place had been a hush-hush affair, a place where nurses tiptoed their way past screened beds, a place where silent forms fought their invisible battles with death. Wrong—combat was all too obvious. Monitors blinked and beeped in every corner, undercut by the rushing of ventilators, the humming of respiration pumps and the occasional high-pitched shriek that drilled into my head and called the nurses into the fray.

Daisy never stirred.

My cousin's vital signs showed as steady blips on a monitor. Her chest moving and falling with the rhythm of the machines, she slept on with hands that were cool but no longer clammy. The only sign of life was her auburn braid snaking from under the cap she was wearing, a cap from which sprouted whitish wires connecting her with yet another machine: the one watching over her brainwaves. Black, the size of a small computer monitor, it displayed a pattern of wriggly multicolored lines which reminded me of a knitting pattern. A sharp odor of disinfectant tickled my nostrils worse than the Clorox Alma and Cecily used at the B&B, but the army of germs would be far more militant here.

Footsteps squeaked across the floor behind me, and I turned around. "We've changed the medication. Ms. Coldron should wake up soon."

Dr. Rasheed, still in rumpled scrubs, made me suspect he had spent another night on this battlefield. "It's amazing. I didn't expect her to come back so quickly. If all goes well, we can move her to the regular ward later."

Dr. Rasheed ran his fingers through his hair and yawned. "Oh, sorry. There was a pileup on the M4 and all the injuries came here."

He gave me the impression that losing even one patient under his wings would hurt and that he would consider it a personal failure. He was that kind of guy. If I ever were severely injured, I would like to have him around. Perhaps the miracle of my cousin's speedy recovery was owed to nothing more sinister than a good doctor and modern medicine.

"Shall I stay?" I asked.

"If you could. It might help your cousin. Touch her, talk to her."

His pager shrilled from within the breast pocket. Dr. Rasheed sagged with defeat.

"Excuse me, please." He shuffled off, making me pray he wouldn't end up in the free bed on Daisy's right.

On Daisy's left, a frail old lady, birdlike bones smothered by a light green sheet, was fading away. The blips on her monitor got more erratic while I watched. I wondered whether I should call for a nurse, then decided against it. The machines would look after the poor woman. I had my cousin to care for.

"Let me tell you what's been going on, okay Daise?" Perhaps she would recognize my voice and would get pissed off enough to wake up and complain. Fine. As long as she woke up.

I tugged at the oversized bile-green coat I had been given. Despite the freezing temperatures in the ward, I sweated underneath, and the pale green bonnet covering my hair itched abominably. A quick scratch under the elastic helped little, so I tried to ignore my unease and clutched Daisy's small hand in mine.

In a way, her unconsciousness was a blessing. I still had

no idea how deeply she might have been involved.

"Well, it appears auntie—mother—has been researching a lot of old families connected through...well, they all have something in common. Or at least they think they do." I refused to use the "M" word. Or the "W" word. Surrounded by hospital high tech, covens, cauldrons, and broomsticks disappeared back into the hole they had flown out of and became part of a fevered dream.

"I wondered why auntie was so fixated on Avebury. I thought it was part of her Wiccan obsession, but it appears our ancestors came from here. And then some of them went—don't ask me where."

Daisy remained motionless.

Another alarm pierced through the din, but it didn't come from Daisy's machine, though the readings for her heartbeat and pulse crept up. Spikes appeared among the wriggly lines creeping across the brainwave monitor.

Attagirl.

"Auntie got attacked because she was guarding something connected with this occult stuff. Said the Coldrons were the keepers. She bricked it up in the attic, then took it out and hid it somewhere else. And gave you a key."

The lines spiked then dropped again. "Daisy? Can you hear me? Press my hand if you can."

No reaction. It appeared I was getting through only to Daisy's subconscious.

"Alan and I found a note of your mother's. Taunting the person after her secret."

The person who had been pulling everybody's strings: Bob Ignatius.

"Daisy, I know it sounds whacky, but I think we're dealing with a cover version of the witch hunts."

Like the little wriggles on the brainwave monitor, Daisy's pulse and heartbeat remained unperturbed. "Who attacked you? Was it Chris?"

No reaction, not even a spike. Like a doomed moth, my heart fluttered with hope.

"Jeff Burns?"

Nothing. Was I fooling myself thinking Daisy was reacting

to my words?

One final name still burned on my tongue. From the timing, it was possible. "Alan? Alan Hunter?"

Again nothing. Daisy had not heard a word.

The monitor showed my cousin's brain activity was back to its previous level. Wondering whether she might be avoiding everything related to the attack, I changed the subject.

"Do you know what it is your mum has hidden?"

On the monitor, the numbers showing pulse and heartbeat were creeping up again.

"Does the key mean anything to you?" The spike was tiny. But it was there.

Shrill ringing exploded in my ears and I jumped to my feet. Machines clamored with alarm; red lights flashed, and nurses dashed from the depths of the ward.

They weren't heading for us. The old lady on my left was losing her fight.

"Sorry, but you must leave." Nurse Baker grabbed my sleeve, but I pulled back.

"Daisy?"

Nothing.

"I'll bring mum home. Then I'll be back. There's only us left. We'll sort things out between us, okay?"

I squeezed those small fingers, willing her to get well. For a fleeting moment, I swear the fingers pressed back, their touch as soft as a kitten's paw before they curled open again.

"Ms. Coldron, please," the nurse said. I saw a flutter of blue figures through my tears and allowed the woman to lead me away from a battle that was already lost.

—

As I drove away, the crescent-shaped hospital building shrank in my rearview mirror. It had rained again, and the smell of damp grass mingled with the exhaust fumes. I set the blinker and turned on to the A342 which, according to my navigation app, would get me to Miller's Funeral Home via the ring-road rather than the roundabout. The events of the last days clamored for attention, but I shoved them back where they belonged. That was another lesson learned: no Sherlocking at the wheel.

I rolled into Miller's car park and turned off the engine. It was high time auntie returned home. It was also high time I faced the truth. Daisy would need somebody to care for her and that somebody could be only me. Early this morning I had made a promise, had offered to stay here if my cousin lived. Now, the debt would get collected.

I rested my head against the steering wheel and groaned. There was no way I could return to my school any time soon. In fact, there was no going back at all. The headmistress had been more than fair, and I ought to return her civility in kind and hand in my resignation without further delay. My decision was made. I was staying in Avebury.

I ripped the key from the ignition, opened the car door, and got yanked back by the seatbelt I had forgotten to remove. Belt released, I climbed out of my Ford and banged its door shut. Auntie had won. But somehow it didn't matter anymore.

My mobile beeped. Sarah had left a message.

"Hi there, Burns is off the hook. He's found a job with Health and Safety in Marlborough. Was there all day yesterday. He refuses to hand over his phone. It might not be easy to confiscate it since technically speaking he hasn't done anything, but I'll try. Will call you later. Take care."

Miller's greeted me with blessed quietness. A young woman, her robust shape almost bursting the seams of her sober blacks, was typing something on a computer. The clacking of the keys was rhythmical, yet muted; she never once stirred, not even when a side door opened, and Mr. Miller appeared. "Ah, Ms. Coldron, welcome back," the funeral director said, *sotto voce*. "If you would please follow me."

He led me through the pine-scented corridor into the wood-paneled room at the back with its images of never-changing seasons decorating the walls. Summer, however, was still missing.

In the middle of the table squatted a sand-colored rounded vase. It contained no flowers. Instead, a flat lid covered the top. Prints of bare feet marched up one side and presumably continued down the back. My pupils would have said it looked kind of cute.

"What's this?" I asked. An uneasiness in my stomach told me I knew the answer.

"Please take a seat," Mr. Miller said and drew a chair for me. "It was of paramount importance to your aunt that we used eco-friendly materials for her burial. This is something I haven't tried before. It comprises sand from the Outer Hebrides and is sturdy yet biodegradable, should you decide on a burial."

He looked at me expectantly. The urn, a word he had circumnavigated aptly, rested between us. From my side of the table I could see that, yes, the footprints continued down the back.

It did look cute. I liked the tiny marks of bare feet and the queasiness ebbed away. "Sand? Will it be stable enough?"

Mr. Miller nodded his enthusiasm. "Absolutely. In fact, you could put this on display if you so wished. The colors are lightproof. They will not fade. Or so I was promised."

He bent, rummaged under the table and brought up a cream-colored carton. "For the journey home, however, I would recommend you use this. We can pad it, to be safe."

Auntie's last trip. In a cardboard box, with my clunker of a car doubling as a hearse. She would've loved that.

Miller looked at me. "Do you like it?"

"Uh, yes, I suppose—it's very tasteful." In a way, it was, as urns went. Not that I had seen many during my lifetime. Three was more than enough.

I swallowed twice, to suppress both the tears and the unsuitable giggle tickling my throat.

Leave nothing but footprints. Aunt Eve had done a lot more than that.

I shook hands with Mr. Miller and pocketed an envelope he had slipped me discretely, which no doubt contained the bill. The funeral director accompanied me outside, carrying auntie for me. We debated over the best temporary resting place for her and decided the footwell of the passenger seat would be safest.

"I've taped the box shut. Don't worry about braking hard if you need to. We don't want you to have an accident."

Nor did I.

My aunt's box beside me, I waved once at Mr. Miller, who returned my goodbye with a smile matching the sun that peeped from behind the clouds. Like the surgeon this morning, he was another person who cared. Unlike Dr. Rasheed, Mr. Miller was not somebody I would want looking after me.

The afternoon rush hour had started, and my cautious progress upset quite a few of the other drivers.

"Yes, to you too," I said, fuming when yet another car shot past me and cut back into the lane straight in front of me, forcing me to stomp on the brakes.

A quick glimpse at the footwell assured me auntie remained unperturbed.

The sun accompanied us on our way home, and the traffic got lighter once I emerged into the countryside. I rolled through a freshly washed Avebury, sparkling in the light of early afternoon. Even the standing stones appeared less morose, set against a serene backdrop of blue spring skies, twittering sparrows zipping between them.

When I crackled across the gravel in front of the Witch's Retreat, I noticed only one car: the German SUV. Once inside, the house greeted me with an unsettling quiet. Something had changed. I could sense it in the atmosphere, which seemed charged with an invisible energy bubbling like bath foam. My scalp tingled in response. The light in the corridor had taken on an odd quality that drew a greenish aura from otherwise mundane objects: the bell on the reception desk, the pigeonholes for the keys and the sideboard with its load of tourist pamphlets. Oddly enough, once I tried to focus the phenomenon evaporated.

A faint, flowery perfume drifted through the hallway, and I wondered whether it was imagined or real. Whatever it might be, it originated from the kitchen, so I traipsed across in trepidation. Auntie's box was amazingly heavy, forcing me to carry it with both arms. I nudged my way sideways through the swing doors and into the kitchen.

My gaze fell on the windowsill. The primula was gone.

The next instant, the doorbell gonged. I turned in confusion, only to swing around again.

The back door stood open and a dead rat lay belly up on the kitchen tiles.

29

POWER FLOWER

With trembling hands, I placed the box containing auntie's ashes on the countertop and knelt down, staying well away from the dead rodent's worm-like tail that snaked across the grouting. The corpse appeared to be fresh. I peeped under the table and in the corners but didn't catch sight of the primula. The doorbell gonged again. Out of time to scout for errant plants, I panted into the corridor and threw open the front door. That turned out to be a wrong move. Jeff Burns exploded into the hallway and I jumped a mile high.

"Hah," he yelled, his bullish face crimson with fury.

He pivoted his chunky head and faced a rake of a man waiting behind him under the pointed roof of the porch. Clad in brownish hues and clutching a clipboard to his chest, the chap was all about verticals, apart from his handlebar mustache. Even to my befuddled mind, it stuck out.

"What do you want?" I asked with a squeaky voice.

"Tell her," Burns said, a triumphant sneer pulling at his fleshy lips.

"Uh, the name's Enderby. From Health and Safety. Mr. Burns you met before, I understand? My new colleague has recently been staying in your establishment and found serious issues of noncompliance with our regulations. He has urged us to act."

The rat popped up in my mind like a bubble in the sludge. With it came anger, a fury so hot it seared through my inner haze.

"Has he indeed? Tell me, Mr. Enderby, is it a Health and Safety business practice to engage in personal vendettas? Did you know Mr. Burns's wife threw out your colleague after he had a go at me? Are you aware Mr. Burns has threatened me with ruin? Has called this place a murder house?" I shut my mouth before the phone calls slipped out. I still had no proof, only a strong suspicion Burns might have been behind them.

"You'll regret that," Burns roared.

"You said the same thing last time. In exactly the same tone."

Enderby swallowed, his Adam's apple sliding up and down his scrawny throat. His gaze darted between us. "Now listen, Jeff, I told you I'm not happy. This establishment always gets top marks and—"

"The woman is new! Told you, there're rats in spaces used for food preparation. Check it out. What are you waiting for? Father Christmas?"

Enderby's mustache quivered with indignation. "Apologies Ms. Coldron, this is not the way we prefer to do our business." He turned to confront his colleague.

About to congratulate myself for getting the upper hand, I spotted the primula, squatting on top of the reception desk complete with pot when I could swear the counter had been empty instants ago. The foolish hope that a Simpkins sister had shifted the blasted plant got shredded when the thing jiggled its greenery.

In a last-ditch effort, I closed my eyes and opened them again. The stalks and leaves of the little plant still fluttered as if shaken by an invisible storm. As if proving a point, the pot lifted and hung in the air before landing again with a soft thud.

My heart clenched and my stomach went on a rollercoaster dip.

Shouts and snarls that must have come from Enderby's and Burns's brawl reached my ear and were dismissed.

This. Was. Not. Possible.

Deep inside, I knew it was.

I took a step aside to block the blasted thing from the view of Health and Safety. Enderby was gesticulating, while Burns brayed at him, spittle foaming in the corners of his mouth.

Rustle.

I swung around. A pink spark plopped from a blossom onto the floor and vanished. A second later, the pot lifted on a trail of embers and zipped across to a spot right behind Jeff Burns's right heel.

My stomach flash-froze, my vision wobbled, and I staggered backward.

Anger burned in Mr. Enderby's pale face while he listened to Burns's bellowing with a derisive sneer. Neither of them noticed the little magical menace at their feet, but it was only a question of time until they did.

Think, Myrtle.

I framed the blasted primula in my vision and willed it to vanish, to move, to do anything that would stop me from exposure. The flower quivered at Burns's heel, giving me the distinct impression it wanted to trip him up.

While the two men continued their stand, I jerked my thumb at the kitchen.

Go. I voiced with my lips.

The leaves of the plant drooped.

Go now.

The primula shot down the corridor, a sparkly blur. Then it doglegged into the kitchen and disappeared from sight.

Enderby swung around. "What was that?"

Burns snorted. "I told you. Rats."

Enderby's long nose quivered and sniffed as if he, well, smelled a rat. "You don't mind if I have a quick look, Ms. Coldron? To help me close the complaint? I'm sure you have nothing to fear."

Oh crap, I had forgotten to remove the rodent.

No sooner had the thought materialized in my brain, did Enderby start along the hallway, following the path taken by the plant.

Burns gave me a triumphant look and stomped after him.

I dashed ahead, narrowly avoiding Burns's outthrust elbow. "Mr. Enderby, I've told you already. The complaint is trumped up. If you find rats, or rather a rat, in my kitchen, it's because somebody put them there."

"You shut up," Burns said.

"Enough of that," Enderby snapped. "I apologize for my new colleague's outrageous behavior. It is uncalled for, and I understand if you wish to raise a complaint. In fact, I'll provide you with the required forms." Politeness didn't stop him from entering the kitchen, though.

The rat was gone.

The terracotta kitchen tiles were as pristine as ever, the appliances reflected the light of the ceiling spots and not a single thumbprint marred the shiny surface of the eggshell cupboards.

"Huh?" said Burns, perplexed.

Enderby ignored him, walked across to the fridge, yanked open the door and pointed at the orderly contents in the fridge's arctic confines with evident satisfaction. "That's how I remember things." His breath came out on a billow of white.

I stared at the windowsill, once more graced with the gaudy primula in its clay pot, a rat's tail dangling over the rim.

———

It was not difficult to get rid of the two inspectors. Burns for once had been thunderstruck into silence, while his colleague was both furious with Burns and apologetic to me. I accompanied them outside and then lurched back to the kitchen, where I sagged onto the nearest chair.

On the sill, the plant gently swished its leaves as if to get my attention. It tilted the pot and displayed the furry body of the dead rodent before straightening again. A giggle burst from my throat, but it was powered by desperation, not mirth.

Through the gap between the back door and the panel, children's laughter rang out, accompanied by the rumble of a lawnmower—the sounds of an ordinary day.

Only mine wasn't. I had the ashes of my aunt parked in the kitchen, my cousin lying in a coma in hospital, witch hunters storming the attic, and a zombie plant with protective instincts prowling the ground floor of my new home.

And those were the more harmless of my problems.

Who am I?

I heaved myself from the chair, ripped off plenty of kitchen paper and reached for the pathetic, little corpse with its exposed yellow incisors. Even through the layers of wadding, the body felt stiff. It wasn't quite so fresh after all. Burns must have planted it at some point when nobody was home. Alma and Cecily would have to learn to close and lock the back door, whether they liked it or not. I walked outside, dumped the corpse in the bin and returned to the kitchen.

I held my breath, yet the plant didn't twitch a leaf or shed a spark. Perhaps it took offense at my lack of appreciation for the botanical acrobatics?

Feeling guilty, I stroked a knobby leaf and found it to be fizzing with energy.

"Thank you," I whispered.

If Great Aunt Petunia was to be believed, I had brought the plant back from the dead. That would explain why it liked me.

Great Aunt Petunia. The recipe book. Surely, I would find explanations in there.

I grabbed the cardboard box with the urn, pushed through the swinging door and stumbled into the sitting room. Glancing around, I wondered what to do with auntie. In my current state, I was likely to drop her urn if I attempted to remove it from the box. I walked to the back and placed her container next to the archway. It would have to do for the moment.

Back at the shelf, my fingers crept toward the battered and stained recipe book, slotted in between Conrad's *Heart of Darkness* and a Regency romance. I hesitated. Now that I knew who I was, would the grimoire—it could only be that—bite the fingers off the magically inept? But then, if the rumors were to be believed, the whole tribe was supernaturally challenged. I snatched the tome from the shelf unbitten and, with the book pressed to my chest, dropped into auntie's armchair. I flicked through the front part of recipes first from my aunt, then my grandmother. The empty bit in the middle came next. I leafed my way through, my heartbeat gathering speed.

The empty pages were only that, empty.

Petunia's curly scrawl, when I hit upon it, sent my heartbeat to a full gallop. Here was her pledge to conserve the lore of a lost people. Her little note about reviving plants. Her warning not to try the trick with things animate. Our so-called "skylles" sucked and as a result, we got stranded.

My eyes fell on auntie's cardboard container.

With a shudder, I turned the page. Aunt Eve was beyond revival.

I read on and hit upon the scary part featuring not recipes and lists of plants but instead weird ceremonies, some of which involved the stone circle. Next came more instructions on how to use one's "skylles," followed by warnings. There were loads of warnings: the old tome contained miles of red tape. Witching must be a hazardous business.

To reduce the danger and to augment the "skylles," hexing was better done *en masse,* or so Petunia claimed. The more practitioners, the merrier. If I recalled correctly, Rosie had said something similar.

I closed the book with a snap. Auntie and Dottie Wytchett between them had attempted to set up a—well, coven was the word that came to mind. They had been shockingly successful.

The window of the sitting room stood open a crack and let in the soft crunch of feet on the gravel. A guest was returning. Surrounded by silence, I welcomed the idea of company. I listened but the car parking had fallen quiet again. Leaden tiredness pressed down on my brain. I sagged into my armchair, closed my eyes and tried to catch my swirling thoughts.

An animated plant with a mind of its own. Impossible, yet all too real. What had my family been guarding? Headstones? Bones? Cauldrons? It had to be something important. Otherwise, Ignatius wouldn't have attempted to steal it, or rather sent somebody to fetch it. The person who had hunted first Aunt Eve and now me. Like the man who caused the death of my parents sixteen years ago and ended up dead in a ditch.

A scraping noise came from the door, and my eyes

snapped open.

The ticking from the ormolu clock on the mantelpiece was the only sound left in the room. The ticking became a roar, surging in my ears as if I had swallowed an ocean. I certainly felt sick enough to have done exactly that.

Something scritched on the door panel, a noise so faint I might have conjured it up. I strained my ears. Hearing nothing at first, I then caught another tiny sound, even more, immaterial than the other.

Would it be the plant in search of company?

The next moment, the handle of the door started moving. It crept downward. Then it stopped, the movement almost indiscernible. But the handle had moved and now it did so again.

Who would be sneaking up on me?

Friends wouldn't use stealth like that. Bile rose in my throat, a silent SOS. I wanted to call out, but I found I had run out of saliva.

I should have run for cover. I didn't. No matter how hard I tried, the raging ocean in my head pressed me down in my seat.

The handle crept down a notch.

Not Burns. He had fired his proverbial gun and shot himself in the foot.

The handle moved again.

Not Ignatius. Not on his own.

The handle stopped moving.

Tension surged through the room in a giant wave, leaving me stranded, a flailing mollusk. There were only two suspects left.

The door panel shifted and whispered across the floor. Alan. Or Chris.

The door swung open, and I was staring at my aunt's killer.

30

SO COLD

Auntie's armchair creaked in protest when I shot up from my seat the same moment the door slammed into the wall and Alan stormed inside, pointing a gun at me.

"Sit," he shouted. Like a well-trained puppy, I dropped back into my chair, my eyes fixed on the muzzle of the weapon. Like an evil eye, it kept tracking my every movement.

A wild thought ricocheted through my brain: British police officers don't carry guns.

Alan squinted over the barrel of the revolver at a point near my left ear. Quiver it might, but his weapon never once strayed from its target: me.

"Enough of your silly games. Where are the plaques?"

Blobs danced through my vision. The expression "at gunpoint" never made more horrible sense.

"No idea what you mean." I licked my dry lips. "No idea at all." It came out as a whimper and I cringed at my weakness.

Alan laughed once, a dry, humorless bark. "Oh, yes you do. I gave you the benefit of the doubt, but when I showed Ignatius the USB stick, he was adamant you're one of them. And your cousin told me you're in on it. So, talk!"

Cousin? The desperate torrent of thoughts gushing through my gray matter froze in mid-rush. "Did you attack

Daisy?"

"Her own fault," Alan snapped. "I overheard her leaving a message on your phone. The witch taunted me, told me she knew where they were, but she refused to tell me anything, which forced me to touch her. She had it coming." His voice flipped, ending on a shrill note.

Salt and iron coated my tongue, and when I touched it, my finger came away red with blood. I must have bitten my lip.

Alan gaped first at me, then at my finger and scratched the wrist of the arm holding the gun. The weapon lowered, but it remained trained on me.

"Stop staring at me like that," he yelled. When his finger tightened on the trigger, my muscles bunched, ready to catapult me from the chair. That was foolish. I would never make it in time.

The hand not holding the gun balled into a fist. "Get up. Get going. Hand them over, and I'll let you live."

*He won't, you know, m*y inner voice said in a conversational tone. *He hates witches. Once you've given him what he wants, you're toast.*

I thought of the primula and screamed in my mind the plant should come, not knowing if the thing would be telepathic. I certainly wasn't. Plus, with my luck, it had wasted all its magical energy on Health and Safety.

"They're in a bank vault, and Sergeant Sarah has confiscated the key," I said. "If you kill me, you'll never get them."

Alan blanched, and his gun arm drooped. If the man pulled the trigger now, he would hit me in the leg. Not good, but not quite so lethal. Unfortunately, he caught himself, and the arm came back up.

I tried again. "If you fail, Ignatius will have you killed because you meddled with his plans and effed things up. You know that, don't you?"

It had been a shot into the dark, but it hit its mark. I could read it in the panic that widened Alan's eyes. It made him edgy, which made him more dangerous. What had I been thinking?

With fake calmness, entirely at odds with the cold terror

gripping my core, I continued. "I need time. And another vault key. Then I can go to the bank and fetch them."

How I wished I knew what I was talking about.

From outside came another crackle and pop of tires on the gravel. Alan must have been torn between his hatred of me and the threat posed by his evil overlord because he seemed not to notice. Once he did, I carried an additional responsibility. What if Alan gunned down a guest? I tried to catch the sounds from outside. And I heard something—a rustle and swishing of leaves in the corridor.

My heart cartwheeled in my chest. I had seen the plant in action. In less than a second, it had reached the kitchen. But would it be faster than a bullet?

Alan scratched his wrist, a little noise that rubbed on my nerves.

Where he stood, he would spot the plant the moment it entered the room. I needed to distract him. Or get him to move.

"I can ring the financial advisor and find out if he has a second key and knows which bank they're at. That means I'll have to rise from this chair."

"Why?"

"Because I don't remember the number and the phone is in my purse. The number might be written down in auntie's address book, but it's next to the computer."

Alan's gaze slipped aside, faced the archway and the den beyond. He wavered just long enough. The primula zipped into the room at floor level a heartbeat before his gaze snapped back to me.

Even without mindreading skills, I could almost see the thoughts rattling through his head. "Ignatius said you lot would part with your life before you gave up the plaques. How come you're so cooperative all of a sudden?" He sneered. "Stupid of your aunt to call her little coven, wasn't it? It's bad enough you aberrations are still running around. Just had to pally up again, did you? Ignatius believes it makes you even stronger."

The presence of the primula sparkling next to the settee gave me courage. "Oh dear, does Mr. Ignatius object to our presence because of his religious principles?"

"Hah. To the contrary, he couldn't give a toss. I do, but that's neither here nor there. No, he wants your magical plaques."

"Ignatius is into hexing?"

Alan's eyes flashed. "He's a businessman, dammit. You lot are nothing but a useful tool. Once he has the plaques, you might get them back if you help him out. He's had a spate of bad luck recently, and he needs somebody to make sure things pan out from now on. Or something like along those lines."

Whatever the plaques were, once Ignatius was in possession of them, he would never take his greedy paws off again.

"If you ask me, your boss crassly overestimates our capabilities."

"No, he doesn't, and I told him precisely what your capabilities are—at least your aunt's. And he's not my boss."

There was too much white in Alan's eyes when he stared in my general direction. Could it be he feared me just as much as his volatile not-boss? What might cause such terror? Unlikely the primula would have gone walkies before today and the plant seemed benign. It reminded me of a friendly imp. Had Alan read the recipe book? I suspected the grimoire would have socked him one if he tried.

"Ignatius decided he needed more leverage to get things moving. That cousin of yours is beyond braindead. People should know there are no such things as double-digit interest for investment schemes. She got greedy and fell for it. The cow even thought I was interested in her as a woman. Got pissy when I gave her the cold shoulder." Disgust twisted his face into an ugly parody of his blond good looks.

Rage lanced my chest. Alan must have been the man my cousin had been about to meet after our dinner in the pub. "You're telling me you tricked Daisy? Is the Wiltshire Police even aware of your extracurricular activities?"

"I've had enough of these bloody exams. They're rigged, or why else do I keep failing them? And a constable's salary is a joke." Alan made shooing movements with his gun. "Stop yabbering and get moving. Make your call, you freak. All I care about are the readies. Of that, Ignatius still has got plenty." He gave his wrist another good scratch, and I wondered about magical fleas.

"Fine," I said, the rage still boiling inside. "I will get up now. Take it easy on the hardware. If you keep waving it around, you'll make me nervous."

I inched from the armchair, forcing myself to ignore the primula. Nowhere in the recipe book had I found explanations on the powers of zombie plants once "revyved." I doubted the plant could inflict much damage. Plus, the pot was rather small. If I got things wrong, I might end up as a witchy sieve. I didn't want to go into the den, though; it was a dead end. No, I had to act now, while I still was close to the door.

The thought was still echoing through my brain when the swing doors to the kitchen whapped. Somebody had gone around the house and entered via the back door, which I had forgotten to lock.

Alan's nostrils widened. "What was that?"

"Drafts." I crab-stepped my way to the backrest of the armchair. "The kitchen entrance is open."

"Stay!" Alan yelled. His voice was like a fist in my midriff.

A cold sweat broke out all over me and my hands shot up, palms out. "Whoa, steady there. How am I going to get the number?"

His forehead glistening with perspiration, Alan's gaze darted to and fro. He teetered on the brink of madness. Once he went over, he would shoot. It was unlikely I would be fast enough to dive behind the chair.

"You stay where you are. I'll check," he said.

The primula rose behind his back on a shower of pink sparks.

With my heart hammering away and my gaze fixed on Alan, I circled my index finger in the air. I mumbled "Abramacabra" under my breath with as sinister a tone as I could muster. Somehow, it didn't sound quite right, but now was not the time for semantics. Although atrocious, my acting produced the desired effect. Alan grunted, took a step backward and collided with the coffee table. He stumbled, and the hand with the gun pointed at the ceiling.

I nose-dived behind the armchair, smacking on to the floor with a solid thump that rattled the fillings in the teeth.

Two deafening bangs and something whizzed over my head, tearing into the mirror above the mantelpiece. Shards exploded all over the place. I curled into a ball.

"Stop." Alan's voice, too close, was drowned in a sudden rush. A howling and flashing engulfed auntie's sitting room as if a storm front had hit. Alan's scream echoed throughout the B&B.

Perhaps, the primula is not so harmless after all.

Ignoring the voice, I speed-crawled along the floor, out of the door and into the corridor. There, I scrambled to my feet. From the room behind me came first a crash, then a shriek, and finally a heavy thump. I raced along the corridor, half expecting to bowl over a guest. But I was alone. The back entrance flaring in my mind like a loadstar gone nova, I threw myself through the swing doors and collided with something firm but warm.

31

REVELATIONS

Somebody gasped before disgustingly muscular arms closed around me and squeezed me tight. How had Alan ever sneaked past me? Where was the gun? I pummeled a wooly chest, but the arms remained locked around my waist.

"Cool it. I've got no idea what is going on here, but I heard gunshots. I suggest we make ourselves scarce."

Concern hung heavy in the soft male voice, which was not like Alan's at all. My befuddled brain searched for buttons to push and took a while to find the right one.

Chris had returned.

Now I was up against two grown men. Fury and panic crested inside me and gave me a strength I never knew I had, and I pushed him against the nearest cupboard.

"Ouch," Chris said, staring at me with an awed expression. "Blimey, so far I've seen nobody whose eyes can actually flash." He grabbed my hand. "Myrtle, we need to get the hell out of here." He propelled me out of the back door and yanked me toward the side passage when running feet racketed along the corridor.

"Crap." Chris pushed me into the rhododendrons. I lost my footing, tumbled over a root and crashed through leathery leaves and spiky twigs with my eyes pinched shut. I held out my hands to break my fall. All that rain had made the ground squelchy, and it softened the impact. It didn't spare me the dagger-sharp agony that shot from my wrists to my elbows.

I half-expected Chris's tall frame to land on top of me, but it didn't. When I opened my eyes, Chris was standing next to the bushes, scrutinizing the back entrance to the kitchen.

"Where is he?" I asked.

"Gone, I think," Chris said. "Somebody slammed the front door. Who are we talking about?"

"Alan, of course. Who else did you expect? Dear Uncle Bob?"

Chris gave me a guarded look. On his cheeks, the bluish stubble ruled supreme, and violet crescents bruised the skin under his eyes. "Who told you?"

I dragged myself off the ground, flicked out my throbbing wrists, and wiped at the mud caking my front. Then I gave up, for there was no point. "I'm not completely useless," I said. "Eventually, I worked things out. Even if it took a tick too long for my taste."

His mouth twitched once. "Who said you were stupid? Anyway, if it's Alan we're dealing with, we've got half a chance. He'll never be one of unc's heavies. It appears he was supposed to act as a scout, but he screwed things up when he killed your aunt." Chris held out his hand, which I grabbed, and he pulled me upright. A cold trickle ran down inside my muddied jeans, but that was not why I was shivering.

"You seem to know an awful lot. Why should I trust you?"

"Before I try to plead my case, you might want to alert your tame copper. She had me dragged into her den and gave me a hard time until I convinced her I'm not on my uncle's payroll."

I wasn't entirely won over. Sarah had slipped up badly with Alan, and, like the confused duckling I wasn't, I had followed her lead. Still, she needed to be involved. Unfortunately, my phone was still in my purse, which could be anywhere, and I could for the life of me not remember Sarah's number. The insides of my head had turned to molasses, and the shivering got more pronounced. Hot tears trickled over my cheeks.

Chris pulled me into his arms and mumbled something

reassuring. His solid body smelled of baby powder and incense and a musk that was entirely his. And mud. The tears dried up. I hiccupped once while warm hands patted my back.

"There, there. I didn't think you were the weepy type." His warm breath tickled my ear.

Idiot.

I broke contact, and my brain checked back in for action.

"My phone is inside. Perhaps you can call 999 on yours?"

"I'll try," Chris said grimly. "I suspect, with Alan gone and no corpses strewn about, they'll hunt for him first and talk to us later."

He tried. He was right. For the moment at least, we were on our own.

"Let me get the phone for you so you can ring Sergeant Wrigglythingy."

"Widdlethorpe. Don't—"

Too late, he was already at the back entrance, where he threw a glance into the kitchen before disappearing inside.

Outside, on the street, a tractor puttered by while I waited. And shivered.

And waited.

I was about to move when Chris's tousled dark mop poked out of the back entrance to the kitchen. He dangled my purse at me. "Found it at reception."

I rushed across and grabbed my bag. "No Alan?"

"Not on the ground floor. I took a quick gander. Told you already—the tosser stampeded along the corridor and the door slammed shut. He must be gone."

I fished for the phone and, with sweaty fingers, dialed Sarah's number. My call went straight to her mailbox. "Sarah? It's Myrtle. Call me. I'm at the Witch's Retreat. Alan has shot at me." That should get her attention. The question was when.

"It appears you got bad bobby with a flowerpot. Well done. Plant's a goner, but I'm sure you can buy another one," Chris said.

What?

I pushed past him and raced back to the sitting room. Clay shards, earth, and plant parts were scattered over the coffee table, spilling onto the floor with yellow and pink petals sprinkled in between.

Blackness rose from my stomach and swallowed me whole. I had brought the primula from the dead, had given her magical life—only to get her killed. I sagged to my knees, and there she was, under the table. What was left of her. I crawled to my miracle plant and cradled the broken bundle of roots, stems and squashed flowers in my hands, my tears wetting the soil.

"Myrtle? What's the problem? It's only a plant." He fell silent. "Isn't it?"

I crept away from the table and rose, nursing the fallen primula in my hands. "When I called her, she came to my rescue." The pain got too sharp to talk.

Chris raised his eyebrows, giving me an inscrutable look. Of course; he was descended from the witch hunters. How could he tolerate such madness?

He swung around and left the room.

I was alone with the remains of my magical plant. And the ashes of my aunt. The weight of an age-old burden settled on my shoulders. Freak, Alan had called me. How right he was. Worse even, I was a freaky failure.

The clock on the mantelpiece ticked the time away.

At first, I thought I had imagined it. But no, something stirred in my hands. Feeble roots tickled my fingers, crushed leaves and blossoms fluttered like Daisy's pulse had done.

The primula was still alive. Or alive again. I was too shattered to feel anything other than gratitude.

The door banged back open and Chris returned carrying a Tupperware box filled with earth, a roll of kitchen paper, and a mug.

"Here, I fetched the soil from the hanging baskets out front. And some water. The hexing I'll leave up to you."

He held out the box, and I eased my botanical bodyguard into its sickbed.

"Please live—Petunia." Saying the name felt right. The primula was a lot more than a small houseplant, just like my ancestor had been a lot more than a Regency herbalist.

Petunia's remaining leaves wriggled once as if in acknowledgment. I placed her on the coffee table before facing him.

"Attagirl. You've done it," he said. "After swearing the oath to your aunt, I was shit-scared about telling you and messing things up."

I dropped onto the beige settee, mud and all. "You swore an oath? What about? When? And why?"

Chris shoved his hands into his pockets, looking sheepish. "As to the what, I was forbidden to tell you who you are. It appears you have to come to terms with your true nature all by yourself. Otherwise, the magic doesn't work. That's the why for you. Your aunt was very concerned she might have been nudging you too much, and it would be her fault if you didn't come into your skills." He rolled his eyes. "Uh, I think that's what she called it. She made me promise I wouldn't pass on her message unless you'd discovered said skills in the meantime. About the when, well, I found her lying up there, all broken." His gaze strayed to the window, but I doubted he saw the car park.

"You're telling me she talked to you?" I whispered.

He heaved a sigh. "Yes. I wanted to help Mrs. Coldron, but she told me to stop. Said she knew she was dying and needed me to pay attention."

It was all too much. My mind was shooting questions like tennis balls out of a machine. I returned the last serve. "But weren't the paramedics listening in?"

"I covered the speaker with a handkerchief, let them babble along and lifted it once in a while to say something. I must have sounded pretty incoherent, but they're probably used to that sort of thing."

"But what did she say? I'm amazed she would have been lucid, with the fever raging inside her. And why did she trust you, of all people?"

He looked me in the eye. "Fever was about the only thing she hadn't got. Seriously. Where did you get that from?"

"The coroner. He said she died from sepsis. He believed Aunt Eve must have been running a high fever and ignored it."

Chris's eyebrows slanted. "She was stressed out, but otherwise fine. The coroner must have misunderstood something. Anyway, let's talk about trust. Uncle Bob learned about the gathering of the last coven, and he saw a business opportunity. Don't ask me how I knew. Just accept that I did. I figured he was up to no good and came here to warn your aunt."

"Why?"

His gaze burned into me. "Who do you take me for?"

I broke eye contact and watched the primula instead. Weak, but definitely moving. With fertilizer on a drip-feed she might soon get back up on her roots.

I sighed and faced him again. "I hardly know you. Can I assume you wanted to make up for the sins of your ancestors?"

The muscles in his jaw bunched. "Something along those lines, yes. I'm amazed Mrs. Coldron accepted me. I wouldn't have been surprised if she'd chucked me out. Some of her new friends were ready to do just that. But she more or less convinced them. Told them I was the logical person to help them build the database of your lore. And I helped her find her friends."

Somebody had mentioned databases recently, but I couldn't recall who it was.

A whisper was all I managed. "Auntie's last words?"

"I'll never forget them. First of all, she wants you to look after her daughter. Then she wants you to continue in her shoes. With one exception, you're the strongest of them all, she said. But you were blocking yourself. I was to make sure you wouldn't come to harm."

"But why did she talk to you?" I asked. "Why not the Ragworts or Dottie Wytchett? Or Jenna? My cousin even. I mean, Auntie involved her."

Chris rubbed at the drying mud on his pullover. "Apart from me being the only one around during her last minutes, I can only guess at her motives. I mean, we weren't exactly bosom buddies. Your aunt struck me as a very private sort of person, and I figure she must have been embarrassed she couldn't get you to accept your skills. I'm not even sure if she kept Mrs. Wytchett in the loop. The two ladies might have had common goals, but to me, it looked like the mating of the hedgehogs. About your cousin, well, your aunt was acutely aware of her daughter's limitations. She fretted about having involved her, but admitted she had no choice." He shrugged. "Anyway, her last words were 'Don't ever tell Myrtle she's got true magic, or she will lose it. We need her.'" Then she fell unconscious."

He raised his hands and dropped them again. "What was I supposed to do?"

"You tried to draw me out at the circle, right? Despite her warnings."

His gaze dipped. "I wanted to help you. I hoped if I got you there, somehow something would happen. My sources claimed unc was obsessing about you, so I couldn't sit on my hands any longer. Once I had left you, I did the unspeakable. I sought out my uncle, tried to explain to him what your aunt confirmed. That their powers were feeble, that they had been left behind for a reason when the Whites exodused through the circle. That he should leave you alone. He appreciated the intel and gave me a bit of tit for tat. That's how I know about Alan."

"The Whites?"

A sad smile hovered on Chris's lips. He reached out and gently tugged at a soggy strawberry strand of hair dangling in front of my eyes. "The top-shelf witches. Bleached by magic or something like that. Don't ask me. My uncle doesn't consider me trustworthy, which is why I don't have access to the family chronicles. My knowledge is limited. They left the Reds behind. Their lesser kin, I mean. Uncle is adamant not all the Whites departed, and their descendants are still around. When I learned Alan was acting as uncle's goon, I tried to warn you. I don't know what Alan told Uncle Bob, but he made it sound as if your aunt was good at the stuff."

Blood cannot really run cold, but mine turned to ice water, nonetheless. "How would he know?"

32

PRICK

"No idea," Chris said. "Perhaps Alan wanted to make the job sound more dangerous than it was. He's always been cutting corners. We met at uni, see? I wish we hadn't." He sat down on auntie's armchair and ripped off a mile of kitchen paper. "Try this. You look like the survivor of a cave in."

"Perhaps I should be grateful it's not soot," I grumbled and wiped my fingers. My new clothes had become a disaster zone kitchen paper could never clear.

"So not funny."

"I still don't understand what those plaques are and how they work."

"We're talking about two Neolithic clay tablets," Chris said. "When the Whites left, they took all their magical gadgets with them. All of them—except these two plaques. That's why they mean the world to the remaining witch folk."

"Yes, but what—"

"I'm not clued up on all the details. It's just that Uncle Bob figured if he were in possession, you lot would jump through hoops to get them back."

"From what I've seen so far, he would soon sack us for paranormal underperformance."

We both regarded the plant, a third of its former size, all flowers gone.

"Well..." Chris said.

Somewhere upstairs, something thudded.

He jumped up. I took a lot longer, my muscles screeching their protest, nausea once more pooling in my stomach.

"What the deuce was that?" Chris asked.

"How about Alan?"

"Unlikely. Let me check what's going on." Chris yanked the door open.

"Why don't you ring the cops again?"

"And if it is a guest? Or your cat?"

I limped toward the window and ripped the curtain aside. Apart from Chris's Beemer, which had joined the German SUV and my clunker, the view appeared unchanged. "No guests in sight. The Ragworts are renovating, and the Germans must be chasing the poor churchwarden."

The words had hardly left my mouth when Rosie and Damian shuffled into the car park. Or rather, she shuffled. He tried to match his pace to hers.

"Cripes."

"What?" Chris said, alarmed.

"The Ragworts have just arrived. I must warn them. They can't come in here until I'm convinced the place is secure."

The next moment, Colonel Elmsworth, Buster in tow, rounded the corner and hurried to catch up with the Ragworts. He was followed by Mrs. Bingham, wearing her Barbour inside out. From the direction of Long Street rushed Linda, the landlady of the Crystal Dawn. Across the road, the curtains in Mrs. Mornings' living room swung back into place and a minute later she too headed for my bed and breakfast. A loud bang on Long Street announced Marty's van. It was accompanied by a few more people I remembered from yesterday.

"What the..."

Chris tilted his head. He reminded me of a big, black, likeable Labrador minus the floppy ears. "Something the matter?" he asked.

"I would say the coven is gathering."

The angle of his head became more pronounced. "You're not wasting your time, are you?"

"I didn't call it. Them, I mean."

The doorbell gonged. A second later, a key turned in the lock and the front door opened to the babble of many voices.

Chris rolled his eyes. "If Alan should still be hanging around, by now he knows something is wrong."

"Myrtle?" Damian hollered into the corridor. His voice was surprisingly penetrating for his age and build.

"What will they think when they see me like this?" I hissed.

"Tell them it's a magical experiment gone wrong. They'll believe that," Chris hissed back. There was a twinkle in his eyes that told me the man might be enjoying himself.

I hobbled into the corridor to face the gathering crowd. "Uh, how can I help you? I'm terribly sorry, I know I look a fright. Spot of bother earlier."

Damian's violet owl eyes blinked behind his bottle-bottom glasses. His wife clung to his arm, panting with exertion. "Gloria said somebody fired a gun," he said. "And there's smoke coming from your chimney."

"The chimneys are blocked," I said, bewildered.

"That's what she said as well," the Colonel cut in. "And that's why she started the call chain."

"Just asking out of interest. Did you use crystal balls?" Chris said from behind me.

Damian faced him with a moue of distaste. "I see you're back."

My head started to ache. "Can you please hold the hostilities until we have sorted this out?"

With a volley of shrill yaps, Buster tore the leash from the Colonel's hands and dashed upstairs.

"Buster," the Colonel thundered. He grabbed the banister and charged after his pet. The yapping became fainter but persisted until another loud thump from upstairs silenced the noise.

"Buster," the Colonel screamed from the first floor and

dashed on.

My muscle pain forgotten, I bolted after him. Chris sprinted past, his long legs eating up the steps. Feet pounded after me, followed by Robbie's (or Johnnie's) high-pitched, "Mum, this is fun."

The inhabitants of Wytchett Farm had joined the fray.

Once I arrived on the first floor, my nostrils twitched at the acrid stink of a thin blue haze drifting down from above. It carried along a menacing warmth. The Witch's Retreat was on fire.

"Call Emergency," Chris yelled from the top floor. The clattering on the steps diminished when at least two of the pursuers stopped to pull out their phones. I, however, raced on, a roaring inferno on my mind. Where I had expected the smoke to thicken and was prepared for the cackling and spitting of flames, the upper corridor bore only a trace of the pungent fumes. It still brought tears to my eyes.

I blinked at Chris, who stood in front of the curtain, peering into the landing.

My lungs and legs decided they didn't like my treatment of them, and I was gasping and staggering by the time I reached him.

The Colonel kneeled next to the dreadful settee, stroking the head of the little dog. I was pleased to see its eyes were open, though it appeared to be rather dazed. To one side lay a scorched nightstand and the old chair, two of its legs broken off, blackened stuffing hanging out.

"I'm going to kill whoever is responsible," Elmsworth bellowed. Then he coughed.

"Stand in line," Chris said. He entered the landing and flapped at the smog pooled in the small space. "Pooh." He dashed into Aunt Eve's room and presumably opened a window, for a breeze of fresh air drifted in from the left, mingling with the acrid draft coming from the attic.

Out of the corner of my eye, I spotted the Wytchetts, Mrs. Bingham, and others, who soon crowded the second-floor corridor.

Chris returned, stared up at the dark rectangle of the opening above, pulled his sweater over his head and climbed the ladder with a grim expression on his face and the garment flung over his shoulder.

"Good man, watch out," the Colonel said, urgency in his voice. "You don't know who's up there and whether he's got a weapon."

Chris didn't respond. He bunched the pullover into a bundle and threw it into the opening.

I sucked in air.

Buster gave a faint whine.

At first, there was no sound from above. A painful breath later, something heavy fell over, fists thumped on muscle, followed by the scream of a child. "Mum!"

My stomach lurched.

"Hello, Myrtle," Alan said from the attic, satisfaction fat in his voice. "I know you're down there. You have one hour to get to the flipping bank vault and fetch me the plaques. And don't even think of calling my esteemed ex-colleagues. Otherwise, the nipper dies."

Events got somewhat rushed after that. Jenna stormed the landing with Johnnie in hand and a wild look on her face. Marty and Chris between them had a hard time stopping her from climbing the ladder and strangling the kidnapper with her bare hands. She only held back when Alan demonstrated he indeed was armed by firing a shot at the clutter upstairs.

"To the curtain," the Colonel urged, Buster under his arm, and we all lunged for the wall with the exit. An instant later, a second shot zinged through the opening and buried itself in the settee with a muffled thud. At least that was where I thought it went. My eyes were squeezed shut, and my nose hovered inches from the nearest wall while my heart sucker-punched the inside of my ribcage.

"I figure I have your attention now," Alan said.

"Mum, can we do that again?" Johnnie asked.

I wondered how his brother might have got up there. I figured Alan must have put the fire escape ladder in place before gracing me with his presence. After the primula attack, he faked his escape and tried to set the attic on fire. For whatever reason, the fire didn't catch. He must have been watching things and, when the conflagration failed to materialize, clambered back up. Robbie must have slipped away from his mother, saw Alan, monkeyed after him and got caught.

With Jenna threatening to go after her son, my brain whirred in overdrive and an idea took shape. It was still sort of fuzzy around the edges, but a hushed exchange with Chris, Marty, and the Colonel clarified things. I started off by fake calling the financial advisor and asking him, or rather my voicemail—loudly, so Alan would get it—about the missing spare key and thanking it for the instructions it had not given me.

"The clock is ticking," said a sing-song voice from the attic.

"You can't seriously consider handing over your heirloom to that wanker," Chris yelled for good measure.

The coven members not in on the conspiracy sent a cacophony of shouts bouncing through the small space of the landing.

"Hear, hear."

"Well said."

"Let's hex him."

"How?"

"I'm leaving now," I hollered at the attic. "It'll take more than an hour to drive to Swindon, park, visit the bank and return."

"How will you be getting them, then?" asked Alan. He sounded relaxed, friendly even. He could have fooled me into believing he was a helpful neighborhood copper and his worst issues were related to stress management. Correction: He had fooled me, and Sarah, into believing just that.

"The finance chap is bringing the spare key to the bank," I improvised. "But don't flip if I'm not back in an hour."

"I never flip," Alan said with indignance. "No tricks. Otherwise, the nipper dies."

"You're repeating yourself." We made sure to trample out of the landing, swearing at the top of our voices. Outside, in the corridor, we shared our battle plan with the others and refined things. Chris, being the resident mountaineer, was to climb the roof and distract Alan, preferably without getting shot. The coven would swarm up the aluminum ladder and vanquish Alan while he was otherwise engaged.

Somehow.

"I know my way around the attic. I'll go first," I said. The sheer thought made my head reel and my abused body ache all over.

"No. I want to strangle the wanker," Jenna spat.

"Let me go with Chris," Marty said with his trademark calm. "You look after Johnnie, otherwise he's up there in no time."

Cops and fire brigades had been called off. We couldn't risk interference. Sarah, however, received another voice message from me, where I explained the situation. I trusted her to do the right thing, hoping she would do it quickly.

With Marty joining Chris, I now had two people to worry about. Marty would send us a text message from the roof before breaking and entering. I considered it to be unnecessary, as there would be noise. There was noise anyway: Robbie, unhappy with his situation, had bitten his kidnapper twice already, so Alan was spitting mad.

The message came, followed by shouting, Robbie's screaming, and a general frantic scramble. I was already doing my own frantic scramble up the ladder and popped into the attic that still reeked of smoldering things. There, I beheld Alan pointing the gun at Chris and Marty, who clasped the wriggling boy in his arms.

Damn it all to hell.

Alan must have seen me, but he held his gun steady. His shirt was torn and soot blackened his jeans.

He stood on the other end of the roof space, coiled like a cobra. "I knew you would try some sort of trick. Who shall I shoot first? You?"

His gun made an infinitesimal flick to the right, where Marty and the kid cowered. "Or you?"

The gun jerked back to Chris. His long, slim fingers grappled for the broom behind him, but it was just out of reach.

I sensed the presence of the coven squashed into the landing and the Colonel hunkering below me on the ladder. The fury boiling inside of me rose and pressed against the inside of my skull until every thought became a painful pulse.

Alan wouldn't dare shoot me, not with the two men closer to him. He would kill them first.

It was all up to me.

The rafters above seemed to fizz and sizzle, and a flowery scent swirled into my nostrils. Or did it exist only in my mind, in a head an instant away from explosion?

How did one do magic?

The pulse in my brain throbbed faster. My vision was tunneling.

It focused on the hand that held the gun.

Again.

I couldn't remember a single spell from the recipe book.

Even if I knew what to do, would I die, like Aunt Eve?

Did I want Alan dead?

No, no, not that.

It is never evil we serve, Petunia had written. Unfortunately, she had left no instructions on what to do when confronted with evil.

My head was killing me.

I remembered the primula and how I had willed her to come. I centered my thoughts on the gun and willed it away.

A shower of blood-red petals exploded from the space where the weapon had been. With a howl, Alan flicked away—a thorny rose. When it landed on the bedsheets, the flower turned back into a gun.

Chris, fury distorting his face, threw himself at Alan.

There had been no noise, no voice, no spell, no nothing.

I didn't even have a wand.

In a starburst of pain, my mind went blank.

I must have been out for the count for a while. When I came to, I stared at a circle of anxious faces.

"Thank the resident deities," Chris said. "You're still with us."

"Next time, you better tell me when you're about to jump," the Colonel said.

"She didn't jump, she fell," Jenna said.

"Yes, I noticed," the Colonel said. "I had a hard time holding on to her and not toppling myself."

"The boy? Alan?" I whispered.

"All is well," Marty said. "We've called the cops again. They were a bit pissed off, so we told them to talk to Sergeant Sarah." He squeezed my hands.

"Don't," Jenna said.

A sharp pain made my palms throb. When I held them in front of my face, they were pink, swollen and dotted with red pinpricks.

"That's magical fallout," Damian's voice breathed into my ear. "At least I think so. I've never experienced live magic."

"Don't gape, man, do something." Rosie dabbed my palms with Sani-wipes. The alcohol stung but cooled the swelling. "Does this help?"

I groaned in response and sat up, holding a head that felt as if a thousand little devils were prodding it with their pitchforks. My hands were not much better, despite Rosie's ministrations. "Where's Alan? I need to talk to him."

"Later." Jenna's voice, cooler than even the Sani-wipes, dampened my brain.

I couldn't let her. "No. Now." With the help of Chris, I stood. He guided me to Alan, lying on the settee, trussed up with so many ripped bedsheets he resembled a disheveled mummy. Only the head and feet poked out. His sneakers were singed.

"It was you all the way, wasn't it?" I said in a light tone that matched neither my mood nor my many aches and pains. "First, you harassed my aunt. Then you went after me, throwing up smokescreens with petals, windows left open, and ladders moving about. Oh, and congratulations, faking the vertigo was a nifty ruse."

"I wasn't acting," Alan snapped. "I can't stand heights and those ladder stunts were an absolute nightmare. But Ignatius threatened to kill me if I didn't deliver. What could I do?"

"You poor darling. You nearly bashed my head in that day, you know?"

"I wish I had." Alan's face was beetroot-red.

"And the ultimatum was a half-cocked effort at making me confide in you, right? Or did you want to spook me into moving the plaques? I wasn't even aware of them."

"I give you half-cocked." He strained, but the ragged ropes held him tight. "You asked for my help, so there. And I got to measure the walls in the bloody attic. Before, the blasted shifts got in the way. The one time I tried in the night, you ruined everything. At least being on the burglary liaison team gave me some flexibility. And you, stupid witch, never guessed."

I resisted the urge to belt him one. My hands still hurt too much. And there was one more thing I needed from him.

"How did you kill my aunt?"

The mummy jerked, the shoes drumming on the faded upholstery. "I didn't kill your aunt. You won't pin that one on me."

"What happened?" I held my breath.

"The cow cursed me. Ignatius said to keep checking the attic, but somebody was always around, and that bloody step ladder makes a racket. That's why I used my special entrance. Next thing I know, she clambered through the trapdoor, screeching like a banshee. Some rubbish about traps and having uncovered the mole. Her eyes were all queer, and she pointed a finger at me."

Here it comes.

The rushing was back in my ears. I couldn't bear to hear this, but I needed to. For my own sake. And the sake of the coven.

"What happened next?" I asked.

Sweat glittered on Alan's forehead. He twitched and twisted as he revisited the past. "She said, 'Die' seven times and kept circling her finger. Thorns flew at me. I held out my hands to ward them off and got stung. Suddenly she stopped, her face went all red and then white. She doubled over, took a few steps backward—and tumbled through the godforsaken trapdoor in a shower of rose petals. My hands hurt like mad, but I couldn't make out any wounds. Then I checked, and she was down there, lying next to the ladder, body all broken up. It's not even that high."

Alan fell silent. When he spoke again, emotion had fled from his voice. "She lay there, with her eyes open. Something like a water bubble, only made of air, spread from her body. I heard rapid footsteps on the staircase—"

"That was me," Chris said.

Alan paid him no heed. "The trapdoor came up, followed by the bolt slamming home. The damn witch must have thought she had trapped me. But I never killed her."

No, he hadn't. However, he was responsible for what happened. But so was my aunt when she tried to kill the hired goon. Would she have lived had she gone after Ignatius?

"Myrtle?" Sarah called from downstairs.

The cavalry had arrived.

33

DEPARTURE

"This is so…" Anticlimactic and humdrum were the words that came to mind. The two rough-hewn squares of stone peeping from the checkered kitchen towel they had been wrapped in reminded me of building rubble. As the priceless magical artifacts my aunt had given her life to protect, they were a disappointment.

As expected, we found them in a bank vault. Mr. Floyd, the financial advisor, kept a spare key to the safe deposit box together with explicit instructions to release the items in question only if two of three people told him to. One had been my aunt. The other two were Daisy and me.

I decided safety was found in numbers and turned up in his office accompanied by Damian, Rosie, Jenna, Marty, and Chris. To do him justice, Mr. Floyd recovered swiftly, accepted Daisy's written authorization, and handed over the key for the safe deposit box.

"We must talk about your plans," he said.

My plans were to run over the hills and far away, but that choice was not on offer. Not with Daisy in hospital, the Simpkinses in need of employment, and a wonky coven mistaking me for the solution to their many problems.

I quit my teaching job and enrolled in a crash course in

hotel management with the temporary landlord of the Whacky Bramble. Greg was bidding on a pub in the neighboring village of Banbury so he could stay in Wiltshire in case the owner of the pub returned in what Greg called fall. Why our cousins from across the big pond insisted on turning a season into an accident had always been beyond me.

Alma and Cecily were as ecstatic about my decision as those laconic ladies could ever be. Not because of the hefty pay raise I arranged for them. At least not entirely. For some odd reason, they liked me as much as they had liked my aunt.

"You're upside," Cecily said, beaming at me.

"Upright," Alma corrected her, for once also beaming.

They meant well. It still didn't transform the grayish lumps I held in my hands into something worth death, a severe head injury, a kidnapped boy, and eight days of madness.

The one member of our small party to disagree was Chris.

"May I?" With his gloved hand, he plucked the bigger of the chalky chunks from the dishrag. He then ogled the piece, which barely covered his palm, in wordless admiration. Wriggly lines, chevrons and what resembled rectangular waves had been scratched into the surface of the little thingy in a veritable Neolithic doodle. The smaller plaque still in the towel showed a more organized chevron pattern but artistic it wasn't.

"I was hoping for a note from our ancestors. You know who I mean?" Rosie said.

"Given the circumstances, 'You know who' is an unfortunate choice in syntax," her husband said. "Folks, let's keep Harry Potter out of this. These thingumajigs are not quite what I expected."

"Chris?" Jenna said.

His face flushed, our tame witch hunter was lost in another world.

I nudged him in the ribs. "You're the resident expert. Care to elaborate on our find?"

Chris resurfaced from his Neolithic dream. "What? Oh, the tablets. Authentic, I dare say. Look at the chevron pattern on yours. The Bronze Age dwellers used it on a lot of their pottery. If you want to be sure, you need to have them tested."

"Nice to hear these lumps are likely the real McCoy, but what have they got to do with seventeenth-century witches?" Marty asked.

Chris stroked his cotton-gloved thumb over the tablet in his hand. "There must be oral records on your side. My knowledge is too sketchy. Somehow, your ancestors must have tapped into the powers of the Neolithic monument. And these plaques played a role."

"You know a lot for somebody who's supposedly not the flavor of the month with your uncle. How can we be sure you're no spy?" Damian pushed out his chin in weak belligerence, reminding me of a scrawny rooster. My aunt had trusted Chris. I did, too. Still, we might be wrong. Just like Sarah had misjudged Alan.

Chris scowled. "Thanks for the warm fuzzies. My uncle doesn't trust me as far as he can throw me. He never gives up, though. He'll continue to have a go at both you and me, there's no doubt about it. He operates with some coaxing here, a bribe there and hopes perhaps something will pop up. And if it doesn't work, there's always blackmail. Or worse. I'm worried about Alan. I hope he stays in jail for a long time."

"About those plaques," I said.

"Ah, sorry. Well, I'll share the few morsels dear Uncle Bob designed to drop me. For what they're worth. To my mind, most of it is sheer fantasy. The Whites migrated straight to hell. These tablets are in reality keys. They contain a curse-to-go that will unlock the gates they passed through."

Chris had raised his voice, and it boomed off the vault's low ceiling. A quick check assured me we were still alone among the rows and rows of shiny bronze doors hiding the strongboxes. There was not much space, which was most likely the reason Chris's statement only caused polite coughs and uneasy shifting and shuffling instead of the full-blown stampede it deserved.

My hand twitched, and I forced myself not to fling the small chalk lump I was holding against the steel walls of the vault.

"What do you mean when you say these tablets contain a curse? Inside?" I could swear the plaque was growing hotter in my hand.

Chris shrugged. "Search me. In any case, the witch hunters turned this world into a living hell. Why bother emigrating to yet another purgatory? Though I'll tell you freely, Uncle Bob will want to try them out."

"If you ask me, they don't look hellish. I've seen these patterns before, in a museum," Jenna said.

"The plaques are our heritage," Rosie said. "Eve died to stop them from falling into the wrong hands. Oops, sorry, Chris."

I wished I could have built a bomb shelter, or rather Uncle Bob-proof shelter, for the blasted plaques, but for the moment the vault was still the safest place.

We restored them to the safe deposit box and went our respective ways in our respective vehicles.

In my case, Chris was driving, since my old clunker had given up its ghost this morning. I needed to raid my bank account for a replacement. Probate hadn't yet been granted and wouldn't be for a while.

"Wrong thinking," said Chris, his hands—slender but strong—guiding the car through the Thursday lunchtime traffic. "You're running a business. Lease a vehicle and slap it on the bed and breakfast."

He had a point there. I would ask Floyd when we met again.

While Chris's Beemer got stalled in traffic, I became aware of his presence. Still, it felt right, as if he belonged there. At my side.

Chris set the indicator and tackled the next roundabout. "Alan is pleading temporary insanity. And he has confessed to killing your aunt."

"But he didn't."

"No." Chris swerved around a cherry-red Mini with the Union Jack painted on its roof. "He's trying to save his life by taking the blame. Perhaps it'll work. Perhaps not."

I thought of the man in the ditch who had killed my

parents. Daisy had explained to me when I visited her in hospital this morning. Despite being chuffed when her mother entrusted her with the key, my cousin had asked some amazingly pertinent questions about its backstory. She should have probed deeper, should have tried to find out how much I knew. But such is life.

My deductions had been correct on most counts. Sixteen years ago, auntie investigated Ignatius's shady business practices and wrote a devastating feature. He researched her right back. Once he realized she belonged to those Coldrons, he gave chase. About to leave the country, she dug up the plaques, which were hidden in the Coldron grave.

The only thing I got wrong was the bit with the headstone. Auntie used it as a red herring when she took the plaques—just in case Ignatius had infiltrated the Farnsworth Agency—and replaced the marker in exactly the same position last November, the reason I found no evidence of recent digging. The rain had washed it away.

Apparently, when Ignatius and Aunt Eve clashed for the first time, he wasn't aware of the true nature of the magical artifacts she was guarding. That's why he fell for the headstone ruse. The witch hunts had happened a while ago, and as with my lot, knowledge was lost. Peeved over his failure, Ignatius read up on things and corrected his oversight. Once the coven was gathered, and he being under what he considered financial pressure, he went after auntie once more.

She had never told her daughter the plaques were hidden over her head for a while. When I mentioned that, Daisy freaked, and the nurse threw me out.

Also, Daisy didn't call Alan on the day of her near-death experience to plead for an extension on the payment deadline as I had suspected. Instead, the bastard had stuck tracking devices on both our cars.

"Myrtle? Wakey, wakey," Chris said with a smile.

"What do you think your uncle will do next?"

Chris raised his right hand in a gesture of mock outrage. He grabbed the steering wheel again rather quickly when we turned a corner and a bus swerved from the curb, belching diesel fumes. "Uncle Bob doesn't like loose ends." He threw me a glance. "That includes the Avebury witches."

"I'm not sure the whole thing is such a good idea. I'd much rather if the gang disbanded. The idea of Schlüsselblum starting up a continental coven I like even less."

"That chap strikes me as being rather determined. So is your lot," Chris said. "Even if they tried, Dottie Wytchett wouldn't let them."

I was so not looking forward to meeting that woman.

We swerved through the s-curve that ran through the henge. What once had seemed sinister had lost its menace. Even the one soot-stained rock no longer weighed on my soul. Daisy had been the one to decorate it with flower chains, and yesterday I had followed her example.

Instead, I dreamt of petal showers, thorny hedges and spooky white beings calling out from among the flames. I shook off the images. This was the twenty-first century. They didn't burn witches anymore. Not even Ignatius wanted that. Instead, he wanted to capitalize on our "skylles."

The tires of the Beemer crunched across the gravel in the front yard of the Witch's Retreat, and the car came to a standstill.

"I've got a job lined up in Wales," Chris said. "I figured it might be better if I stay away for a while. Until you have got on top of things." He jerked his head at a curtain twitching in Mrs. Mornings' house across the road.

There was no reason his comment should kick me in the stomach like it did. We weren't even an item.

A few deep but silent breaths later, I was ready to respond in what one might call a civilized fashion. "Fine. Unless you're leaving right now, you could join me for a cup of tea. With some apple pie? I made it myself."

"I'd love to. About my job, well, Wales is not far." Chris sent me a smoldering look that zinged straight into a region south of my navel. It reminded me of the fizz I experienced when baby-stepping my way through the hexing. But this was a different kind of magic.

I had bought the ingredients for the pie myself. Following auntie's recipe word for word resulted in a flattish cowpat, slightly burned at the edges and the middle a tick on the slushy side. Not to Chris's standards of cooking but not bad for a start. He seemed to agree, munching a slice doused with cream as he wandered through the sitting room.

"Neat," he pronounced rather thickly through a mouthful of pie and pointed his fork at the bookshelf. "Uh, why is this slice sitting beside the vase?"

"Oh, that." Among all the rush to view the infamous plaques, I had forgotten the first piece of pie, which I had placed next to the urn with auntie's ashes. At the time it had seemed the right thing to do.

But Chris had wandered on and was examining the primula on the windowsill. "It still looks rather scruffy, but I dare say the primula might make it." He fingered a bud peeping from underneath the frayed leaves. Pink buds only this time.

A faint rustle of disgust. A pink spark.

"Petunia is no 'it.'"

Chris put his empty plate aside and eyed me over the rim of his teacup. "Petunia? Methinks this is primula vulgaris. Ah, yes, you gave her that name, didn't you?"

Something tickled my bare ankles. Energetic lapping confirmed Tiddles had joined the tea party and found the cream.

There was one question I still needed to ask. "Why do you keep a copy of the witch hunter's bible in your room?"

Chris placed his cup on the mantelpiece. "How would you even know I had one?"

"Cleaners get everywhere."

"Ah, I see." Chris stapled his long fingers, his dark gaze intense under those straight eyebrows that only slanted when he frowned. Or grinned, like he did now.

He had a cute grin.

"My uncle hands them out to his minions," he continued. "I got hold of one. Just so I would never forget where I come from."

As if either of us could ever do that.

"Let me guess, you didn't 'clean' in Alan's room?"

I shook my head.

"I strongly suspect you would have found another copy."

Did I want to delve deeper into my magical heritage? Was it even worth trying to find out what happened all those years ago, who the Whites might have been, and why they abandoned their relatives? It was so rotten of them to run and take all the magic away. They had left us the plaques, though they still didn't wow me.

Then there was the recipe book. Written during the Regency period, yes. But the more I looked at it, the more I was convinced the tome must be much older. And what about those empty pages in the middle?

So many secrets. So many mysteries.

For the moment, I was content to snuggle into my armchair, safe in my new home, with my new friends, my housekeepers, my cousin, my cat and my zombie primula all close by.

My aunt died in a magical accident, and I inherited her life.

Aunt Eve was a witch.

So was I.

Acknowledgments

Oodles of thanks are owed to my husband, Keith, without whom this novel would never have got finished. Thank you for your patience, your staunch support, and for believing in me when I did not. I love you.

I'm also indebted to the great people in Wattpad, without them this novel would never have got started. To my fellow Wattpad authors, Stars, and the wonderful critique group on The Writer's Edge – thank you for making me see the light.

Special thanks go to Sharon Salonen, for editorial input as incisive as it was inspired, and to Susie Brooks, Chief Editor of Literary Wanderlust, for calming down a budding author in the small hours. You both rock.

And last but no way least, a huge big thankyou goes to my parents, for introducing me to books in the first place. (They immediately regretted it afterwards, when I tore through every reading matter thrown my way at lightning speed).

About the Author

Lina Hansen has been a freelance travel journalist, teacher, bellydancer, postal clerk and communication specialist stranded in the space sector. Numbed by factoid technical texts, she set out to write the stories she loves to read— cozy and romantic mysteries with a dollop of humour and a magical twist. After living and working in the UK, Lina, her husband, and their feline companion now share a home in the foothills of Castle Frankenstein. Lina is a double Watty Award Winner, Featured Author, and a Wattpad Star.

In My Attic is the first of the Magical Misfits series of mysteries. More information and Lina's blog can be found at www.linahansenauthor.com or connect via Twitter
@lhansenauthor or Facebook @linahansenauthor.

Lightning Source UK Ltd.
Milton Keynes UK
UKHW040716140820
368251UK00002B/508